KAITLYN AND THE HIGHLANDER

DIANA KNIGHTLEY

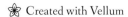

For Kevin, I will...

CHAPTER 1

*J*ames said, "You know what I miss doing with you?"

I giggled. "I can guess but I want to hear you say it." We were sitting on two lawn chairs, red cups on the ground beside us, facing the beach even though it was too dark to see what was out there — undulating sand dunes, whispering sea grass, and rolling waves beyond. I could hear them, the distant crash and splash through the darkness.

"Skinny-dipping."

I was mystically transported back to high school days when the smile of James Cook could make my knees buckle. I giggled again.

"Want to go now?"

Tipsy didn't begin to describe how I felt. I had gone past tipsy an hour before and had since entered Drunk as Hell.

As we walked together along the boardwalk over the dunes, I kept bumping into James who laughed and stumbled into me. He said, "I think I'm drunk."

"Me too."

I stood still at the end of the walk and wiggled my toes down deep into the sand. It was the consistency of coarse raw sugar and I had really missed its feel on my feet.

James joked, "You first."

I teased, "You think I'm going to chicken out?" I stripped my shirt off over my head, unclasped my bra and dropped it off my arms.

James said, "Okay then," and began working on his pants button, dropping them to the ground. He took off his shirt but I was already streaking by him. "See you in the water!"

My feet hit the ocean, warm, lapping. I ran with big leaping steps, splashing all around, and dropped face down into the water. I popped my head up in time to see James, running naked, his dick flopping side to side. I giggled even more.

He dove under and came up right in front of me with a whoosh, water dripping down his forehead. "Hi Katie."

"Hi."

His hand, his big hand, big football-playing hand of bigness, reached out and pulled my ass closer. A small wave lifted and gently dropped us. There was barely a swell. Like bathwater really, another thing I had missed.

He said, "You've been gone a long time."

"I have." My legs were treading, sliding around his slippery skin and groping hands.

He kissed me.

"I missed you, Katie."

I kissed him back because this was entirely too much talking and if he got nostalgic I might cry. Or heck, I might cry if he said one more word and I wasn't doing that anymore. I was going to be flirty, wild Katie, who didn't give a shit anymore.

Lightning arced across the sky.

"What the—?" James looked up. "Oh shit, we better get out." The sky north of us was dark, growing darker, and moving our way fast. Lightning sparked from the middle of it, hitting the beach.

"Crap!" We both raced from the water. He scooped up his clothes and tossed a towel at me. "Run!"

I had never seen anything like this storm before. The clouds banked high, black as coal, climbing and roiling. Lightning sparked and flashed. The air sizzled around us.

He grabbed my arm. "Katie, you're going to get killed, move it!"

The storm had a fury to it, wind and roar. The sky darkening, the air thickening, and the — "There are people in it!" I yanked away from his grip. "Look, people in the middle of it." I froze for a second, then yelled, "Hey!" and waved my arms.

James grabbed me by my arms and tugged. "Katie, I will drag you out of here if you don't come on." A sharp bolt of lightning arced from the storm to the sand right between me and the people under the storm.

I yelled, "They'll be killed!"

A clap of thunder, so loud, so terrifying, so startling; I clapped my hands to my ears.

"It's just a shadow, run, now!"

I stumbled over a dip in the sand, landing on all fours, my hair flinging around my head, the wind whipping behind me. James pulled me up and pushed me toward the boardwalk stairs. As soon as my feet hit the steps, I sprinted, wrapping the towel around my naked body.

James was just behind, between me and the storm, yelling, "Run! Run! Run!"

The dozen or so other party guests had sheltered in James's living room, and Hayley watched for us through the glass door. We slid the door open and rushed in, flushed, wet, and mostly naked.

James said, "Where the hell did that storm come from?"

"You guys — naked running!" Hayley doubled over laughing.

"James's junk was flopping all over." Michael mimicked James across the living room floor.

"Very funny, guys."

Hayley and Michael stopped and looked quizzically toward the boardwalk.

Two cloaked figures, one very tall, the other much smaller, were approaching the house. Their footsteps thudded on the boards. The storm was wild behind them, the wind blowing them forward, pushing their hoods over their faces, wrapping their cloaks around. They were so dark. The porch lights were on but they remained unlit, like shadows, as if they didn't have light waves emanating from them. Like they were the opposite of light. It was hard to explain and I was also very drunk.

As the two mysterious people shuffled toward us down James's boardwalk, huddled and oh so dark, not dressed but costumed in cloaks that were thick, heavy, antique-looking, I decided to stay right there. Why go to the bathroom to change? Why not just pull my clothes on while hiding behind Hayley?

James didn't leave either. He pulled his pants up with familiar tugs and shifts and ran a hand through his hair like the sexy teenage quarterback he once was.

I looked away and down, noticing that my shirt's tag was hanging just under my chin. How did that even happen, inside out and backwards? I got my giggles back as James slid open the door.

"Can I help you?"

The ocean breeze whipped through sending a chill around the room. The smaller cloaked figure, a woman, stepped behind the larger man. She huddled there much like I huddled behind Hayley, which made me giggle more.

Hayley said, "Shush girlfriend, are you seeing this guy?" I peeked over her shoulder.

This guy was big. His face shadowed by the extremely dark cloak. The outline of his nose was strong, his jaw, chiseled. His clothing — both of their costumes — was full on cos-play. Like at Ren Faire. Like from a Hollywood movie. Like some of this made sense if I was in Los Angeles but I wasn't. I was in North East Florida, Fernandina Beach on tiny Amelia Island. There wasn't even a costume shop. Plus, this looked authentic, weirdly authentic. Specifically intricately detailed authentic.

Jeez, I was drunk.

He spoke. "Good evenin', sir. I am Magnus Archibald Caelhin Campbell. The Lady Delapointe and I find ourselves in need of fair lodging."

Hayley nudged me in my ribs but she didn't need to get my attention. Gotten, thank you. Because that voice was hot. It rumbled through the room like Chris Hemsworth's Thor voice, deep and accented and awesome, setting my insides all wiggly.

It sounded Scottish. Round, rolling along. The rumble stepping down from the beginning of the sentence to the end with a leap. I whispered to Hayley, "Jeez Louise, he's hella hawt."

"You said it girl."

But this is the strangest part — the smell that wafted in around them. It was thick but not bad, just different — electrified storm mixed with incense. It was enough for me to come out entirely from behind Hayley because yes, maybe I'd just breathe that in a bit.

I picked up a red cup that had 'Katie' scrawled around the top in sharpie pen and drank deeply. I wiped my chin on my arm because of spilling.

James seemed confused, but he was also drunk. He was probably thinking, "Off my porch, out of my house," but also if he was at all like me, it was hard to think. The stranger was big, dark, breathtaking, and something jutted up behind his head under his cloak that must have been a weapon. Did he have a freaking sword under there? This was all hard to mentally deal with and all I needed to do was stand and stare. I didn't have to be the person to call the cops. Or give them a ride to the hotel. Or call them an Uber. Or whatever this situation called for.

James asked, "Where did you come from?"

The man seemed to consider, then said, "We have only just arrived from Scotland, sir." Those Rs rolled through the word 'arrived' with a resonance that made me need to remind myself to breathe.

James said, "I see that." He looked around at us all with a look that meant, *are you kidding me with this?* He said, "I don't have room for you. There's a hotel down the street."

The man turned, met the eyes of the woman behind him, and turned back. "Tis far? We — we have traveled verra far this day and we haena horses."

"It's about two miles up on Sadler."

The man stood, head bowed, considering for a moment. "Pray, would ye be kind enough tae give us haven here under your protection, on your lands, tae rest until morning?"

James stifled a laugh. "Uh, yeah, my protection. Sure. Look, if y'all need to sleep you can do that under the house next door. It's empty, a short-term rental. The car park has some lawn chairs you can sleep in tonight." James looked out the door and scanned the sky. "It looks like the storm passed, so it will be dry enough."

He disappeared down the hallway and returned with two blankets and two pillows and awkwardly held them out.

The man continued to stand there, seemingly confused by what had transpired.

James looked confused too.

I said, "James, I think you should show them the chairs."

The man met my eyes. His were deep as night. His brow dark. He looked away.

"Yeah, good idea." James stepped through the sliding door to the porch and gestured with his head. "Follow me. And where about in Scotland did you say you were from?"

The man followed. "We hail from Argyll some of the year but more recently, Castle Balloch, the home of my uncle, the south bank of the River Tay."

The woman followed silently behind him, head demurely down.

When they left the porch, we all let out a collective breath of air.

"What the hell was that?" asked Michael.

A few minutes later James returned and repeated Michael, "What the hell was — did you see those people? Where'd they come from?" He went to the pitcher which was empty, but he tried to pour some, anyway. "Y'all drank all the Pirate's Punch?"

Hayley laughed. "I think you helped."

He swung open the fridge, found some orange juice, pulled a bottle of rum down from his liquor cabinet, unscrewed the cap, and poured himself a Screwdriver. "I notice y'all didn't send someone with me. Did you see the sword?"

Michael said, "Is that what was under his cloak?"

"That shit looked real. When he shifted, he opened his cape thing enough for me to see it. Shit, now I've given him a place to sleep a few feet away. What if he's a murderer?"

I laughed. "Murderers don't usually travel around in Ren Faire costumes. Kind of noticeable."

A song I liked came on and my rattled brain lost track of our conversation. I reached for James's drink and swigged some. "Hayley, dance?"

"You know it, girlfriend. I love me some Tay-Tay." We danced in the center of the room, by ourselves, creating a full-blown spectacle with our overly sexy gyrating and occasional stumbling. "I love you Hayley," I said as I accidentally tripped over the coffee table.

"I love you too, girl. I'm so glad you're home. We're going to have so much fun!"

The song wound down. We joined everyone else around the center island in the kitchen. I was flushed and hot and wind-blown and rather proud of myself for how attractive I felt.

James asked, "So Katie, you went to Los Angeles and you didn't make it into the movies. I'm surprised."

"There are a lot of pretty girls out there—"

Hayley, like a good friend, said, "Bullshit, you're beautiful. You were our prom queen. And you've got that whole thing — you look just like... What is her name? The one from that show where they all go to the coffee shop?"

I let her suffer for a moment trying to remember. Then to help her out I said, "Friends?"

"Yes! The one with the light brown hair, the really pretty one."

"Rachel?"

"Exactly, I've always said it."

James said, "You do, you look just like her. Beautiful."

I blushed, grabbed James's cup and took a long drink.

James asked, "Then what else do people do in Los Angeles if they aren't filming themselves?"

"Oxygen bars, yoga classes, vegan restaurants."

James joked, "Well, LA Girl, maybe in the morning I can remind you how delicious bacon is."

I slurred, "Oh I remember your bacon." And pretty much the whole party died laughing.

And then I vomited all over the floor.

Everyone screamed, gagged, and jumped out of my way.

I collapsed down and threw up again.

Last thing I remember, Hayley was holding my hair while I said, "I'm so sorry, I'm a huge—" I threw up more; it was probably time for me to go to sleep.

CHAPTER 2

I woke up the next morning on the floor of James's bathroom. My head rested on a rolled-up towel, a beach towel covered me. How old was I? Oh right, twenty-three. This had been a dumbass move.

What was I doing?

Being a dumbass.

And what a weird night. What a crazy storm.

And that Scottish guy was so hot. And mysterious. And — probably just a hallucination. My brain definitely wasn't functioning. Because of head pain, parched tongue, ugh, my skin hurt. Someone's red cup was beside the sink. I poured out the stale punch, filled it with water, and drank it down. Forgot how island water tasted — not great. Drank a second, then a third.

I looked like hell. Not good at all. I shuffled into the kitchen, finding my way easily having spent much of my youth here. I found my purse. My toothbrush was in there because I had suspected I might stay the night with James. I had planned, just not well enough because this was one of those Be Careful What You Wish For kind of things. I brushed my teeth, smeared on some lip balm, and wrapped my hair up in a messy bun, spot cleaning the vomit off my shirt.

I tiptoed through the house looking for anyone else awake. Hayley and Michael were sleeping in the extra bedroom. James's door was closed. Quentin snored on the couch. I couldn't figure out why I was up so early. I also couldn't agree with myself about whether I was still too drunk to drive. Probably. Maybe not. I tiptoed to the front door with my keys in my hand.

The heat of the day was in a full blaze, and it was only nine o'clock.

And whoa, there he was, the Scottish man from last night standing underneath the neighbor's house facing the dunes, cloaked, broad-shouldered, his stance firm. Hot. Definitely not a hallucination. His hood covered most of his face. The woman huddled on a lawn chair with her cloak wrapped around, clutching a large tapestry bag on her lap.

I paused for a moment. What was their deal?

The man called out, "Good mornin', Mistress..." I stopped walking as he drew closer. "Pray, where might I hire a horse, or — obtain a meal and lodging after our travels?" He glanced over his shoulder at his companion, seeming concerned about leaving her alone.

"There's a hotel, it has a restaurant." He watched my lips as I spoke. His brow knit, seeming confused, as if he was translating my words. I spoke the same language though, just not using the words in quite the same way, and without the same beautiful sexy lilt. "I could give you a ride."

"Aye," he nodded and returned for his companion. He led her across the sandy landscape with a steadying hand at her elbow.

I jingled my keys. My head was banging. My eyes were burning. It was sweltering hot out. My mouth tasted like a big wad of cotton had been dipped in a garbage can and stuffed into the spaces around my tongue. "My car is over here."

He followed me down the driveway, to the street where my Prius was parked all by itself on the shoulder like it had been abandoned. The man stared at it for a long and awkward pause. I guessed they wanted to sit together, so I opened the back door and gestured them in like a chauffeur.

They climbed in on the same side. She slid over and he threw his cloak off his shoulder, slid a long sword out from the harness across his back, and pulled himself in. He was big and had to duck uncomfortably, sliding the sword across my car's floorboards. When that didn't work he situated it diagonally. He wore a kilt, not the usual kind, small, pleated, and fitting, this one looked like wrapped fabric, draped, gathered, part of it twisted up over his shoulder. So much fabric he must have been sweltering.

Me too because every red-blooded American woman knows a kilt is the most goddamned sexy thing in the world and this was no exception.

His companion tucked into his shoulder her eyes clamped shut.

"I thank ye most heartily, mistress."

"No worries." I climbed in the driver's side, started the car, and pulled onto the beach road. When I glanced into the rearview mirror, his eyes were clamped shut too.

I didn't really have the mental health to strike up a conversation but it felt awkward to sit in silence so I started with, "You said you were from Scotland?"

He didn't open his eyes. "Aye, Argyll, the Highlands, and..."

"Will you be staying here long?"

He didn't answer but shook his head. Then his head lolled as if he was seasick and weak. I drove up to the hotel entrance. "This is the hotel — wait, oh, it looks like the restaurant is closed today. Are you hungry?"

He opened his eyes and looked around. "We are verra

famished, Mistress. Pray, if ye could spare a meal, it has been many long days since we have eaten."

"Yeah, I need a coffee and a muffin sandwich or eight. Do you like McDonalds?"

He scowled. "Mistress, I winna be welcome in the lands of Donald, our clans have been feudin' for many long years."

This cos-play thing was getting pretty weird. He was seriously immersed in his character; was he a method actor? But wouldn't he go to Scotland instead of Amelia Island? We had windswept dunes, not moors.

"Well, your feud won't matter, they'll give you something to eat no matter what, and I need it for my hangover. My name is Kaitlyn Sheffield, by the way." I wasn't sure why I gave him my full first name but his stiff formalities made me embarrassed to call myself Katie.

"I am Magnus Archibald Caelhin Campbell, this is Lady Mairead Campbell." He glanced at the woman beside him and added, "Lady Mairead Delapointe."

"Do I call you Magnus then?"

"Och, aye, Magnus." He made it sound like Mah-g-nus.

"Nice to meet you." I pulled my Prius to the road, headed toward the McDonalds, and looked back to see Magnus's eyes clamped shut again.

It dawned on me as I turned on Eighth Street that I should have checked to see if they had any money. Maybe they were homeless, or gypsies, or was that even a thing anymore?

Or what if this was part of a reality show? Maybe the cos-players were involving me because I was the notorious former YouTuber, KatieMakeSTuff, the girl that had that complete breakdown on Facebook Live. The girl who took her career and flushed it down the toilet by calling her fiancé a cocksucker while lunging at his face and trying to kick his ass pretty good.

Of course, it was the fault of the Mimosas I had been

drinking all morning while we tasted wedding cake samples. Just before he told me he didn't want to marry me because he had fallen in love with another YouTuber named Yummybabe.

I sighed. My user-name, KatieMakeSTuff, was an awesome play on words but beside sexy, cute Yummybabe I came off as pretty shrill and a lot psychotic. An embarrassment.

Braden fell in love with someone else but she was cute so no one blamed him. I took all the blame because I lunged across the table cursing like a pirate.

I was no longer fit to be on video.

Wait, was this a prank? Could Braden have sent this guy to embarrass me more? His ratings were slipping because ultimately he was hot but not very bright. He didn't have the abilities.

I really hoped he would fail, and I'm sure he knew it.

But ultimately he wasn't smart enough to prank me this good. Yummybabe wasn't either. She was dumb as rocks.

I pulled the Prius into the McDonalds drive-thru. "What do you want to eat?" I asked over my shoulder. His hands were gripped into tight fists. I turned my music down; maybe Katy Perry was too much this early in the morning.

His eyes met mine and held them, focused deep. "I dinna ken, Mistress Sheffield, though I am hungry enough tae eat a bear."

"They don't have bear — you've never had a McDonalds breakfast before? I can recommend the muffin sandwich, and their coffee is good. Would you like me to order something for you?"

His voice came up from his chest like a rumbling wave. "Aye, Mistress Sheffield, I haena been tae a place as this, I would be verra grateful."

"Okay then." I pulled into the drive-thru and ordered: seven muffin sandwiches, three coffees, three milks, and three waters. I didn't have nearly enough cup holders for this many drinks, but I was going to drain most of mine right there, anyway.

My two guests sat quietly in the back staring down at their hands. I asked, "Do you have any money?"

He looked at me quizzically, his brow pulled down in a question. Then he whispered with the woman beside him. Her voice was too low for me to hear what she was saying, but I didn't think it would matter because her words sounded unrecognizable.

Finally, Lady Mairead Delapointe yanked at the rope of the very large and full tapestry bag and from inside it pulled a coin. I call it a coin but it was clearly gold. And very old. And probably worth very much more than this meal.

"That's okay, wait, put that away. I mean, um, man—" I paid for our meal with my debit card. I pulled to the next window, received the food, and then considering the two did not look like they knew what to do with a bag of McDonalds food, pulled under the shade of an oak tree and kept the engine and AC running.

The two of them were still so dark and mysterious, was it soot? In contrast, everything around my car was lit in the full bright sun of a Florida summer morning. A morning that was already steaming and about to become scorching. I turned and passed them drinks. "Careful, very hot coffee." They both still seemed confused by everything about the meal, so I ate with big flourishes, opened my coffee, stirred it, blew into it, then closed the lid and showed them how to drink from it. Then I unwrapped a muffin sandwich and ate it with big copyable gestures. It was a lot like what I used to do on YouTube. I had forgotten his answer before so I asked again, "So where in Scotland are you from?"

He furrowed his brow. "You know of Scotland?"

"I do. I've seen Braveheart." I grinned.

He said, "My new residence is Balloch Castle, the home of

my uncle, the Earl of Breadalbane. Tis on the south bank of the River Tay."

"Oh," I said, as if that explained it.

While he spoke the woman's hood slid off the back of her head exposing her full face to me for the first time. She was really beautiful but her cheeks were marred by deep, jagged, red scars. Magnus carefully helped her unwrap her sandwich. It dawned on me he could have been the person who scarred her.

Maybe I was involved in a kidnapping, or people trafficking — crap. My heart raced. I needed to get them to a police station. Plus the sword. Any man who walked around in 2017 with a sword probably had a lot of baggage.

Magnus ate like he was famished. Devoured the sandwich, opened another one, and then a third. I built up my nerve, my phone in my lap, finger poised on 911. Then, while he was chewing, I looked directly at her and jumped in, "Lady Mairead, um — do you need help? Is this the man who hurt you?"

"Magnus has rescued me from my second husband, Lord Delapointe. You have nocht tae fear from my son, I promise ye."

"You're sure?" I watched her face for any sign of stress.

"I am sure."

"Oh, good, thank you. My apologies."

She said, "Thank ye for your kindness."

Magnus had been looking between my face and Lady Delapointe's during our exchange. His brow drew down but he didn't seem overly bothered by my accusation.

I relaxed and ate a few more bites of a second muffin while stealing glances at Magnus. He was handsome, broad-shouldered; that knee jutting up without a cover was a seriously sexy knee. And what was wrong with me? I shouldn't have been this desperate. How long had it been, less than a month since I loved Braden and thought he loved me back?

I was planning to marry him, and then he didn't want me anymore.

Our wedding date would have been next weekend.

I scowled.

Magnus said, "You dinna like your muffins, Mistress Sheffield? Tis a braw feast ye laid out for us." He licked his fingers, grinned, picked up his coffee cup, and drank deeply.

I smiled back. "I like it. It's my favorite meal to fix a hangover." Then I segued. "I know this is a tricky question but that gold piece you showed me, do you have a lot of it?"

His hand edged closer to his thigh. He had another weapon there, probably. The hilt of his sword, laying on the floorboards of my Prius looked precious too, antique and authentic looking. Perhaps a family heirloom? If so, it needed to be in a museum, not laying under the bed at the local hotel.

"I mean, if you have a lot of it, gold, you can't just check into a hotel like that. You'll get robbed. Seriously. I mean they'll have a safe box for you but if you have more than a few pieces it needs to be in a bank. For protection."

"This bank would have men guardin' it?"

"Sure. Enough. My dad works there."

Magnus nodded. "Aye. Will ye passage us tae the bank, Mistress Sheffield?"

I started the car and drove it out of the lot and pointed it in the direction of the First Coast of the United Bank.

At the receptionist's desk I asked for my dad. He came to the lobby under the impression that it was a personal visit but it wasn't. "Dad, these are um..." How to explain these strange strangers, wearing a sword and carrying a bag of gold? "This is Lady Mairead Delapointe and, um—"

The woman interrupted to correct me, "I am Lady Dela-pointe, or Lady Mairead, which I prefer."

"Yes, and Magnus Campbell, they need to make a deposit." I gestured toward the tapestry bag Lady Mairead was carrying and introduced my father. "This is John Sheffield."

My dad looked flustered at their costumes but led them through to his office. I opted to stay in the lobby, waiting. It was none of my business, plus I had three missed calls from Hayley. "What's up?"

"Where'd you go, girl? We woke up and you were gone."

"Funny thing about that. I was going to pick everyone up some muffins and coffee but that couple from last night—"

"What? Who — oh the hunka hunka Scotsman? I almost forgot them in the fog. That was fun, huh, and so weird. James keeps asking for you."

"Yeah, yeah, tell him I'm sorry I ran out this morning and sorry I didn't bring the muffins back, but I'm at the bank with that couple. They needed a ride and food and now a place to store their money..."

"So you're hung-over, driving the weirdos around the island, being a tour guide? How LA of you."

"Yeah, I guess so—"

"James wants you to meet us tonight at the Turtle in down-town. Isn't that awesome? We can all four of us hang out together all the time."

My dad stepped out of his office heading across the lobby towards me. "I have to go Hayley, I'll see if I can make it tonight. I haven't even showered yet so it's hard to imagine doing anything. I'll call you back later."

His face was flushed, excited, but he held his voice down. "Where did you find these people?"

I answered vaguely, "Friends of friends."

"You were right to bring them here, have you seen what they have?"

"It looked like gold."

"Piles of gold, also jewels, also a ring that looks very, very old. It will all need to be appraised of course but market value on the gold is at least $200,000." My dad had a habit of taking off his glasses and rubbing where they pressed on his nose when he was attempting to control his excitement. He slid his glasses back on. "I've called your mother, she's on her way—"

"Mom, what does — Dad, is Mom coming to sell them a house?"

"She has a house that will do for them, I think. She can short-term lease it to them. It's on the beach, very ritzy."

"I was going to take them to a hotel."

"Don't be ridiculous. Have you heard where they're from? They lived in a castle, Katie. Let your mother and I do our jobs."

I blew out a breath of air. "Fine, but it seems kind of unethical..."

"To get them in a home, like they're used — here comes your mother now."

My mom blew in through the front doors headed straight for us. "Hello Katie. John, are they in your office?"

My parents bustled into dad's office together. At this point I was not needed at all but felt sort of responsible for Magnus and Lady Mairead, so I lurked around, playing on my phone until they all walked out of the office together. My parents were dressed in their Summer Suits for Selling People Big Expensive Things. Magnus and Lady Mairead were in their dark cloaks, hoods up. The tapestry bag looked empty and light. Magnus's sword remained, jutting up, behind his head. No one had convinced him to put it into the safe, so maybe it was a fake after all.

My mother said, "I didn't know you'd still be here, Katie."

"I wanted to make sure Magnus and Lady Mairead didn't need a ride to—"

My mother said, "Oh dear, no, I'll take them. I need to give them the keys and show them the amenities, anyway."

She headed toward the parking lot with a follow me gesture but before he left Magnus stood in front of me to speak. "Thank ye, Mistress Sheffield, most heartily for the food and the care this morning. I hope tae meet ye again someday." He offered Lady Mairead his arm and they swept into the bright heat of a Florida day.

CHAPTER 3

On Monday, after a weekend of going out with Hayley, Michael, and James, I woke up bored. Everyone I knew had to work. I was tempted to go by and see what Magnus was doing because he was new to the island after all. I could be a tour guide. But also, why? I had given them a ride; how creepy would that be?

But boredom won out. I decided to use the beach access closest to their new house to look for shark teeth. That way if I saw Magnus or Lady Mairead I could pretend to be 'just walking by.'

I took a baggie for collecting shark teeth and shells and parked my Prius on the shoulder of the road. I walked out on the beach and checked out the house.

It was different from the classic beach houses that used to line the shore here. Those had been built up on stilts in case of floodwater. With thin legs, wind-pummeled wood, and low slung roofs, they seemed a part of the landscape. The stilts gave them lift, as if the wind could carry them if it wanted to, it just had to decide to.

This one was newer, hulking, huge. Built. Like it was daring the wind to try to carry it away, just try.

After Mom had unloaded her biggest house on them, we celebrated that night at dinner, with Mom and Dad congratulatory toasting and clinking their wineglasses. I found it troubling. There was nothing wrong with leasing a mansion to the rich foreigner but there was something about Magnus that made me think he deserved better. His manners? Maybe it was because I'd never been involved in my mother's business deals before. She was often described as a shark, and I didn't believe the term to be unfair.

The beach was beautiful, warm, full sun, a bit cooler than last Thursday by degrees. It was still a June summer in Florida of course, ninety-two degrees instead of soaring over a hundred.

The sand was so pretty, white and glistening. The tide was heading low revealing bounteous beautiful unbroken shells. I crouched in the wet sand at the edge of the warm, gently lapping waves, searching, occasionally scooping — there! A shark tooth. Small, but perfect, and I had found it within the first three minutes. After the first one they would be easy to find because my brain could focus.

I felt so happy to be home suddenly, in this beautiful place. Where better to walk and think through what went wrong? And my role in the whole debacle? I hadn't done that much.

Instead I had regressed into my past self: daughter, party girl, bestie. I supposed that was common, after a world-wide embarrassment, *regressing*. What did celebrities do — check into rehab? Go to a spa? Or in the case of minor celebrities, like me, less famous, more viral, especially now I had bared my teeth and drunkenly slashed across my fiancé's face on live video — go to their parents' beach town and hide away.

I approached the boardwalk entrance of Magnus's house. It didn't look like anyone was — wait, the entire front of the house was glass and someone was sitting in the top left window.

This was awkward.

Could I make myself look casual and not weird at all? I stepped on the stairs, then took my foot back to the sand, changing my mind. But Magnus turned and peered through the window.

I was seen.

He gestured me to the house, then met me at the sliding door but didn't open it. He pushed awkwardly, a little desperately, at the handle then shrugged.

I peered in through the glass for the lock. Every one of these door handles was different but this one was basic. I mimed pushing the lever up. Then pointed at the top of the door where there would be a second lock and pantomimed how to unlock it as well.

I slid the door wide with a smile. "How are you Magnus Campbell?"

"Nae good, Mistress Sheffield. I daena feel well, and Lady Mairead is verra ill." He was agitated and sweaty. No wonder, the place was stifling hot. "Will ye see her? I haena been tae hunt yet. I canna leave her side these many days."

"Oh, oh no, Magnus, yes, where is she?"

He rushed up the steps, with me a second behind. He pushed open the door of a bedroom, and I rushed to the edge of the bed. "Lady Mairead?"

She moaned. Her face was red hot, her breathing labored.

Magnus said, "I dinna ken what tae do. She needs food..."

"You don't have any food?"

He looked at his feet. "I dinna dare leave her."

"Oh." A full sweat dripped down my face. Was the AC broken? I checked her forehead. It was very hot, definitely fever-ish. She convulsed with a scary sounding cough.

"She has been coughin' for two days past."

"We need to get her to the hospital."

"A physician?"

"Yes." My heart raced as I dialed 911 on my phone and explained to the dispatcher that I needed an ambulance. I didn't know the address, so I guessed at the street number, the road name, and the description of the front of the house. I told them I would meet them outside.

I hung up, my hands shaking.

He hung his head. "I must go with her. I have sworn tae protect her."

"You can, but wait here now. I'll go downstairs and wait for the ambulance. Then we can all ride to the hospital together."

He nodded gratefully and returned to the chair pulled alongside the bed. I raced down the stairs.

The house was huge, modern, very, very white, stark glass and metal, with accents of colored modernist plastic. The furniture was spare. Giant dried starfish hung on the tall living room wall. How did the Scottish man in traditional Scottish clothes feel about his new castle? I located the AC controls near the laundry room door off the kitchen. It was a sleek box, mostly hidden, with digital controls. I punched quite a few numbers before the central air conditioning purred to life, thank god. I lifted my shirt and fanned my belly. How long had they been sweltering in here? I glanced around and yanked open the refrigerator. It was off. Empty.

I was going to kill my mom.

CHAPTER 4

The ambulance arrived about fifteen minutes later and bundled Lady Mairead into the back. Magnus and I followed in my Prius and arrived just behind it. I wanted to handle the paperwork but knew nothing past her name. I asked Magnus for their passports but at his confused expression invented a back story: "They were robbed when they left the airport. His new passport hasn't arrived yet, but he's a UK citizen. He's leasing a beachfront — you know, here — call my father. He'll vouch for him." I gave them my dad's private phone number, then my mom's.

Magnus and I sat in the hallway, side by side. He looked very worried and haggard.

"She'll be okay. They'll treat her for infection, help her rest, then she can go home."

He nodded quietly. Then dropped his head back to the wall. "I am verra much starv'd."

"Oh, right, stay here in case they need to speak to you. I'll run and get you something." I hustled down to the cafeteria and bought Magnus a club sandwich, chips, and a soda. Also a water.

I handed him the food but then took it again, twisted the cap off the cola, and opened the packaging on his sandwich because he looked at everything as if seeing if for the first time.

After he devoured the food, I asked, "Do you need me to stay?"

"Aye, Mistress Sheffield. If you could remain while I wait, I would be verra indebted."

"You know, you can call me Kaitlyn, thanking Mistress Sheffield sounds too formal."

"Aye, Mistress Kaitlyn, then. I thank ye for your kindness both formally and informally." The edge of his mouth went up a bit in a smile.

It was about five o'clock when the doctor finally spoke with us about her case. He looked Magnus up and down, much the way everyone looked him up and down because of that freaking kilt. I had urged him to wrap his sword in his cloak but the large bundle was there beside him. His boots were leather, wrapped with more leather. Even the bottoms were not formed so much as molded to his foot, much like baby shoes.

Yet even with these ancient trappings, he was tall and attractive so people seemed to move quickly past his oddities. Case in point: I was helping him. Though in my defense he had a way of speaking, low and intense, plus a way of looking kind of lost that made me keep on helping.

"We have stabilized her and are treating the viral infection and the dehydration. She has what amounts to the flu, and her immune system is very weak." He squinted his eyes. "It doesn't say on her records what her age is, this is your wife?"

"Nae, the Lady Delapointe is my mother."

"Ah. She must be at least forty-five then? Can you explain the scars on her cheeks?"

"Her husband has done it."

I added, "That's why they're here, I think."

The doctor asked, "You're Katie Sheffield, your father is John Sheffield at the bank?"

"That's me, I grew up here. This is my friend." Then to give him some information that might make sense, I added, "I've been living in LA."

He said, "Oh, right. That makes sense. All right then, the Lady Delapointe needs to stay overnight—"

Magnus interrupted, "She canna, I need tae—"

I put a staying hand on his arm. "It's all right Magnus, she's protected here." I turned to the doctor. "Will she sleep all night?"

"Yes, until morning. You can return tomorrow during visiting hours, and if she's better she may go home tomorrow evening."

Magnus turned to me, his face drawn and worried. "There are many windows, a road just beyond the walls. Would it be possible for him tae station guards?"

The doctor looked from me to Magnus. "No, but I can have someone close the curtains."

"It will be okay, Magnus. I can drive you home and you'll be back tomorrow when she wakes up."

He stared at the door of the room. "How far away would I be then?"

"About ten minutes."

He looked like he was calculating the distance. "Aye, t'would be an acceptable distance. I shall return tae my house."

The doctor said, "Good, visiting hours begin at nine o'clock." He strolled away.

Magnus's mind still seemed worried, but he said, "Pray, Mistress Kaitlyn, where would I forage for more food? My middle is achin', and I'm afeared my tartan is loosenin' and may fall tae my knees. T'would be a scandal. My hunger dinna cease with these — what did ye say they are called?"

I smirked. "Pre-packaged, institutional, vending machine junk food. Yes, we can get better."

CHAPTER 5

$\mathcal{T}$he heat hit like a wall when we stepped out of the hospital. I half expected it to be night but it was only six pm, a summery six. It dawned on me we might go out and eat at a restaurant but also his mother was in the hospital. And he hadn't even turned on his AC at home yet, so I figured the nicest thing would be to take him to a grocery store. As my grandmother would have said, "Help that man get his feet under him. So you can climb him like a tree."

I tried to hide my amusement as I held the Prius's passenger door open because Magnus seemed confused by the handles, the doors, the seats. As I started the car, he flicked the vents on the air conditioning up and down. He pushed a button and startled when his window slid open and closed. As soon as I pulled onto the road, he clamped his eyes tight and held the dashboard.

I tried to think of reasons why he was so weird about my car. The door handle might be explained because he usually rode with a chauffeur. The AC — maybe it was always cold in Scotland? The windows — Scottish cars must be very different. He mentioned horses, right? Maybe he was a farmer. Probably old-timey, like the Amish.

I turned on the radio, one of my favorite old songs, and watched him peripherally. His eyes were closed tight, his head lolling loosely as I drove onto 12th Street and sped to thirty-five miles per hour.

At the grocery store I parked under a blaring street lamp. "This is an American grocery store. Ever been in one?"

He peered up at the giant sign and quickly at the cars and people and shook his head slowly. "I have never even seen one."

"You are in for a treat. What is your favorite thing to eat?"

He didn't think at all. "I verra much like leg of lamb, though I am famished enough for the whole sheep."

"Well that might not be available in the deli department. I was planning to get an assortment of readymade food and take it to your house. I'm a good cook but maybe not leg-of-lamb good."

We entered through the front doors and were hit in the face by a blast of cold air. Also the collective gasp of the store's entire customer base. Everyone stared at Magnus and then glanced warily at me. He was indifferent, going back out through the door and coming in again, looking around at the signs, up at the electric mechanism, up at the drop-tile ceiling, and dazedly around at the whole store. Which made everyone stare even harder.

I couldn't blame them — he had that unexplainable darkness, shadowy and mysterious — the cloak, the sword, the leather shoes. Plus he smelled like that combination of incense, dust, and old church. And Kilt. And Big. And Hot, like really, really hot.

I led him to the deli and began ordering: roasted chicken, fried chicken, pulled pork, a couple of baked potatoes, a tub of macaroni and cheese. He reached for a dark pumpernickel bread, a kind that did not look appetizing to me at all, watching me for cues, then placed it in our cart too.

I picked some spreadable cheeses and another loaf of bread,

French. "More my style." I scooped a tub of olives into the cart. Then, after all of that asked, "Do you like ice cream?"

He blinked and thought for a moment. When he was considering information he wasn't sure about, he squinted. "Aye?"

"Good answer." I pushed the cart, leading him toward the frozen food section, noticing that he jingled under his cloak. There must have been a buckle near his sword, adding to his oddness, causing people to step out of his way and point.

I chose a gallon of salted caramel ice cream, a gallon of chocolate-chocolate brownie surprise, and two gallons of plain vanilla because that seemed like it would be his style, though he didn't seem to know what any of it was.

I led him down an aisle past the paper products, grabbing toilet paper, soap, and paper towels while he stood idly by, to the alcohol section. "Beer, ale, wine."

His eyes went wide. "Ah, this I recognize." He eagerly looked up and down the coolers.

I pointed to the middle shelf. "There's a Scottish ale here."

His eyes widened as he read the labels. He lifted three six packs, four liters, and a growler into the cart. "We just carry this all away with us?"

"After we pay for it. Wait, did the bank give you a way to pay for things?"

He swept his cloak aside revealing a fur pouch hanging just below his waist. He opened it and pulled out a credit card, bright green, plastic. "I have entrusted the bank with an entire fortune and in exchange they have given me the use of this small green tile."

I grinned. "That's as good as money and better than carrying the gold around, I promise. I'll show you how it works."

I let him push because the cart was piled very high. Plus, he needed something to do besides gawking at everything. Other customers made way for us as I led him to the register.

The cashier said, "Katie? Katie Sheffield?"

"Yep, that's me."

She scanned some ice cream. "I was ahead of you in school. When did you graduate?" I told her and she said, "I was three classes ahead of you."

"Oh, sure. I think I remember you."

She stopped scanning, her hand resting on the toilet paper. "I'm Sandy Adams, remember?"

"Oh yeah, of course," I lied.

"That super sucks what happened to you. We were all so proud of our Katie making it big time in Los Angeles and then — that was crazy. My friend Stella, remember her, Stella Winger?"

I shook my head.

"Well she thinks you deserved to lose everything but I said no way that guy was a total asshole. Oops, sorry. He deserved what you did to him. He posted a video today; did you know he still has marks on his face? Anyway, are you living here now?"

Her eyes darted up to Magnus.

I sighed, "I'm staying here for a bit that's all." I found myself looking around for an escape route, but sadly I couldn't leave Magnus here with a pile of food and a plastic tile he didn't know how to use. She finished scanning our food and then I slid his card through the machine and asked him for his PIN number.

He answered, "One. Seven. Nocht. Two."

"Nocht means zero right?"

We hefted the sacks of food into the trunk of my car. My mood had grown sour; the conversation with the cashier embarrassed me, and I hated that Magnus heard it.

Why though? Why was I here, doing this? Sympathy? Charity? Because he was wearing a freaking skirt?

I figured it was because he was the one guy in the whole universe who didn't know about my YouTube fiasco but now, guess what? He knew.

CHAPTER 6

*W*e lugged groceries up to the kitchen and Magnus made another trip to the car while I turned on the refrigerator and loaded food onto the shelves. I had almost forgotten how much I loved this kind of thing, unpacking into an empty house. When I unpacked into my dorm room it had been so exciting, my first time away from my parents. When I unloaded boxes of my things and Braden's things into our Los Angeles apartment, we were embarking on a life together. After the stress of a move it was fun to open boxes, unpack, and decide where to put everything, creating order out of chaos. Maybe this was a good life-calling for me, unpacking boxes — what would that career be, a mover?

I found dishes, salt and pepper, and spread our meal on the kitchen island.

"A cold wind is blowin' through." He watched a plume of air blowing from a vent.

"I turned your AC on before I left."

"Och, ye are Mistress Kaitlyn of the North Winds. I will

invite ye here every day tae cool my castle." We pulled legs off the roasted chicken and ate with our fingers. He ate as if he was starved and followed each bite with big thirsty gulps of beer. His smile was warm and inviting.

"So how did the American grocery store and food compare to your stores at home?"

"The stores here lack much in the way of dirt and grime. A loaf of bread such as this would have required a thorough dusting, perhaps a washing. And I dinna need tae argue for the price either. Just last week I had tae haggle with Auld Woman McGeene, she was fitful and ornery as a bear. Had a beard like one too." I laughed as he licked chicken grease off his thumb with a contented grin. "After this meal I might become more my former self."

"Might?"

"Aye, my temples ache from the brightness of this eternal flame."

"Oh." I glanced around the bottom floor of his house. It had soaring ceilings, giant windows, and though darkening now, with shadow and sunset, had been bright as the surface of the sun and almost as hot when I had walked in earlier that day. Now, this evening, I had turned on every overhead light I could find and pushed the dimmers all the way up. It was very bright.

"Here, let me show you." I brought him to the light switches on the kitchen wall and showed him which dimmer worked for which lights. I turned them all down except for the under-cabinet lights. It was much nicer. Then I led him to the wall of windows looking over the beach. There, beside the sliding glass doors, was a control box. "Not sure how this works actually but we'll push buttons until we figure it out."

I tried a few combinations until the windows tinted dark. Then I found another combination that caused screens to slide down.

Magnus watched as the wall of windows darkened. Quietly he said, "Pray, shew me the buttons again, Mistress Kaitlyn."

I did the combination again. The screen slid up. I did it a third time and the screen went down. He watched carefully each time. "This was past my understandin'."

I said, "No worries, Magnus. You try it."

He pushed the buttons. The screen slid up and then back down. This time though he didn't watch it slide. Instead he stared at the box, his brow drawn. He shook his head. "You must think me as dim-witted as a bairn."

"A bairn?"

"A child."

"Ah. You know, if you need to know something, just ask. I'll tell you. Without judgement. I love to show people how to do things. I'm quite bossy actually, and it's kind of what my job was before."

"What do ye mean, your job?" We returned to the kitchen island.

"I used to make videos where I explained how to do things." I glanced around the kitchen, took a big swill of heather ale, and assembled a few things for a demonstration. There was a microwave hidden within a cupboard. A cutting board in a drawer. I had bought a four pack of ivory soap bars.

I arranged them on the counter, and paused first, like I was filming. "Hi, This is KatieMakeSTuff and today I'm going to teach you how to make an erupting lava magical soap cloud..." I grinned widely, held up the bar of soap, and slowly and enthusiastically peeled the paper off. "For this magic, Ivory soap is the only soap that works. I don't know why — I should probably research that, but trust me." I held the soap up right by my eyes and did my trademark 'cute' grin. Then I placed the soap on a paper plate on the spinner, closed the microwave door with a slam, and set the power on high for two minutes. "Now watch the magic happen." Magnus stood beside me as the soap spun, bubbled, and then burst up in a puffing cloud. "Awesome, huh?"

He peered through the window. "Tis extraordinary."

When the soap finished erupting, I pushed the cancel button and pulled out the plate. Magnus poked the cloud of soap. "What other magic can this box do?"

"It heats up food." I tossed a piece of bread in, warmed it for a few seconds, and gave it to him to eat. "Anyway, that's the gist of my videos — showing how to do things."

"I have something — tis indelicate but most imperative."

"Yes?"

"Where does one relieve themselves here in the New World?"

"Magnus, did you not have running water in your castle in Scotland?"

He laughed. "You answered a question with another question. In a situation that requires action ye may wish tae speak more swiftly than this."

I jumped from my seat. "Follow me." The bathroom closest to the kitchen was, as my mom would have said, too tiny by half, so I rushed him through the downstairs master bedroom to the gigantic full bathroom beyond. He appraised the room as if he'd never seen it before.

"Have you never been in here — wait, no more questions, here's how it works. This is the toilet. You relieve yourself here, standing, like this." I mimicked how he would stand there, even pretending to hike a skirt because I was feeling silly as hell, plus pretty buzzed.

He laughed, so that was good.

"Then you flush here." I pushed the handle down. He watched dutifully.

"If you need to do something more, or if you're a woman, like me, you sit like this. You flush the same though. Then you wash your hands here. And, oh wait, here's toilet paper." I wound a bit and mimed wiping with it. I knew some Europeans used bidets, so I felt safe assuming it was foreign to him.

I really needed to look up Scotland and figure out why I knew nothing about how backwards it was. I had been living in LA for a while though; it was easy to forget every place on earth wasn't as cosmopolitan. Plus, I was on a self-imposed 'break' from looking things up. Whenever I went online, something reminded me of that day with Braden when my whole world went to hell.

"You put it in the toilet, flush it, and then wash your hands."

I paused for a second appraising the room and enjoying how awesome my explanation had been and how thorough.

He asked, "I am expected tae do this with company?"

"Oh no! Close the door, lock it for privacy. Here, on the handle." I showed him the handle lock and scooted out.

I was seated at the kitchen island, giggling, when he emerged a few minutes later because the toilet flushed six times. I joked, "Everything turn out okay?"

He chuckled.

"Have you been holding it for four days Magnus?"

"No, I haena the stamina but we winna discuss the how or where of my earlier necessities."

I laughed again. "Sounds good. I will ask no questions, except — inside or out?"

"Out."

"Well, it can't be helped. If anyone asks, tell them teenagers did it before you arrived. You'd be surprised how much trouble people will ignore if you say 'teenagers' with just the right amount of incredulousness."

"Teenagers?"

"People aged thirteen to nineteen."

"Ah. Notorious troublemakers but excellent fighters. They daena fear death. My cousin is aichteen, I am verra worried about him that I am nae in London tae see tae him. How old are ye, Mistress Kaitlyn?"

"I'm twenty-three."

"And you belong tae the man I met the other night?"

I coughed out a spray of beer. "What? Who, James? Oh my god, *belong*? Magnus, I don't know how it works in the hinterlands of Scotland but here in America women don't belong to men; we're equals."

He raised his brow with a chuckle. "I only meant are ye married tae him?"

"God no." I sighed. "No, just — I don't know... We used to date. We were very serious at one time, but no, not married. Can we put this on a list of things I don't feel like talking about? Let's change the subject."

Magnus nodded and swigged from a beer. "Pray tell me more about your job."

"Let's see, well, my videos would get millions of views. My most popular video was..." To be truthful, my most popular video was when I leapt across the table full of sample wedding cake slices. They smeared all over my dress but I didn't care. I was too busy aiming my fingernails at my fiancé's face. But instead of mentioning that one, I told Magnus about my second most popular video. "I devised three questions to ask on a first date that will tell you all you need to know about someone. People loved that video. A lot of my viewers told me it helped them, so that was great." I swigged some more ale and sighed. "You know, I don't really want to talk about it?"

"Aye, Mistress Kaitlyn, your list of unwanted conversations is quite long."

"It is, embarrassingly long." My phone interrupted us with a series of notifications, one after another, Snapchats from Hayley and James.

Hayley's said: Are you coming?
   And: When will you get here?
   Then: You promised!
   And: Where are you?

Until finally: Okay if you don't answer, I'm calling your mom. I'll tell her I saw you in a crop-top hanging out at Main Beach partying with some really wild Georgia boys and you'll be grounded for a week like the good old days.

James's said: Can't wait to see you tonight.

They were all at the Turtle already, Monday night drinking, their weekly meet-up. I had told them I would come and now it was 8:30 already.

I answered back: Something came up. Can't make it tonight. I'll see you later in the week?

James sent back: Friday night? I'd like to take you out to dinner. A date?

. . .

I glanced quickly at Magnus but there was no reason to feel weird. This was just a sympathy bedside visit while "someone's mom was sick" kind of thing. Not a date, of course. Whatever.

I answered back: I'd like that.

To Hayley I sent a selfie cross-eyed with my tongue out that said: Can't come, feeling too peculiar. Will call tomorrow.

When I glanced up Magnus was watching me closely his eyes squinted, confused again.

I explained, "My friend Hayley is asking if I will come to the Turtle tonight. It's like a pub. I was telling her I couldn't come, the photo was to be funny."

"Och, aye." He chuckled. "It looked as if ye had gone like Auld Man McGeene. He is afflicted with one eye that rolls away, so his mind goes runnin' in search of it. Tis nae easy tae converse with him."

I laughed.

Magnus said, "I like having ye here. I daena like being alone in this house. But you have somewhere tae be, so I winna keep ye."

I blushed a bit. "It's not that important. Plus I've probably had too much to drink to be driving downtown anyway..." I changed the subject. "You aren't the biggest fan of this house?"

"The biggest fan?"

"You don't like it?"

"Ah." He looked up and around at the overly tall flat walls, the endless windows, the faraway ceilings, and back at me. "This house has improved tenfold since ye arrived. One hundred-fold since ye spread the table with food. Verra much more since ye taught me where tae relieve myself."

We both laughed but his meaning was plain: this house didn't suit him at all. "I feel partly responsible for your situation with this house because it was my mom who leased it to you. How about we make a list of what you need to make it livable?" I fished in a drawer for the pad I knew would be there — a notepad with a photo of my mom above her motto, "Buying and selling dreams!" I found a pen at the bottom of my purse. A bank pen. From Dad. I looked expectantly at Magnus. "What's wrong with this house?"

"Hot as a demon's breath with nae fire tae dampen."

I wrote too hot and placed a check mark beside it. I liked to list things and check them off. It made me feel successful. "Too hot, we fixed that with the AC setting. Next."

"I had a pain in my head because of the blaring lights."

"Too bright. Got it. Now you know how to close the screens and dim the lights." I checked that off too.

"I was most desperately starv'd."

"Check." I grinned and gestured at the counter covered with deli food trash and empty beer bottles.

He said, "Mistress Kaitlyn, ye have saved my life."

"You sir, are over-dramatic."

He chuckled, low and rumbling. "Well, I need nocht else but Lady Mairead will need someone tae help her dress."

My pen stopped in midair. "To dress? Is she an invalid?"

"She is used tae many comforts. Dressing is but one of them and I canna be the one."

I blinked. "Well, you probably need a staff, I mean, you have the money. Lady Mairead is used to having someone take care of her. Do either of you know how to cook?"

"Nae need. I will ride tae the food stores each day."

"Ugh. I mean this is great mac and cheese, but I promise you won't be able to eat it for four days before you're sick and tired of it. It's the same as McDonalds, can't eat it every day. You'll need a personal chef. Also a maid. Do you clean house?"

"Nae. I daena care for it."

"Exactly. So if you hired a staff to give Lady Mairead the comforts she's used to, how many people would you need?"

He listed on his fingers. "Cook, laundry, clean, tae market, dressing. I will need a man tae be in charge of the stables. Also, weapons. Would I be able tae find some men tae protect the walls?"

"Security you mean? And hold on, a stable?"

"For my horses. And security, tae protect Lady Mairead."

I dropped the pen. "Is she in danger? Who is she in danger from, her husband?"

His brow furrowed. "I dinna mean tae worry ye. Twill take time for Lord Delapointe tae find us but tis my duty tae protect her. I will need men day and night."

I added that to the bottom of the list and circled it. "But I'm safe here, right?"

His hand rested on the handle of a long knife he wore at his hip. "Aye," he met my eyes and held them. "Nocht will happen tae ye."

I looked away to count down the list. He would need at least five people, maybe more.

"Hayley runs her family's temp agency. I'll call her and ask if she has any people." I pulled up my phone and called Hayley right then.

She answered, "Hey girl! You should come, I'm doing shots!"

"What kind?"

"Absolut Legspreaders!" She giggled wildly.

"Awesome. Hey, you know that guy from the other night, the one in the kilt?"

It was loud where she was; she yelled, "The hottie in the kilt?"

Her voice carried through the phone causing Magnus's brow to draw together.

"His mother is in the hospital, so I'm helping him arrange for when she comes home tomorrow. I wanted to know if—"

"You're with the hottie in the skirt right now? You blew us off for a skirt-wearing Scottish guy?"

"Can James hear you right now?"

"No, I got up from the table before you said all this crazy bullshit. You have a date with James in a few days right?"

"I do. This is just business."

"What kind of business? Are you YouTube videoing him? Are you making porn with the kilt guy?" She giggled drunkenly. "I mean, there are worse things, of course, but if you go being a porn star with MacDickson, you won't marry James and have babies at the same time as me. Our babies need to grow up together—" I put my hand over the phone to cut off her words, stood up, and left for the laundry room. I lowered my voice to a whisper. "I'm not marrying James. We have one date planned. Plus, if you remember, he *played* me last time. Played me hard. Broke my heart."

"He's changed though, Katie. He really has."

"Bullshit. Where are you right now?"

"The sidewalk out front."

"Look through the window. What's James Cook doing right now?"

"Um..."

"Exactly. Who is he talking to?"

"Christina, you remember her from school? She's in my seat."

"Is she flipping her hair, Hayley? Is he spinning his beer bottle and doing that lopsided smile thing?"

"Katie, I'm going to kill you. Just don't make porn with the Scottish guy, and please give James a chance on Friday, for me, *please*?"

"I am going on the date. And this is just business. And I need you to call me when you get to the office tomorrow. I need to hire about..." I had forgotten how many people, so I quickly counted. "Five people. Possibly more."

"Crap girl, that will make my quota. I'll call first thing. Don't do anything I wouldn't do!"

"Doesn't leave much."

I walked back into the kitchen. It was awkward to go from talking about Magnus when he could hear me, to speaking to him directly. "Sorry about that, my friend Hayley has opinions she likes to share, loudly. I'll organize it with her though, and she'll send some people tomorrow.

He was standing beside his barstool. I was standing beside mine.

He said, "T'would establish me verra well tae have more men. Tis been a long and arduous week. I dinna ken what I would do without your assistance."

"You probably need to rest...I should probably go..." I pulled my purse off the back of my chair. Trouble was I didn't really want to. This was the most relaxed I'd been in days. I loved meeting someone new, especially when they were like this, nonjudgmental.

He said, "I know ye have somewhere tae be but if ye dinna — would ye stay here tonight? I have rooms aplenty. I daena much like the idea of being alone — the house is verra strange still but your presence has improved it measurably."

He looked uncomfortable and that had been really sweet. And my other options weren't great. If I went home now, Mom and Dad would still be up. They'd talk to me about my "plans" and I was a little too tipsy for that. Or the inverse, they would ignore me and act like I was in their space. Which I was. Eating their food. Watching TV in their living room. Sleeping in the guest room because my old room had been turned into their gym.

As Mom helpfully pointed out, "You were getting married that means you don't live here anymore."

I could show up at the Turtle. That would be pretty funny since James was flirting with someone, but also, Hayley sounded full-blown buzzed. That would not be fun to walk into the middle of. Also, how much had I been drinking? Probably a lot. I supposed I might as well stay. In a separate room of course.

"Okay, yeah, I mean, I could stay in the guest room that would be okay." I put my purse over the back of the chair again. He opened another bottle of heather ale and set it in front of me.

"Besides, I still haven't given you a full tour of the house yet, with extra instructions. Let's start here." We were facing the living room. "What do you see that doesn't make sense?"

He walked around the room looking at things closely and making a hmm noise, as if studying it, rubbing his fingers along his square jaw, contemplating. Nodding. Finally, he said, "'Tis all mysterious, nae familiarity in anythin'. My grandfather, Archibald, told me, 'Magnus, if ye see something ye haena seen afore just scratch your balls—" He glanced at me and corrected himself with a chuckle. "Hae a bit o'ale and keep mum on it. Tis better tae make no noise than tae chirp like a corncrake.' My grandmother though, said, "Tis better tae question and know the meanin' of it, than tae suffer like a fool.' They were verra often more adversaries than friends."

"My grandmother told me, 'If you don't know what something is, pretend like you do while you figure it out.'"

Magnus laughed a low booming laugh. "Your grandmother would have gotten along with my grandfather quite well."

"I'll tell her next time I speak to her."

"She still lives?"

"Yes, far away though, in Maine."

"Mine died during a battle with some of clan Donald."

"Scotland is definitely different than I thought. It's in the EU, or it was until Brexit, but I guessed it was much more cosmopolitan than you're describing."

Magnus tipped his glass, drank to the bottom, and then poured another. "What is this big black thing on the wall?"

"The television? Seriously, even the Amish know what a TV is..." I walked toward it shaking my head.

He laughed. "I am telling ye a story, Mistress Kaitlyn. I know tis a teev but haena seen this kind afore."

I eyed him suspiciously. "Good, because TV is as basic as rock-and-roll at this point." I hit the power on and switched through channels. Nothing looked good. I glanced peripherally at Magnus, who was wincing. "Too loud?"

"Everythin' here buzzes, as if bees were swarmin' inside. Tis verra loud. You canna hear it?"

I shook my head and turned off the TV. "What about music? I turned on a speaker, hooked my phone to it, and turned on my 'Chill for a Sec You Dumbass' playlist — created just after I assaulted Braden. On camera. The playlist had lots of Lana Del Ray, so I deemed it quiet enough. I switched the volume way down.

I dropped onto the comfy couch. That was one good thing about Beach Modern decorating, giant overstuffed sofas with a surplus of decorative pillows. I tucked my feet up under me and lounged.

Magnus asked, "Would ye like another ale?"

I already had a very nice buzz, but now that I didn't need to drive, why not? "Sure."

He grabbed two ales by the bottle necks and joined me in the living room dropping into a chair beside the couch. "This music is beautiful."

"It's Lana Del Rey, one of my favorites." I sang a couple of lines, very low like a whisper, because my singing voice was terrible. Everyone thought so. A friend in middle school once told me

I sounded like a baby hippo crying when I sang along to Rihanna. It was true, so I didn't mind. I caught Magnus furtively glancing at me, so I quit singing. "You and your mother must be very close."

He said, "No, I haena known her most of my life. I was sent away verra young tae be raised by my uncle John in London."

"But you're protecting her now?"

"I have sworn tae protect her by oath. No matter what comes. Wherever it takes us."

"Oh, that makes sense." I said it though I didn't really understand it. "And you said her husband was going to come for her?"

"Aye, Lord Delapointe. She has taken something he verra much wants."

I was enjoying this story. It was like the plot of a movie — easy to forget it was real life because so much about Magnus had a weird fantasy vibe about it, not seeming real at all. I swigged from my bottle.

Then I thought of something. "What did she take, was it the gold and jewels? Are we caught up in a museum robbery or something?"

"Nae the jewels belong tae Lady Mairead. He wants something else entirely."

"Oh."

"I would rather nae speak of it, if ye dinna mind, Mistress Kaitlyn. I find myself in the New World, at the dawn of a new life, with new friends," he lifted his bottle in salute to me. "I prefer nae tae dwell in the past."

"Hear hear." I raised my bottle too. "And that's a good reminder, dwelling in the past sucks. New World, dawn of a new life, new friends." I yawned, a big yawn, the kind that cracks your face wide with embarrassing noises.

"You are fatigued?"

"I am, I was up late last night watching TV. How about you?"

"Much the same but I can make do on little. You may retire, Mistress Kaitlyn. You will be safe enough, I'll keep watch."

"Lady Mairead's room is upstairs, which is yours? I mean, I'm wondering which room I should take?"

"You may have the grand room." He gestured toward the door of the master bedroom. "I'll make my bed here." He bounced up and down on the cushions of the overstuffed chair. "What name would ye call this?"

"A chair?"

He chuckled. "I had hoped for somethin' fancier. I shall sleep in this heaven-stuff'd chair."

I hadn't known him for long but his face had so many expressions, most often intense and deep. But then when he was amused his smile spread and crinkled the corner of his eyes. I drained my beer and stood to grab my purse and head into the bedroom.

He asked, "Will ye turn off the lights? I have forgotten your first lesson, Mistress Kaitlyn. Ye may need tae shew me again on the morrow."

"Happy to." I turned the switches off throwing the entire bottom floor into darkness, but only for a moment. Once my eyes adjusted, through the sliding glass door, the boardwalk glowed faintly in the moonlight. The sea grass beyond stood still on the dunes.

"Tis peaceful, ye made it just right."

"Goodnight, Magnus."

"Good night, Mistress Kaitlyn, thank ye for welcoming me tae the New World."

My room was luxurious, large, with a full wall of glass. I didn't close the blinds to look out at the beach, at night, from my bed. It was awesome. I had never had a view like this, undulating dunes covered in sparse sea grass.

The bed covers were silk. The pillows so large I was sure to throw a neck out by morning. Why did luxurious beds always have neck injuring pillows? I tucked one between my legs, wrapped around another one, tucked into the covers and was asleep in minutes.

CHAPTER 7

The next morning I woke at eight-thirty. Crap. Visiting hours started at nine. I raced to the living room and found Magnus standing on the back porch. A bit of breezy wind blew a curl on the nape of his neck. At my footsteps, he turned, and his face lit up.

He slid open the door and met me in the living room. "Did ye sleep well, Mistress Kaitlyn?"

"Nice, you've got the doors figured out already. And yes, I did." I checked my phone. "We need to get you to the hospital. Coffee first though." I went to the kitchen, filled a glass with water from the refrigerator, and took some big gulps. "Dehydrated."

"We go tae the lands of the Donalds then?"

"Definitely."

"Good, because I could eat a horse."

In the drive-thru Magnus ordered four muffins and two coffees. I ordered two muffins and one coffee. I rather liked watching him fish the card or, as he called it, his tile from his leather pouch. He was scrunched in the seat, knees splayed, shoulders taking up most of the freaking room. His jawline taking all of my air. We ate while I drove and then carried our coffees and breakfast into the hospital to check on Lady Mairead. She was still sleeping, so we ate outside on a bench.

Then I left to go to Hayley's place of business, the Temps on Top Agency. I told her years ago it sounded like she was running a prostitution ring to which she said, "Exactly. I'm not but if that gets me some phone calls I can say, 'No, I don't have someone to service your sexual desires but perhaps you'd like a girl to come over and polish your silverware.'"

I laughed. "Is 'polishing your silverware' a euphemism for sex; are you running a prostitution ring?" And the sign always made me laugh.

I entered the small, well-appointed, empty, waiting room. She called me through to her office, and I sat on the opposite side of her desk like a customer.

"So tell me all about it." Her eyes squinted. "You're holding a coffee from Mackydoos so obviously you're hungover. Did you bed the wild Scotsman? I hope not because James was pining for you all night."

"I am. I did not. And no he wasn't."

"If not pining, he's really looking forward to your date. So what are you doing with the dude in the skirt?"

"I don't know, nothing. I spent the night—"

She gasped, "Katie!"

"Let me finish, I spent the night in the guest room. His mom is in the hospital, and he doesn't know his way around — anything, and... We're friends."

She looked suspicious. "You should keep it that way. He

looks like nothing but trouble. He carries a sword for Pete's sake, it's 2017. Is that even legal?"

"There are guys who carry big guns strapped to their backs around a Starbucks in Texas. I saw it on Facebook."

"Yes, but you don't want to date one, Katie. I've known you since you were five. You've never once dreamed of a man with a gun strapped to his back. Maybe a prince on a horse but I don't think weapons had any part of it. Besides that, what does he think about your on-air tantrum?"

"He's never seen it."

"Ah girl," Hayley cocked her head to the side with a sympathetic pout. "See? That's what this is. What are you going to do, nervously wait until he has? Hope he finds it funny when he does? That's what's so great about James, he's seen the video, he thought it was funny, and he still likes you."

"And he'd punch anyone in the face who would say otherwise."

"Exactly. He's your prince."

I chuckled. "I wouldn't go that far. He did break my heart pretty good back in the day. Plus, he's not the only man in the world."

"You should know that everyone deserves a second chance. I'm just saying I'm glad you're going out on a date Friday night. Second chance him. Then second chance him again. The third time you second chance him, ask yourself, do I want to second chance him forever? And whatever, there's a great band at Sliders, you can dance with him first, then second chance him later." She laughed. "Then if you don't like it, go do your other men."

I pretended to be irritated and huffed. "So the business at hand." I placed the pad on her desk, leaned on my elbows, fishing a pen out of her desk jar. "The Scotsman needs..."

"What's his name?"

"Magnus Campbell."

"Magnus." She jokingly shifted in her seat, then said it with a sultry voice. "Mahg-nus. Oh, Magnus. Oh yes."

"Are you going to be able to do this, Hayley, or are you going to sexually harass your client?"

"Here at Temp on Top, we are totally professional. What kind of staff does he need?"

"A full time, twenty-four-seven, security team. A maid. Someone to dress Lady Mairead, maybe a nurse? Or a personal assistant? He wants a stable boy but I don't have the heart to tell him he doesn't have a stable. And a cook."

Hayley's eyes went wide. "Seriously? He has the money for this?"

"My dad says yes. Dad has decided to personally handle Magnus's money and says he's very, very rich."

"Whoa. Okay then. A staff that large definitely fills my quota. Does Lady Mairead really need someone to dress her?"

"I think she's royalty and is used to having everything done for her."

"Okay then, I have a—" Hayley turned to her computer and started clicking and typing and talking to herself and me.

"I'll call Jim Sanders, you know him, Declan's uncle? He runs Island Security. I've got one guy who temps security, but I'll need more."

"Sounds good. I barely remember Declan, definitely don't remember his uncle."

"A stable boy? Doesn't he live in a beach house?"

"I'm just telling you what he wants."

Hayley scrolled through the list, muttering to herself. "I'll call Debbie over at Amelia Stables and see if she has any ideas. Remember her? We worked for her for two weeks that summer when we were twelve?"

"I do, barely."

"For nurse I have Elizabeth Macklinberg, she's great. She

moved here from Brunswick, is a nurse, and worked in eldercare hospice. I think she can dress a royal."

"And that leaves the best for last, Michael's very own big brother, Zach, is a chef. He works over at the Inn as a line cook, but he's so great. Do you think Magnus would mind that he's covered in tattoos and uses foul language just about every other word — his food is amazing?"

"He probably won't mind, just tell him to keep it down in front of Lady Mairead."

"Best part, Zach's girlfriend is out of work, Emma. She used to clean houses for Maids for Hire in Jax. So there's the house-keeper. Zach will be thrilled they can work together." She leaned back in her chair and said, "Done. When do you need them by?"

I grinned. "This afternoon."

She looked shocked. "That's just a few hours."

I skimmed the list. "I think the security is very important. He's willing to pay extra to have that in place now. He hasn't slept in days."

Hayley leaned forward. "I told you he was trouble. What is he hiding from?"

"I don't know, but I think it has more to do with Lady Mairead. I also think the cook is very important, and the nurse. If those were in place by tonight that would make you the greatest living temp agency boss in the world."

"Good, because that's the title I've been dreaming of."

"When they're ready to start, I can meet them at his house and show them around."

"Maybe you should be the house manager, I'll hire you?"

I scoffed. "Me? I'm sure I don't have the skills for that."

Hayley joked, "Yeah, you've only been playing house, orga-nizing, party-planning, obsessing, and making videos where you explain how to do things since you were four years old."

I leaned back in my chair. "Yeah. But I don't know... I need to get my head together."

"Yeah, yeah. You've lost your I'm-an-epic-human-being confidence. Braden is a dick for stealing that from you. If I could fly to LA and punch him in the face, I would."

"Thank you sweetie. I'm going back to the hospital. Lady Mairead will be released today."

"And a staff will be waiting for her. Hopefully." She laughed and picked up her phone to start making calls, waving her hand at me to send me from the room.

CHAPTER 8

When Magnus and I pulled up to his house with Lady Mairead and her new nurse, Beth, at 6:30, some of the staff was already in place because Hayley was a miracle worker. She was still there showing security around, making lists, and organizing schedules.

Magnus's house that had been so empty before was now bustling. Lady Mairead was helped to her upstairs bedroom, and her nurse moved into the room next door. She would stay there full time until Lady Mairead felt better. Magnus stood on the porch outside and went over the security plan with Jim Sanders and one other man because that was all Hayley could get on short notice. But Magnus seemed relieved enough. That was good.

Best part, Zach, and his girlfriend, Emma, were in the kitchen making dinner for everyone. It smelled delicious. After a few minutes of introductions and last-minute instructions, Hayley left promising she would return in the morning to check in, making Zach promise not to curse like a pirate, and hugging me goodbye.

Then I waited awkwardly. Through the sliding glass door Magnus stood in front of his men, feet planted, the sword at his side, broad shoulders, hair blowing a little in the hot breeze. The two men wore T-shirts that said "Security" on the back, had tight-clipped hair, guns at their hips. They all mimicked each other with their strong stance, standing in a circle, strategizing.

Zach and Emma were in a cooking groove making magic, smells wafting around them, smiling at each other, and giggling at inside jokes.

Why was I still there? No reason. I was just the lady who wouldn't leave. So I asked Emma to let Magnus know I was going home and left. My job was done. People were there to take care of the Scotsman and his royal mother. I had done my non-job duty — perfectly, I might add. I did have a knack for this. There just wasn't a lot of need for it here on the Island.

If this *was* my thing, I'd probably need to move back to Los Angeles to do it. People there needed personal assistants or organizers. Trouble was, who would hire the notorious KatieMake-STuff? Maybe a rock star? Was Marilyn Manson hiring a personal assistant? He might be the only person—Ozzy Osbourne?

I went back to Mom and Dad's house.

CHAPTER 9

It was Friday night, the night of my date with James. It had been a long boring end of the week. Hayley had been busy with all the extra work of Magnus's staff. Mom and Dad were going out a lot, still gloating over their score with Magnus's estate. And James was busy at work after taking the long weekend the week before. So I watched TV, walked on the beach, not near Magnus's estate, and generally felt sorry for myself.

For a long, long time Braden had been my best friend. We moved to Los Angeles together, did everything together until he pulled away doing other stuff, and then suddenly he was gone. I had been so busy mourning the loss of my fiancé that I hadn't much noticed I lost my friend too. I was lonely and hurting.

I heard somewhere that it takes eleven weeks to get over someone. I was on week five. I knew I would live on, but how, when? And the loss was so much bigger because I had lost everything — my Braden, my apartment, my business. It sucked.

All those years of building a career and now because I lost my shit over Braden's announcement — "Hey Katie, I've been thinking, I'd really rather not marry you" — my business wasn't mine anymore. Because I was a screaming banshee. He called it assault. I called it, "Why the hell did you tell me you didn't love me anymore, that you loved someone else, while we were live on Facebook?"

That hella sucked.

All it had taken was a week of videos where Braden replayed my scene, while he showed the world claw marks on his cheek, and I was done. I think he added makeup to make it look worse. I could have, of course, refused to surrender. I could have carried on with a new channel, with three subscribers who all shared my own last name but, to be honest, Mom and Dad didn't even watch YouTube. They didn't know how to work anything but their Facebook feed. Starting over with zero subscribers felt like the end of the world. So this was me now: grown ass woman living in parents' house. Trying to find her next life path.

I spent a lot of time searching for shark teeth. Most of the time crying.

So when Friday rolled around I was pretty lonely and definitely ready for the date. James called to check in on Friday morning, and I agreed he could pick me up. We would go early, eat, talk, and then everyone else would show up once the live music started. We'd party with them and then, he hadn't asked, but I figured I might spend the night, maybe, probably.

I got really dolled up. My makeup was on point. I was wearing strappy heels and a dress that was tight and short and showed a lot of skin. It was hot out, so yeah, skin was good. I looked epic.

Mom, who was really excited about my date with James, said, "Well, I guess you aren't planning to come home tonight." Which made me roll my eyes even though it was true. That thing a week ago, where I wanted to sleep with James so he could kiss me, tell me I was beautiful, and make me feel like someone might want me again? It was worse now. I was desperate for someone to think I was great. Even passable.

Probably, if I had a therapist on call, the therapist would tell me that going on a date this desperate for love was a terrible idea; that I needed to love myself first but also — whatever. James liked me. Wanted me. Was going to buy me dinner. So yeah, this might not be smart, but it was going to happen.

James helped me into his truck with a joke about my short skirt. He had always owned big trucks for the statement of it. But now as a successful contractor, his truck was even bigger, requiring steps to climb into it. Worse on gas.

My Prius was a statement too, just not the right kind as far as he was concerned.

James was a regular at Sliders. On the way to our table he talked to just about everyone in the restaurant. I, on the other hand, was treated familiarly but also delicately. I had been a local for a long time. My parents were very local. I had left though, the high-speed, see-ya-later, I'm out-of-here kind of left. And now I had changed from Local Girl Done Good to Local Girl Gone Wrong. The waitress said, "James, sweetie," and kissed him on the cheek. "Who's this? Oh, is that you, Katie Sheffield? I barely recognized you though the last time I saw you was on that vid—"

James interrupted, "I'd like to order a beer. How 'bout you, Katie?"

"Same."

She walked away. I took a deep breath and tried some internal pep-talking to get back to sexy, glamorous, fabulous, confident.

"I'm glad you could do this tonight." He leaned across the

table and held my hand, gentle and sweet. "And I'm really glad you came back to town."

"Thanks, it's beginning to feel good to be home." I was lying, but I hoped it would be true someday.

He reminded me about a night together when we went to a concert, bought a kitschy toilet plunger from a gas station, found $12, drank too much, and slept on a sand dune. Reminiscing with him about it got us both really laughing.

After a few minutes he said, "I missed your laugh."

"James you're making me blush."

He leaned back with a shrug. "What am I going to do, not tell you? You need to know."

Then he reminded me of the time we played poker with the gang and then it turned into strip poker. The guys let Hayley, Emily, Tracy, and me win, while they were butt-naked wearing the pillows off Tracy's couch. James had worn Tupperware on his penis. It was a good memory, silly. Our food arrived and we ate and talked and laughed, and I'd have to say it was one of the better dates of my life. Easy and comfortable. He was charming, I had forgotten how much.

By the end of the dinner I was a little smitten, maybe enough smitten. I had some lovely flirtation going. He had some adoring looks. He was really good at this.

He received a text and glanced down at it. "Mike and Hayley are headed here now with Quentin, Sarah, and a few others." He reached out and held my hand again. "This is nice."

"It is."

"Just like the good old days."

"The good old days before you messed around with the girl from Valdosta." I'm not sure why I said it. It was supposed to be flirty and easy but didn't sound as teasing and cute as I intended.

He looked up at me, still holding my hand. "You know, I was really young back then and stupid. I've grown up a lot. Also, I'd like to point out, you were leaving, Katie, headed off to school. You had been planning it for months, and what was I going to do, live here, take over Dad's business, and wait for you? Would you have come back? You were going away. So I left you first. Hoping it wouldn't hurt so bad."

"Oh."

"Yeah, oh."

This was a point I never considered. I would need to do some serious reflecting. Was this the bullshit of an f-boy or the truth?

"I'm a changed man. I promise. Give us a chance and you'll see."

There was no time to think about any of this now because in walked the gang. They piled around our table laughing, talking loudly, and disrupting the whole dining room. James ordered another round, and we carried our drinks out to the wide back porch with a separate bar surrounded by sand, a stage, and the beach beyond. A live band was set up to play.

Hayley yelled, "Woo-hoo! We'll be dancing tonight!"

We did dance. First me and Hayley. Then Hayley and Michael and me and James to the song, Banana Pancakes. It was a lovely rendition, and I had a nice buzz. Also, when we danced, James put his hand right on my hip and that was nice. The breeze was warm. Between songs you could hear the ocean waves crashing and see the sea grass lit by moonlight waving on the crests of the white dunes.

We were sitting at three tall tables pulled together with barstools all around, some full of friends, some empty. The tabletop was covered in beer bottles and cups and pitchers, empty, full, partially full. James excused himself to go to the bathroom. Michael went to the bar to get another round. Hayley and I were giggling and talking about how much fun we used to have here years ago when we would stash wine coolers on the beach and would steal out to chug them and sneak back to dance.

Suddenly Hayley stopped. "Oh my god, girl."

I followed her eyes down the length of the boardwalk to the dark beach beyond, and there was a man riding up the beach, on a horse. It was unmistakably Magnus. That was the only person it could be. The strangest sight in the world but also, the way he rode that horse, completely natural and reasonable. He was lit by the moon, dark, big, his hair rustling in the wind. Magnus. On a horse.

Hayley asked, "Is he on a horse? Did he just ride a horse up to Sliders?"

He dismounted in the sand, tied the reins to the railing, and headed up the path toward us. He was wearing a black linen shirt with a collar buttoned up the front. It was untucked. With his kilt. His sword was strapped on his back. He had a knife hanging from a belt. Hayley asked, "Is he walking this way?"

I lost my ability to speak in sentences or to have logical answers. I gulped, straightened in my chair and tried to pretend like I didn't notice but oh man I was noticing. From the periphery I could see he was looking directly at me. He walked straight to our table. It was all very excruciatingly slow but also surprisingly, totally discombobulating how quickly he appeared.

He bowed his head. "Good evening, Mistress Hayley." Then he leaned in and spoke to me "I wanted tae — I was unsure how tae speak tae ye, Mistress Kaitlyn. You went afore takin' your leave."

He was standing in front of the space that had been James's seat, now pushed back and vacated, looking directly at me, and Hayley was staring from his face to mine, eyes wide. He seemed, what is the word, intent.

I said, "I thought you were busy, so I didn't want to bother you. Is Lady Mairead better?"

"She is healing well. Her nurse, Madame Macklinberg, is excellent for comfort and health."

Hayley interceded, drawing his attention from me. "I'm glad she's working out — how did you find us?"

"I asked Chef Zach if he might help me in locating Mistress Kaitlyn, and he directed me here." He returned to speaking solely to me. "He stated ye were oft here on a Friday night."

I inhaled because there was some seriously awesome smell emanating from the shadowy darkness that was Magnus because he was hot and handsome, but he smelled faintly of the back room of a candle shop.

Hayley seemed amused by his focus on me. She asked, "Speaking of Chef Zach, he's almost a brother to me, what do you think about his cooking?"

Magnus smiled and turned his attention to her. "Ah, Chef Zach is a master of tastes. I am well pleased with the meals he conjures. And Mistress Emma takes verra good care of me."

I felt a small pang of jealousy that someone else was taking 'verra good' care of him.

He returned his attention to me. "I wanted tae ask if ye—"

Just then Michael returned to the table, passing out bottles. He seemed amused by the appearance of the Scotsman.

Then James walked up. He paused with his hand on the back of his chair, grinning incredulously. "We meet again, first in my house, now in my chair." James slid his barstool back, closer to me, sat down on it, and took my hand.

Magnus stole a tiny, almost imperceptible, glance at my hand now encapsulated in James's and moved farther away from me to the other side of James.

James's smile broadened. "I know we met the other night, but my name is James Cook. Mike, go grab our friend here a beer. And remind me your name?"

"Much obliged. I am Magnus Campbell." They shook hands while James did this thing where he appraised Magnus down his nose as if Magnus was beneath him. I had seen James do this many times. It was a move he had been using since he was thirteen and the most popular kid at school because half of popularity was letting everyone know you were at the top and they were at the bottom. James moved his hand to my thigh, which was mostly bare because my dress was so short.

Magnus glanced down at James's hand.

Michael returned with a beer for Magnus, they were introduced, Magnus was offered a chair, and everyone resumed their seats.

Hayley said, "Magnus was just going to ask Katie a question."

I noted to myself to kill her later and looked down at my beer.

"Ah, do tell," said James, rubbing my thigh.

Everyone waited for Magnus to speak.

"I have learned from my guards there are legal impediments tae riding my horse on the roads and if tis necessary for me tae travel farther, I will need tae acquire a car."

Magnus was speaking directly, intently, to me again.

And James was watching him, his face even more incredulous, appraising, and arrogant.

I said, "You want me to help you buy a—"

James interrupted. "Have you seen Katie's car? It's a Prius; it barely even has a horsepower rating." I rolled my eyes at Hayley. She giggled. James said, "A man like Magnus Campbell needs a real vehicle. I've got the day off tomorrow. I'll take you to the Ford dealership over in Jacksonville. I can introduce you to John. He'll get you set up right away."

Magnus appraised James in return. "I would be verra indebted to ye Master Cook."

"No worries, we're friends, right? You've been to my home. You're a friend of my girl. We're sharing a beer. It's all good, besides I don't mind a good car buying excursion."

I took another deep breath. "I don't think Magnus has a license though, right? To drive?"

"A man like Magnus Campbell doesn't have a license? Do you know how to drive?"

Magnus shook his head. "Nae, I dinna ken."

"I'll take that as a negative. Okay, car first, then we teach you to drive. What are you doing tomorrow, Mike? Want to drive to Jax with me and my friend Magnus to buy him a car he can't drive?"

Michael was finding the whole thing very amusing. "Sounds good to me." He turned to Magnus. "James and I will pick you up about 10:30."

Magnus said, "T'would be verra helpful. I look forward tae our journey."

James pushed back his seat. "Stay awhile, but Katie promised me a dance and our song just came on."

I asked, "What song is that?"

"I'll fix you. Coldplay. Remember prom?" He pulled me to the dance floor. We rocked back and forth. The music was lovely. The breeze was warm. If this moment happened before Magnus arrived it might have been very romantic and sweet but now it all felt so proprietary, like James was establishing ownership. Sorry, but I hadn't agreed to anything, not really.

When we returned to the table, Magnus was laughing with Hayley and Michael.

"What's so funny?"

Hayley said, "Michael was acting out how nervous Zach is about his new chef job. Apparently whenever Magnus asks for something specific from Scotland, Zach googles recipes in a panic. He's scared to death he's not good enough."

Magnus chuckled. "When I met Chef Zach, I was close to starv'd. He might have burnt the food tae blackened chips, and I would have still devoured it. Pray, don't divulge this tae him. I enjoy his cooking verra much, but I also appreciate his enthusiasm."

James leaned in and started telling me about a new project he was working on. I suffered missing out on the better, more interesting, more fun conversation at the other end of the table.

I was fascinated by Magnus but also on a date with James.

And James had been my thing for so long that even now, when he was acting jealous and uncool, I was capable of letting it pass. He was insecure. About me. And like Hayley said, maybe I needed to give him a second chance. Especially in light of this new news — he had been unfaithful back in the day because he was upset I was leaving him. I had promised to come back but would I have? I would have met Braden. Would it have made a difference if I had been in a long distance relationship with James at the time? If the past had been different would my present be the same?

For the next couple of beers, James continued being testy with Magnus and taking up all my attention. Then when he left for the bathroom again, Magnus stood to leave. I watched him go, wishing I could talk to him for a minute more. Then I figured, what the hell, and jumped up to follow him to the boardwalk. "Magnus, wait up."

He pulled short. He was tall and imposing but his eyes were soft when he looked at me causing my heart to race. I wondered if I could simply rise to my tiptoes and kiss him, maybe climb on the back of his horse and ride away down the beach with him, like in a romance novel.

Sadly, there were real problems with this scenario.

First, he hadn't given me any indication beyond 'being hot' that he wanted me to kiss him.

Second, I didn't know anything about horses. I could imagine that the whole thing would be much more awkward than romantic.

"You okay with going to Jacksonville tomorrow with James?"

"Aye," his eyes had a mischievous twinkle. "He seems a braw fellow, I greatly look forward tae a day in his company."

"Yeah, about that. He's not usually like that. I think he's worried about our friendship. And you know, just—"

"Mistress Kaitlyn, you daena need tae explain him tae me. I might nae know how tae work things but my whole life I have lived with men, brothers, uncles, cousins. I understand the workings of a man such as James Cook."

"Okay. Good."

He watched my face for a moment. "I'll see you on the morrow Mistress Kaitlyn." He turned down the boardwalk to his horse. I watched him, entranced, as he mounted it to ride south down the beach.

When I returned to the table, I told James I had a terrible headache and needed to go home. There was a lot going on that I needed to think about. I kept him from being too disappointed with a promise that I'd meet him the next night for dinner at the restaurant under the bridge.

CHAPTER 10

*H*ayley and I met at the restaurant. James and Michael spent the whole day helping Magnus buy a car and promised to meet us there at six for dinner. But then James kept sending me texts explaining they were running late with the car purchase. Michael texted Hayley that they would pull in around seven-thirty.

Hayley and I got a table in the back of the noisy bar area and drank a few beers while we waited. She grilled me about the night before. "Just please tell me you went home because of a headache and not because of the Scottish guy, please."

I said, "I did because of a headache but also why is this so important to you?"

"Because I think you're great, and I think he's great, and I literally have to see him. All. The. Time. If he's not seeing you, that I love, he'll be seeing some other crazy chick, and I'll have to pretend to like her and it will suck. Michael and I almost broke up when James was dating some girl named Rebecca because she was such a nightmare."

"So what you're saying is that your relationship with Michael depends on me? Well that just sucks because even though you're so much better than him, and he's basically a fourteen-year-old wrapped in a man's body, you two have been in love for forever. And he knows in his bones he's the lucky one. I can't be responsible for messing that up. Whenever he looks at you I think that's what I need, someone who adores me and knows I'm better than him."

"Exactly! James will adore you like Michael adores me." Her phone lit with a notification. "They're pulling up now."

"Good, because I'm starved. I can't believe we've been waiting for them for an hour and a half."

"Two hours, it's almost eight."

We went to stand at the edge of the parking lot. I had chosen an excellent dress for the night, flowered, silky, a sweet and sexy summer dress in shades of blue that I knew looked good on me. While dressing though I couldn't figure out who I was trying to be pretty for: James, because we were dating now, or Magnus, because I hoped he would notice me?

Under the bridge with a plume of dust came a Ford Mustang convertible. Matte black. Its top down. Quentin was driving, James sat in the passenger seat, Michael and Magnus rode in the back.

Magnus's shoulders were so wide they filled the space between them. His eyes were closed, which made me happy. He had spent the day with the boys but maybe he still needed my help after all—

I stopped short and made myself look at James. I was waiting for James. One hundred percent.

Quentin pulled the car up right in front of us as James turned to look in the backseat. "You've got your eyes closed again, Mags. I told you when we went under the bridge to keep your eyes open so you would look cool for the girls." He opened his door, stepped out, and kissed me hello. "I mean sheesh, he's got this freaking cool car and..." He kissed me again. He sounded buzzed and his lips tasted of alcohol.

Magnus spread his arms across the back seat. "On horses one should sit tight and controlled, yet in my Mustang I must sit wide like a roosting hen?"

"Yes, but you aren't moving now. So you can relax.." James kissed me again. "Cool car, huh babe?"

"Very nice car."

Magnus said, "Tis a verra braw car, though I canna keep my eyes open when movin' along the highways."

I said, "Then you'll definitely need a driver because you have to be able to see."

He jumped up, so he was sitting on the back of the seat then swept his legs over the side to the ground in one effortless move.

James, Quentin, and Michael all seemed to like Magnus. They patted his back and teased him like old friends. Their day must have gone well. I caught Magnus looking me up and down but James stepped between us and maneuvered me into the front door of the restaurant. His hand was on my back rubbing my skin through my silky dress.

Hayley and I had saved a big long table and everyone slid in and filled chairs. Magnus and Quentin took the far end and talked about the car. Quentin had the manual open between them and was pointing, discussing, and patiently, only sometimes incredulously, explaining the details of the new car.

I didn't have a lot of time to watch though because James was in a want-to-love-me mood. His hand caressed my side and every few minutes he nuzzled into my neck, kissing my throat. He whispered how much he missed me into my ear. It was sweet how much he liked me and getting kind of hot how much he wanted me.

We had been stuck in the friend-zone after our first night was ruined by my drunken vomiting. Our relationship thus far had been pretty boring but this was a little — he nibbled my ear — a lot hot.

I breathed in his smell, a zingy cologne with floral undertones, combined with alcohol.

"You coming home with me?"

I laughed and said, "Yes."

"Yes? You're coming home with me, awesome."

The waitress interrupted us, moving around the table taking our orders. Hayley and I both ordered full meals, but James only ordered a beer and an appetizer.

Then Michael said he wasn't hungry and only ordered a beer. So I asked, "Wait, did you guys stop for dinner somewhere?" And James said, "Just a bite," and changed the subject back to nibbling on my neck.

Magnus scowled toward my end of the table. A real scowl. The kind that meant jealousy.

A thrill rushed through me.

Suddenly, all I could think about was Magnus. Was he thinking about me? Was he thinking about me 'in that way'? And if he was, did I think about him that way too? And finally, most importantly, *should I get up right now and walk by his end of the table, so maybe he could see how cute I was in this dress?*

Yes, definitely.

So I stood, but as I turned to go to the bathroom James grabbed me by my hips and brought me down hard on his lap. He started kissing my neck and pulling me down and really, there was a moment there, where I was held down, too hard.

I struggled to get up. I had to push his hands away. "Stop it James."

I brushed past him as he slurred something like, "Baby, don't go away mad, come back I want to talk some more."

Michael laughed because he always thought everything James did was hilarious.

I was so pissed I forgot to notice if Magnus was checking me out and really hoped he wasn't because that had been super awful-embarrassing.

I fixed my makeup. Two steps out of the bathroom door, returning to our table, I saw Magnus leaving the restaurant. James and Michael were laughing.

"What was that about, why did he leave?"

"No reason baby. Come back."

I said, "I'm going to check on him. He doesn't know how to drive to get home. Who's driving him by the way?" Everyone shrugged.

CHAPTER 11

*M*agnus was sitting in the backseat of his convertible, head back, eyes closed. I leaned on the side without saying anything. He opened one eye to see that it was me and then closed them again.

I asked, "Are you okay?"

"How can ye—?" He shook his head. "This day has been verra long, verra loud. I needed tae rest my eyes."

"Ah," I said and watched him for a moment, quiet, still. I turned toward the restaurant, loud music, clanging dishes, excited voices. Through the window James was looking around. He stood, Michael behind him, and they all headed toward the front door looking for me.

None of them had eaten dinner though we had met for dinner. They didn't seem to mind that my dinner and Hayley's dinner hadn't even been delivered to the table yet. They ate dinner out even though we had plans...

Everyone came out to the front of the restaurant, where I stood leaned on Magnus's car. James said, "Katie, come back inside."

I turned to Quentin and very casually asked, "Are you hungry Quentin or did the restaurant in Jax fill you up too much to eat?"

He slurred, "Oh it got me full up all right. Restaurants in Jax always fill me up," and broke down laughing.

I squinted my eyes at him.

He stopped laughing and looked sheepishly at James.

James said, "Dammit Quentin, you weren't supposed to... Wait — Magnus, did you say something?"

Magnus opened his eyes. "I have spoken tae Mistress Kaitlyn enough tae say I am exhausted from the day."

James said, "Yeah, well we agreed not to bring it up, right Quentin?"

"Why not?" I asked James. "You just got hungry, right? Grabbed a bite? You can tell me these..." I looked around at all the men.

Magnus wouldn't meet my eyes. Quentin was fidgeting nervously. James was doing his thing, the big smile, the sense of humor, the charm, trying to cool everyone down. Even though he was the one causing the drama. In the past thirty minutes I had drastically changed my mind about this guy. The only reason why I was still talking to him was because now I wanted to get to the bottom of this. I needed to.

"I don't know why you're all acting so weird — so you stopped for a bite to eat? I couldn't care less."

James put his hands up. "Because you know how you get."

My breath grew quick and I tried to calm it down. "How I get?"

"Yeah," he was slurring and kind of wiggly on his feet. "You get crazy when you think I've been lying to you."

"Not when I think it, when you *are* lying to me. And hiding shit, information. This is all a form of lying. That's the truth."

"I knew it, I knew you were going to go ballistic if you found out."

"Found out what?" I was so mad my hands were balling into fists. "Found out what, that you got hungry, that you and your bros got a bite to eat? What the hell, James?"

From the corner of my eye I saw Quentin mouth, "Sorry man."

Hayley said, "Katie, it's okay, they went to get a meal—"

"That's what I'm saying, it's okay. Why the hell are you hiding it from me? Don't you trust me?"

A laugh burst from Quentin's sealed lips. He bent over hysterical. Then he attempted to stand and hide his laughing. I saw it already. Plainly.

I could not figure out what was going on.

I glanced at Magnus. He had climbed up on the back of the seat as if he was ready to jump from the car. His elbows were on his knees, his eyes down, not looking at me. Worst part there was another scowl on his face.

I was making a scene. I was a freaking embarrassment.

I came here tonight thinking I was cute and sexy and that not just one but two guys were a little into me and now those two guys spent the day together. They were friends. There was that code again. That stupid bro-code that kept them from telling Katie the truth.

I was having trouble getting air and noises were thudding in my ears. Maybe I was a lot drunk. Out of the corner of my eye I caught a glimpse of something fluorescent pink on the brake handle. My eyes fixed on it. It was a paper bracelet, black writing on the side. I tried to read it but had to — I leaned over the door and fished it off, turning it to read all the words. Then I had to turn it again to understand what they said: Little PussyCat Full-Nude Men's Club — Dinner Served All Day.

Then I started to laugh.

I laughed hard.

I had to cross my legs because I was laughing so hard and it would suck to pee my pants. "Oh my god, you went to a strip club, James?"

Quentin snickered. "Watch her Magnus, we told you this would happen, like the video she gonna go ballistic."

They had told Magnus about me. Maybe even showed him the video. Great. The one person in the world who hadn't seen my meltdown and now that was ruined. No wonder he wouldn't look at me.

I wiped my eyes. "I'm not going to go ballistic. I'd just like to point out that you went to a strip club the day after you told me you were a different person and that you were going to make it up to me."

Michael said, "Magnus had never been to one."

"Magnus has never been to one, but James has. James goes all the time. James is on a first name basis with the ladies at the front. So the thing is, me and you," I waggled my finger in between us, "this, it's over."

"Aw, come on Katie, it's just a place to get dinner. It's no big deal." James had his arms out, a big smile spread across his face.

I dropped the bracelet back in the car. "You're right, it's not a big deal. You were meeting me for dinner but instead you ate dinner with a stripper on your lap. How many layers of fabric were between you and a stripper tonight James? Two?"

Quentin held his sides laughing and burst out, "One, when he was excited."

James said, "Dude, I'm going to kill you."

Quentin shook his head. "She already knows, man. She figured it out."

I said, "Yeah, one question, were you wearing those same pants?"

James looked down as if he had to check.

I added, "Great. Now I have to go home and take a shower. Dumbass."

James said, "Come inside, eat."

"Not feeling it."

"So, me and you, I blew it?"

I let out a deep breath of air. "Yeah. Because you're a walking cock without the brain power of an actual rooster."

Quentin doubled over again laughing.

"But, to be truthful, we blew it years ago. I don't know what I was doing trying to start it back up again. I think I was just kind of lost." He had his hands in his pockets, his face arranged in a fake-forlorn expression.

I shook my head. "But hey, we can still be friends."

He nodded. "That would be good. Let me buy you your dinner."

"You know, the more I think about it, the more I need that shower I mentioned. Plus, this much truth and drama requires a bit of thoughtful reflection, with ice cream. So I'll pass."

"But I'll see you? Tomorrow we were going to get together for kickball. You in?"

I smiled because he sounded kind of desperate, and I wasn't at all. I was actually more than relieved. This was exactly what needed to happen. I was going to be fine. After some ice cream of course. "I don't know if I'll be able to make it tomorrow, all I know is I'm going home now."

I turned and walked for my car and yanked on the door handle but it was locked. And I didn't have my keys or my purse or anything. Great. I turned back to the restaurant, Hayley, James, Michael, Quentin, and even Magnus were headed into the restaurant. I would have to walk up to the table, all eyes on me, to get my purse.

Maybe Hayley would bring it to me but she had been sitting

KAITLYN AND THE HIGHLANDER | 77

on the other side and my purse was on the ground out of sight. I leaned on my car swinging my foot through the gravel in frustration.

And then Magnus appeared, carrying my purse and my keys. Oh.

He walked across the parking lot. Out of the ordinary, big, dark, he walked like he owned walking. "I believed ye might be needin' these."

I dropped my eyes. "Thank you. I'm sorry about the scene. That was embarrassing." My hand shook as I put the key in the door and dropped into the driver's seat.

"Nae, this troublin' winna your fault, Mistress Kaitlyn. Master Cook, Master Greene, Master Peters, and I must bear the weight of the shame."

"It's the bro-code, whatever. It's my fault for believing I could trust him."

He solemnly shook his head. "Twas nae your fault at all."

"Thank you but I find myself in this position so often... There must be something really wrong with me. Like I'm broken or something..."

His brow drew down. "You art a braw lass and mighty capable, tis nocht wrong with ye, Mistress Kaitlyn of the North Winds." The corner of his mouth went up in a smile. "I found your description of Master Cook tae be a fine use of language."

"Well act like a rooster, I call you a rooster."

He stood in the space between my car and my door. I just met him, yet he was the only one still around. "How are you going to get your car home?"

He looked over his arm at his new car sitting under a light post. "Tis been many a year since I owned a horse I couldna ride."

I dropped my head on the seat back. I did really want to get home to sitting around, watching television, and feeling sorry for myself. There wasn't anyone in that restaurant though that could help Magnus get his car home without killing themselves. It was up to me. "What if I called Zach, got him to come with Emma. He could drive your car home for you?"

"Aye, t'would be a gracious favor."

I texted Hayley: Need Zach's phone number for Magnus.

She texted back: Girlfriend that sucked. I'm going to kill Michael. I'm so sorry James was an ass.

No worries. It's good to know he's the same guy. Kind of comforting actually. He's consistent.

Will you come tomorrow, kickball?

Doubt it. Need some time to get my head together.

Okay, not too long though.

She gave me Zach's number. I called and arranged for him to catch a ride to the restaurant and drive Magnus's car back. I hung up and dropped the phone in my lap. "They're on their way."

"Thank ye Mistress Kaitlyn."

"You're welcome." He gently closed the door, kept his hands there for a second longer and then returned to his car.

I started mine and pulled out of the parking lot looking back over my shoulder. Magnus had returned to the backseat of his car facing the restaurant. The crowded dining room was noisy, bright, and hectic. He was dark, in a pool of light, watching as I drove away.

CHAPTER 12

That night I ate a whole pint of Ben and Jerry's Americone Dream while I watched episodes of The Walking Dead. I was wrapped in a blanket because mom kept the AC on 68 degrees. It was frigid but truth be told I needed the blanket because the show was getting all dramatic, zombie gore and mayhem, plus ice cream.

Mom came into the room at one point. "How was your date with James?"

Dad followed her and disappeared into the kitchen.

I paused the show at the exact moment a zombie was ripping cheek skin off one of the regular characters. A gruesome freeze frame. "Not good. He was late. The ladies at the strip club kept him longer than usual."

Mom clucked. "He's a good catch, just tell him what your rules are and make him stick to them."

Dad added, while looking through the freezer, probably for the ice cream I just finished off. "Men go to strip clubs."

"Gross Dad, do you go to strip clubs? Mom do you know Dad goes to strip clubs?"

"I went to one back at John's bachelor party in 1999. Your mom knows."

I said, "Exactly, a bachelor party. Not on a Saturday when your date is waiting for you at a restaurant. Me and James are done."

Mom said, "Well, I'm sorry to hear that. First Braden, now this. What are you going to do?"

I huffed. "What do you mean what am I going to do? I'm going to be a grown-ass woman with a fabulous life, a good career, and whatevs — maybe I'll become a lesbian."

Mom looked shocked which was entirely my point. "I'm not sure that's a good idea. And also, my point is, you don't have a fab life, a career, or even seem much like a grownup, so maybe you need to work towards one of those goals."

"Yeah, yeah, I'll get right on it." I shoved my spoon into the pint carton.

"I can help you if you want to get your real estate license."

"Yes, I know, but mom it was a really hard day. Can I go back to the TV?"

CHAPTER 13

I slept like a stone and woke up early and groggy-headed. I was shuffling around the kitchen in boxers and a T-shirt, scratching and smacking, and hoping for some Nutella to magically appear, when my phone notified me of a text.

I glanced down and from Zach's phone the message said:

Aye MahgnusCambel

I laughed to myself. *Jeez, was he illiterate too?*

I texted back: Hi.

He texted: MistresKatlin

. . .

This is Kaitlyn. What can I do for you MahgnusCambel?

I couldn't help smiling at the thought of him holding Zach's tiny iPhone in a hand built for sword fighting, learning to text on it.

The dots appeared and stayed there and stayed there and stayed there. So I decided to help a man out and FaceTime him. The phone dialed and he answered, the camera aimed at the ceiling. The phone jiggled. The camera swept around aiming at everything but his face.

I said, "Magnus?

"Och, nae!" He dropped the phone with a cracking noise.

"Magnus? It's me, Katie. Just pick up the phone. Look down on it."

More muffled exclamations and voices emitted from the phone. The video jiggled up, dizzily swept around, and I was looking up at his face from very far below. He must have put the phone on the bed or something and was now looking down on it. Zach was laughing in the background.

"Magnus, did you break the phone?"

"Aye, there is a spiderweb upon it. You gave my heart a scare when your voice came from the inside."

"Tell Zach you'll buy him a new one."

"Aye, tis much the worse than when he lent it tae me."

"Why are you calling?"

"James Cook has invited me tae the games this day. I hoped ye would come. You might drive my Mustang, if ye are pleased tae." Zach cracked up in the background. Magnus's face turned to speak to someone off-screen. "Did I ask it well?"

A voice I assumed was Emma, Zach's girlfriend, said, "Totally."

I said, "I kind of thought I would stay home."

"Nae one else can attend. I would verra much like tae go."

I sighed. The hot Scot needed a chauffeur. I ought to tell Hayley to add it to his list of employees, but would I be okay with him not needing me at all? I said, "Okay, I'll be there at 2:30."

CHAPTER 14

$\mathcal{M}$agnus was waiting beside his car wearing his white loose shirt untied at the neck, his kilt, and leather boots. His very long sword was strapped across his back and his long knife was slung at his hip He handed me the keys, laid the sword across the back seats, and climbed into the passenger seat. It took a moment but I figured out how to put the top down. Once I pulled the car onto the road toward town, I sped it up to 45 mph.

"Tis a great many horses," said Magnus as he clamped his eyes shut. I opened it up to 50 mph, just for fun, but his death grip on his knees made me rethink. I dropped it down to 35 mph. It was an excellent car. A lot more power than my Prius. I liked power, oh yes, I did, and it was beautiful inside, leather and wood, very luxurious.

Even though I was going slower, he kept his eyes tightly closed. "You still haven't gotten used to riding?"

"Nae, I have grown used tae the blaring lights and clamorous sounds but traveling with this speed and roar I canna get comfortable with. The rush seems verra foolhardy. Master Peters explained twas quite safe, but did ye know tis combusting? There is a fire below us we canna see?"

As the car entered a roundabout at 12 mph, he held on to the dash and the door.

"Master Peters? Oh, that's right, Quentin."

"Aye, he's a good man, knowledgeable about armaments and fortresses."

"I suppose so, he was in the military." I kept the car at about 25 mph. "You ride a horse though? That's fast right?"

"Aye, but I understand my horse. It has a spirit I can tame. Tis under my control."

"You'll probably like this car once you learn to drive it."

"Will ye shew me?"

"Me?" I chuckled. "I think James would disagree. He thinks I'm a terrible driver."

"Master Cook may be in considerable error about a great many things."

We pulled up in front of the park. There were about eighteen people sitting on coolers, blankets, and in beach chairs. James was already standing in front of the group, commanding the audience. When I walked up, he held out a fist to bump mine. "Friends?"

I smiled. "Yep, friends."

He asked, "Occasionally more if you get drunk enough?"

"Jeez, you're incorrigible."

"Don't know what that means but I'll take it as a compliment."

James turned his focus to Magnus. "Magnus Campbell, you wore a skirt!"

Magnus lifted it enough to expose his knees with a laugh. "A wise man wants movement when performing feats of strength."

"Not really feats of strength, we'll be chasing this rubber ball around."

Magnus joked, "A wee ball is enough to impress your women?"

"Our women play too. How do you do it in Scotland?"

"We duel." He unsheathed his sword and allowed it to glint in the sun. "We toss caber and stone. Play our pipes. Tis quite manly."

"Have you ever played kickball before?"

"Nae."

"It's a lot like baseball. It's a bit like soccer, or football, as you call it. Different rules though and you can use your hands."

Magnus looked confused.

James asked, "Like football?"

"Ah, I have never played."

So James went through the rules of kickball. Then we divided up into teams. Magnus and I ended up on James's.

We had been gathering for kickball once a month in the summer since we were all about fifteen years old. Once we were old enough to find someone to buy alcohol the game included beer drinking. And once we were able to afford eating out, we would head to the Turtle for appetizers after. It was tradition, yet many of the faces were new. I supposed that was good news, it meant the tradition would carry on.

Magnus and I sat on the grass. I explained rules in the beginning but it only took him about five minutes to get the gist. And first try he was very good. When it was his turn to kick, he flew around the bases. When he was in the field he had such a good arm on him that by the second inning James put him on first base.

The first time I kicked I made it to third and with the next kicker speedily made it home for our team's second run. Magnus and James were both watching me appreciatively. Magnus especially. I had picked a great outfit, short shorts and a crop top, specifically for a little jealousy on James part but had grown used to believing that Magnus considered me the hired help. Un-hired help. Basically his chauffeur.

But his eyes followed me around the bases. That was awesome.

Because when he raced around the bases my eyes definitely followed him. He moved smooth, sure, like an athlete, someone who was used to moving, walking, running. He was laughing, joking, clapping people on the back, and fitting in, light-spirited, but then I glanced down at the sword beside me, big, heavy, menacing. It was hard to jibe the two.

James dropped beside me in the grass and watching Magnus run said, "So you like the Scotsman, huh? I see how it is."

"Don't go fooling yourself that he's why we're not together. That was all you."

"Yeah, I get it, but you're eyeing him like he's a prize and as your friend—"

"Friend advice already? Because I'm not eyeing him." I glanced up to see what he was doing, talking to Hayley. Yep, I was eyeing him.

James followed my gaze and joked, "Okay, you aren't but still if you decide to, be careful. I mean, he's a great guy, we all like him. He's a riot to hang out with but I'm worried for your sake that he's not what he seems. There's something off about him. He doesn't even know soccer. At all. You can't be from the UK and not know soccer. So who is he and what's he hiding? That's all I'm saying. Be careful."

"Finished?"

"Yep I'm finished, and here he comes anyway."

Magnus walked over and collapsed on the grass beside me. "Master Cook, tis a great game."

"You've got a knack for it. You sure you've never played it before? But you've definitely played soccer right?"

Magnus shook his head. "I canna say I have played it, but I would try it some—"

A great big whirling wind, a building cloud, and a giant storm grew right above us, just over the park. It was suddenly loud, yet we hadn't noticed it advance. It covered the sun. The kickball field was beside a large marsh and lightning struck a tree just on the edge of it, not sixty feet from where we were standing.

James yelled, "Go, go, go to the cars!"

Someone screamed because of the bolts, the energy, the darkness, as they raced to their cars. I grabbed my purse as I ran by, Another bolt of lightning arced through the sky just behind me. I broke stride gaping at it.

The surrounding cars were a flurry of activity as everyone yanked open doors and piled in on top of each other, lights on. Passengers huddled inside, sitting on laps, crammed in. Magnus shoved me from behind. "Get to the car, Kaitlyn, the car!" I raced for it, skidded around the back, yanked the door open, jumped in, and shoved the key in the ignition. I pressed the button to raise the roof. "Come on, come on!"

I looked back for Magnus. He was surrounded by upended coolers and tossed over chairs, staring up at the storm.

It was as if he was searching the storm cloud. Grey sky, blackened clouds, howling wind, electric arcs of light and thunderous booms, and Magnus, his hand on the hilt of his sword, peering up as if about to fight the darkness.

He stood amidst the lightning arcs, his hair and shirt and kilt whipping as he bent against the wind. The cloud built higher into the sky like a wall.

Magnus turned, running sideways, hand still on his hilt, looking back over his shoulder, racing to the car. He tore open the door, unsheathed his sword, dropped into the seat, and slammed it closed.

I asked, "What was that storm? That was crazy. Did you see something?"

He peered out the window, looking up at the sky. "Perchance I saw — something — but nae," he shook his head, "tis only a storm."

He pushed his sword into the seat behind him. "But did ye feel any difference in it?"

It had been a weird storm. Electric, loud, and it came up so fast. "Yes, it wasn't normal, there's no rain. And it was so sudden."

My phone startled me with a vibration.

Hayley texted: OMG What the hell was that crazy storm?

I looked over at James's truck. She was huddled on Michael's lap.

James texted a group of us: We're just going to sit here until it passes. That was insane. Hold your seats. No one get out of the cars. Katie tell Magnus sword fighting it won't help.

Hayley again: Tell Magnus he's going to get struck standing in a storm like that.

I said, "James and Hayley want you to know that standing in a storm is dangerous."

"Aye, tell them I know much the danger of a storm." He continued staring up at the sky. "This storm is more dangerous than most, tis a warning."

"Like an omen?"

"Aye." He peered out through the back window. "The storm is beginning tae abate." The clouds rolled up on themselves, smaller and smaller, until they disappeared as quickly as they came.

Magnus opened the door and stood outside of the car watching the sky, then he returned to his seat. "Tis gone, yet I would rather nae remain. Might ye drive me home, Mistress Kaitlyn?"

I texted the group: Well, the storm is gone, but we're not going to make it to the Turtle tonight. I'm going to drive Magnus home.

CHAPTER 15

I pulled the car into the garage right beside the newly contrived pen with a horse standing in it.

Magnus said, "Pray, come inside, Mistress Kaitlyn, I am still uncertain tis safe and I would like tae consult my men."

"I don't know, I haven't had a full day of feeling sorry for myself yet."

"I owe ye a dinner."

"True."

As I climbed the steps to his front door, Magnus was just behind, hand on the smaller knife at his waist, turning to look down the steps, watching that we weren't followed.

When Magnus crossed the threshold to the house, he announced, "Lights out." Behind me he locked the door. Zach had been bent over a baking sheet but stopped mid-movement, wiped his hands on his apron, and turned off the music. Then the kitchen lights. The house was full of the rich smells of steamed tomatoes and what was that, capers? Anchovies? I inhaled. It smelled of Puttanesca, my favorite. Zach and Emma both dropped down between the counter and the island in the shadow of the afternoon.

Lady Mairead had been sitting on the couch. She asked, "Twas a storm, like ours?"

Magnus said, "Aye, much like it. From nocht, accompanied with lightning and great gusts of wind."

"This means he has found it — in time he will decipher how tae use it." Lady Mairead swept up the stairs to the upper floors with her nurse following her.

Magnus turned off all the light switches, easily I might add. "Mistress Kaitlyn, pray join Chef Zach in the larder." At the wall controls he activated the window screens, then stepped out to the back deck. The last thing I saw before I settled below the counter was Magnus, his kilt flapping in the breeze of a coming storm, speaking with his security team on the back porch. They were checking the sky.

The house wasn't completely dark because it was afternoon but I marveled how the house and so many people had gone completely still and hidden.

Zach reached up and carefully, quietly, clicked off his sauce simmering on the stovetop.

All told, we stayed hidden for about five minutes. Then Magnus quietly opened the sliding door. He appeared in the kitchen a moment later and offered his hand to help me stand. "Many apologies, Mistress Kaitlyn, for causing ye worry. Tis all clear. I must ascend tae Lady Mairead's rooms for a moment. Pray Chef Zach, continue cooking, just nae music for a time."

Zach chuckled. "Yes sir, I'll keep it down." He stood and helped Emma up and they both turned on lights and the oven. Zach wiped his hands again, set the stove temperature back to simmering, and returned to his baking as Magnus climbed the stairs.

I took a seat on the barstool at the kitchen island and watched

Zach and Emma resume their baking, nonchalant, and seemingly unworried.

"What was that about?" I whispered.

Zach said, "We're not sure. The man that Lady Mairead was married to is looking for her. That's all we know. Magnus ran us through some drills the first day and," he grinned at Emma. "I think we were fucking perfect. Like these pastry puffs."

Emma stood on tiptoe to kiss his cheek. Chef Zach was tall and wiry, about six foot six and a hundred and sixty pounds wet.

I asked, "Her husband is coming by storm?"

Zach shrugged. "I think it's more like an omen but hey, believe what you want."

"I'm sorry about this. If I had known about the danger I wouldn't have put your name forward for the job."

Zach said, "Are you kidding me? This is the best fucking job I've ever had. I cook literally anything I want all day long, and Magnus acts like it's the best thing he's ever tasted. Emma and I go shopping and buy whatever looks good, cook enough for eight people, and basically hang out all day with each other, listening to music and watching television. The occasional lights-out-drill isn't going to send me packing."

Emma said, "Lady Mairead is quiet, doesn't talk much but seems to like our food and doesn't care either way what we do, but Magnus is so nice. Just like the nicest guy. Do you like him Katie?"

I looked up the stairs where he had gone. "We're just friends."

Zach asked, "Will you be staying to dinner? I'm making pasta. Get this, Magnus said he isn't familiar with Italian food, isn't that crazy?"

Suddenly our attention was drawn to the top of the stairs and hushed, arguing voices. Magnus and Lady Mairead were discussing something, heatedly.

"Nae, you canna return Magnus, I winna allow for it."

Magnus said, "I must, I need tae fight this battle there, rather than here. What would you have me do, nest as a field mouse in a log while he is a hawk circling, about tae dive down—"

"Twas dangerous traveling here but we find ourselves in this place. We must make do. When the time comes we will take it but now is nae the time."

"I can kill him. Let me return. I beg of you, Mairead. I should have done with this, allow me."

"Nae, tis my answer. You have sworn tae uphold my word and I say, nae. Tis a command, ye understand?"

"Aye."

A few minutes later Magnus entered the kitchen, shaking his head and muttering. Distracted, he asked, "Pray, what meal have ye prepared tonight, Chef Zach?"

"Italian food."

"Och aye, tis what ye explained this morn." He perched on a barstool beside me. "Mistress Kaitlyn, have ye eaten the cuisine of Italy? Chef Zach has assur'd me tis delicious."

Zach stifled a laugh.

"I have had Italian. It's one of my favorites. But Magnus, I know I keep asking this, is it safe? This is all really scary. You're talking about bad omens and we're all hiding in the kitchen…"

"Nocht will happen. We were nae followed, and my guard is on the walls. I promise tis safe." He glanced back up the stairs.

We went out on the deck to wait for dinner. Magnus assured me that the boardwalk would be safe, and when I looked back at the house a security guard was standing on an upper deck. We walked out halfway to the sand dunes.

"It's such a beautiful stretch of dunes here. Do you come here often?" I asked.

"I ride here every day, but I daena walk much."

"If I lived here, I would sit on these dunes for hours every day. And then I'd hunt shark teeth for a couple hours — I guess what I'm saying is I would pretty much live out here." I grinned at him. "How did you get the horse by the way?"

He sighed. "Tis nae really mine. Madame Debbie is loaning him tae me. She explains that I daena have permission tae keep it, so tis a matter of time afore the officials will require I relinquish him. There are a great many inscrutable rules."

"Yes, there are. Not a lot of horses."

"I am of a mind tae ignore them." He smiled. "And tis a braw horse by the name of Sunny. A name which fits his disposition, so I daena walk verra often."

I leaned my forearms on the railing and spotted a small turtle very near the neighbor's walkway about thirty feet away. It was traveling toward the beach. I pointed it out to Magnus. "It's one of the reasons we built these boardwalks to protect the dunes for the animals."

"For the turtles — you have gone tae all this effort?"

"Well, not me, specifically, but yes. All along here — this is sea grass. It's so pretty, isn't it, blowing and bending in the breeze? It looks light and airy and only decorative but the truth is it has roots that grow down into the dunes. The grasses hold the dunes in place, protecting them from the wind and water, and if the dunes are in place then the whole island stays in place. So we protect the sea grass."

Magnus nodded slowly. "You know much of this land."

"I grew up here. I moved away, but I came back." I pushed my shoes off, kicked them to the side, and wiggled my toes happy to have them off. "I came back to get some solid ground under my feet but there's not a lot about Amelia Island that's solid ground.

It's all sand shifting, marsh ebbing and flowing, ocean rising and falling, and wind blowing."

"There is also a great deal of torrential rain."

"Well, you sir, are visiting during one of our wettest months. It seems like a storm every other day."

"When the storm clouds part though, tis beautiful. In Scotland we have a word, turadh, a break in the clouds."

I tried to say it. "Turad?"

He smiled and said it again. "Turadh. Aye. In Scotland though we have far fewer breaks in our clouds."

"So it's gray there?" I turned to lean my back against the rail. His shirt was pulled tight across his shoulders, a curl of his hair fluttering a bit on his cheek in the wind. Our shoulders had been almost touching and now I regretted turning and making the gap between our arms wider. "That would be hard on me. I grew up in sunny Florida and lived for a while in sunnier California. I like a bright blue sky overhead."

"You would nae like it much then, tis verra dreich weather."

"What does dreek mean?"

"Tis Gaelic for miserable weather. In Scotland tis dreich and terrible because ye must wander about in it anyway."

The light was changing. The sunset dropping behind the house. The sky a luminous pink, a bright blue overhead meeting deep black from the edge of the ocean. Black pushing against blue pushing against pink. Sea grass bowed toward the sunsetting side. Security stood watch at the end of the deck, and Magnus, big, still, secure, and warm as the breeze, leaning on the railing with a smile at the edge of his mouth, his jawline within kissing distance. "Do ye see this sky Mistress Kaitlyn? Tis as if the sun is pulling a blanket of stars over your land."

"Over your land and your house."

He chuckled but seemed as if there was a hint of sadness to it.

"I have only borrowed the land, the house, the time, tis nae truly mine."

"It hasn't been mine for a long while either, I was living in Los Angeles until just a couple of weeks ago."

"And where is this Los Angeles?"

I searched his expression for a sign that he was joking but his eyes were serious. "It's in California. The west coast. One of the biggest cities in the world. Where movies are made?"

Magnus nodded. "Och aye, of course, Los Angeles."

We were quiet for a moment watching the sky as the light met dark and battled for supremacy in the middle.

Magnus asked, "What happened tae ye, Mistress Kaitlyn?"

I laughed a bit. "You saw the video, right? Quentin and James showed you?"

"Aye, they have shewed me, but they shewed me much that needed further explanations. I have grown used to your teachings and would consider it a great favor for ye tae give me the history of it."

"You know... I really, really, really don't want to talk about it."

"Tis your prerogative. I winna do ye a disservice and press further on the subject."

"Good."

But he had already seen it. He was forming opinions on it with or without my explanations. I sighed. "Are we friends?"

"Aye, we have shared a beer and a laugh."

"If I show you the video, you might..." Tears welled up a bit. I was able to blink them back but couldn't trust myself to keep talking. I took a couple of deep breaths.

"Might what?"

"Think I'm awful. Terrible. An old vengeful hag or something."

"How auld do ye take me for, Mistress Kaitlyn?"

"I don't know, same as me, twenty-three or so?"

"Twenty-one. I suppose a grown man of twenty-one might yet know how tae wipe his arse and where tae relieve himself in a civilized manner, yet I found myself in a cruel predicament just a few days back. Twas a woman, much like ye'self that shewed me how tae perform those duties, and she did it with much good humor and grace without any malice. I would wish tae repay her with the same good faith and humor if she found herself in need of my opinion."

I screwed my face up considering. "You promise? You won't think I'm terrible?"

"Nae, and I have already seen the story."

"Okay, fine, but after dinner."

CHAPTER 16

The smells of Zach's sauce wafted around us as Magnus sat between Lady Mairead and me at one end of their new extremely long dining room table. As Zach and Emma placed the plates in front of us, Magnus stared hungrily at his. "As usual, the history of this meal, please Chef Zach?"

Zach chuckled. "It's pretty scandalous, Magnus, sir."

"I've an appetite for scandalous histories." Magnus winked at me. "How about ye'self Lady Mairead?"

She said, "Tis good tae hear the misfortunes and scandals of another. Will make our own seem comparatively small, and we might learn something as well through our blushes."

Magnus tucked his napkin into the top of his shirt and motioned for Zach to get on with it. "We are ready."

Emma laughed. "I told you he would make you say it, Zach."

Zach said, "The story goes that in Naples, Italy, brothels would cook this very robust and fragrant sauce to entice the Italian gentleman inside to partake of their, um, services. The men would do their business and get a bonus of hearty pasta to energize them after. The taste and smell would um, cover the taste and smell. Thus in some circles, Puttanesca is referred to as whore sauce."

Magnus boomed with laughter. "Ah, tis truly scandalous."

Lady Mairead smiled. "And I have learned a new art, spices as a cover for intrigue."

"It should serve ye well in your contrivances." Magnus grinned mischievously and ate with enthusiasm.

Zach and Emma sat at the opposite end of the table after shuttling plates of food out to the deck for the security men. And a plate upstairs for the nurse.

Magnus asked for double helpings, twice. Zach or Emma jumped to retrieve the platters from the kitchen to serve it. He complimented and thanked and wanted us all to agree. "Tis delicious! Do you like it Mistress Kaitlyn?"

"One of my favorites."

"Good, good. Lady Mairead, do ye like the meal our Chef Zach has cooked?"

"I do, verra much."

Magnus called across the table to the kitchen where Zach and Emma, having finished their dinner, were washing dishes. "Chef Zach, best meal so far, well done."

"Thank you, sir."

Magnus patted his flat stomach. "I am much satiated. We should retire tae the grand room. Mistress Kaitlyn has promised tae shew a — what is the phrasing?"

"A video. But in front of everyone?"

Magnus asked, "Chef Zach, have ye seen the video of Mistress Kaitlyn?"

Zach met my eyes for a second. "Um, I have. That guy was a total pribbling ill-bred maggot-mouth." He grinned at Magnus, who smiled widely. "Magnus has asked me to take up more creative cursing than my usual f-bombs."

Magnus headed to the living room settling in the big chair he slept in that first night. "See, ye are among friends. Lady Mairead, would ye like tae see the video of Mistress Kaitlyn's downfall?"

Lady Mairead sat on the couch and smoothed her skirts. "I have an inordinate appreciation of the dramatic."

I sighed, turned on the TV, connected my phone to it, and sat in one of the overstuffed chairs. It was a pale yellow so I was pretty sure I shouldn't tuck up my feet having been barefoot for about an hour. "Fine, but I'm going to start with a video where I'm awesome." I found my old YouTube channel, KatieMakeSTuff, and scrolled through the best, most popular videos to one of my favorites: an ice cream sundae tutorial. Braden was in it, so I had to look at the lying sack of shit but figured it would help in explaining the whole sordid tale. I could feel Zach and Emma behind me. It was hard enough showing the video to Magnus and Lady Mairead when they knew nothing about YouTube and pop culture but Emma and Zach knew how hard and how far I had fallen.

The sundae tutorial was twelve minutes long and I was cute and funny in it. Braden was adoring and a little incompetent which made our viewers believe he was sweet, honest, and the vulnerable one. In it I made a three-layer sundae with caramel sauce, hot fudge sauce, and raspberry sauce, plus I placed a bit of dry ice in each so that fog poured over the edge of the bowls, covering the table.

Magnus watched the video wide-eyed. Then when it was over asked, "Chef Zach, could ye make a concoction such as this?"

"Right now?"

"Och aye, with a wee bit of cloud inside the bowl?"

"I can. Emma, would you go to the store for some dry ice and more ice cream?" Zach and Emma stood in the kitchen looking through the freezer and the cabinets for the ingredients.

Lady Mairead asked me, "So this is your work, Mistress Kaitlyn?"

"Yes, I mean, it was. I don't do it anymore."

"And this man is?"

"He was the man I was going to marry."

Lady Mairead sat up straighter. "Well now, this is an interesting history." A second video began playing automatically. This one was very popular — Braden and I were picking out the invitations for our wedding. I started to click it off but Lady Mairead said, "I would verra much like tae watch this one as well."

I glanced at Magnus, who nodded. "Aye, but if it contains more recipes we may need Zach tae sit with us tae list it down."

Emma zoomed out the door with a laugh.

Zach joked, "Magnus sir, I can't make anything else, Emma already left."

Magnus sighed jokingly. "I must settle with magical foggy ice cream then. Mistress Kaitlyn, pray continue."

In the video Braden and I sat staring into the camera, giggling into each other's ears, bumping shoulders, and joking with each other. It was so sweet how he deferred to me in the decisions, telling me I was beautiful and so great. At one point he said he loved me.

I turned the remote control over and over in my hands as tears welled up again. I blinked them down watching as my video-self held up invitation samples, thinking, *this was such a big decision, the typeface, the color of the paper, the style of the embossing* — it felt important.

I had been stressed out by the decision and Braden had been so kind and considerate and loving through it. Yet at the time he was already in love with someone else. I had been so happy in this video, so in love. And he was such a good liar.

I tried to wipe an escaped tear from my cheek without anyone seeing.

Lady Mairead had a look in her eye of deep scrutiny. "What happened tae this man ye were tae marry?"

I said, "He decided to marry someone else."

Lady Mairead blinked. "Well — tis unforgivable."

Magnus said, "Let's see then."

I went to Braden's channel, BradenthenedarB, glancing at his subscriber numbers, 2.1 million. Great, growing bigger every day, and there it was, his most popular video: the day of my freak out.

Zach said, "Have you ever personally shown this to anyone before?"

I said, "Nope. Haven't needed to, everyone's seen it already. Plus, as you can imagine, I don't really like to watch it. Anymore." I glanced at their faces. Magnus's looked expectant. Lady Mairead's seemed curious. Zach's seemed concerned. "Are you sure you want to see it?"

Magnus said, "Aye. Let us see it, Mistress Kaitlyn. I promise it will be better than nocht."

I pushed play.

There I was waiting at a table, talking to the camera, explaining that we were there for our wedding cake tasting and filming it on Facebook Live. Then Braden appeared and I was thrilled. I threw my arms around his neck and kissed him hello, knowing our audience would love it.

The bakery was upscale, exclusive, and trendy. We had a special table because this was excellent PR for the bakery; we broke records for how many people were viewing. Something about our cute personas, our 'in love' romantic gestures, our playful teasing, and upbeat personalities. Our channel was getting a lot of traffic and money was rolling in, so our wedding would have the best of everything, which tied us into the lucrative wedding market.

I was wearing a beautiful sun dress. It was white because — bride, and it had a wide skirt and lace. My hair was up in a twist and I had daisies placed in the back. I looked beautiful and my smile was wide. I loved Braden so much.

He and I drank four mimosas before the first bite of cake hit my mouth. I was giggling and pretty gosh darned buzzed. What I didn't notice then but anyone could see plainly now was that he was leaned back in his chair, distracted. I reached out for his hand and he shifted it away. I had watched this so many times since it happened, obsessed with the details of it.

There was a moment where I asked, "Isn't this one so scrumptious Braden?" And he didn't respond. Instead he scowled and asked for another Mimosa.

Finally, after so much awkwardness that my heart wanted to break watching it, he said, in front of the whole wide world, "I don't want to marry you, Katie. I'm in love with another girl," and my heart flooded my brain with a tsunami of crazy.

I glanced at the couch. Lady Mairead's eyes were wide.

Magnus's eyes were squinted in concentration.

Zach was perched on the arm of the couch, hand over his mouth, suppressing all facial reactions to be polite because we had reached that moment where I flung myself across the table, squashed cake into the front of my dress, and clawed his face in my fury.

I was not proud of this and wanted to run from the room in shame. Magnus stood and crossed to the screen. He watched up-close turning his head from side to side. "Stop, there, if ye will, Mistress Kaitlyn." He tapped the screen next to my right arm as I was about to reach out with my claws. "I wonder ye dinna have a weapon. You might have killed him."

Lady Mairead said, "You should have killed him. Never attend a dinner with a man ye haena married without a blade — here," she pointed between her breasts, "or here." She daintily lifted her skirts and patted her ankle.

Magnus said, "Och aye, tis true. Right here." He pointed at

my thigh on the screen. "If ye had been wearin' a dirk under your skirt, there, ye might have had it at the rascal's throat afore he finished speakin'."

I laughed. "But then I would be a murderer! I'd be in jail!"

Lady Mairead said, "Nonsense, surely they winna jail a woman when the scoundrel hath deserv'd the blade."

"Yes, they would." I opened my eyes wide, incredulous, but also pretty amused. Zach was stifling a giggle.

Lady Mairead said, "If there are laws, then fine, daena run him through with a blade. Instead you would add a bit o'hemlock to his food day by day."

My eyes went even wider. "You think I should have killed him?"

Both Magnus and Lady Mairead answered in unison, "Aye."

I let the video play out. I looked insane of course but Magnus and Lady Mairead didn't seem bothered by it. He asked me to pause again. "How many people have watched this?"

I said, "Millions."

Lady Mairead kept her eyes on the screen. "And this was your work, do ye still perform these duties?"

I said, "No, public opinion took his side. While I was lying in bed feeling sorry for myself, he created a video showcasing his injuries—"

Magnus said, "What? That wee scratch upon his cheek? Any real man would bear more in silence."

Zach said, "If you think about it, he killed you, your good name. Whose idea was it to do the cake-tasting on Facebook Live, anyway?"

I said, "His."

Zach said, "So he premeditated it too. That sucks, Katie."

Emma walked in just then with three bags of groceries. Zach jumped up and helped her carry them to the kitchen. Emma glanced at the screen and looked at me sadly from across the room.

Magnus said, "Thank ye for shewin' me."

I gave him a half-smile. "Yeah, no problem. You know, I actually feel a little bit better. I felt so ashamed of my behavior. It's kind of nice to know someone on earth believes I didn't go far enough."

Lady Mairead said, "He must consider himself graced he winna whipped for his behavior. How did the church stand on this breach of divine law?"

"Um, I don't think the church had any say in it."

"Well, tis unfortunate. I believe his priest should have weighed in on the matter."

I smiled. "Had the church been involved they might have forced him to marry me, then I'd be stuck with him. I consider myself lucky." It was the first time I uttered something like that out loud.

Magnus said, "I would like tae know how Mistress Kaitlyn, with so much wit and good sense, came tae be entangled with two such foolish men?"

"I ask myself that every day."

Zach and Emma clanked dishes while making our sundaes. Lady Mairead asked, "What do ye mean, Magnus, 'two such men'? Twas another one?"

Magnus said, "The man who gave us shelter the first night we arrived, James Cook. I have seen him behave much the same as this tae Mistress Kaitlyn. She then called him a brainless cock."

An imperious smile spread across Lady Mairead's face. "Well done, but Mistress Kaitlyn, I urge ye tae carry a weapon. And ye must marry. Women have considerable amounts tae manage already without applying so much effort in building an alliance. You should pick a man who suits ye, who furthers your aims, and ye must marry him. Then ye might apply your wisdom tae other duties such as ruling your household. And your husband would carry a weapon on your behalf."

"Generally speaking that is the exact opposite of most advice I receive. I hear I need to grow up and become independent."

"Tis true that women must grow up. But what foolishness is this, independence? We are the unifying force of the family. Without us our men are merely roosters, crowing about in the dirt, strutting and fighting."

Magnus laughed. "I am nae sure if the comparison of manhood tae a rooster is deserv'd or nocht, but tis happenin' verra regular."

Lady Mairead raised her brow. "You art less cock, more bull."

Magnus laughed again. "Aye, now this comparison is deserv'd."

Zach said, "Sundaes are served."

As Magnus rose to lead me to the dining room table again, he said, "Chef Zach is playing music for me each night at dessert. Last night was...What music was it?"

"Last night it was the Beatles."

Magnus said, "Verra loud and strong."

Zach said, "Tonight sir, I was planning to play you a band called Nirvana."

I laughed. "If you thought the Beatles were loud..."

I sat down to my bowl of smoking ice cream. Magnus agreed it was magical. Lady Mairead declared it too sweet for her tastes. I felt lighter than I had in weeks and asked for seconds.

CHAPTER 17

The following day I was in my parents' living room curled up on the couch watching the third episode in a row of The Handmaid's Tale at ten in the morning. I didn't know why I was watching something so dark. I had woken up that morning fresh, with clarity. Listening to Magnus and Lady Mairead talk about murdering Braden had put everything in perspective.

He had deserved an epic beating. I had let him off easy, considering. Hell, I had showed restraint. Maybe most of the world didn't agree, but the two weirdly anachronistic Scots I found myself hanging out with thought my only failure had been in not being more dangerous.

I switched the show off and watched a New Girl episode instead. I had watched this one before, but it made me laugh and laughter was a relief. I actually felt a little like I had gained some of my confidence.

I still had a little money in the bank.

I could go back to college if I wanted to, or get a job if I felt like it.

I was living rent free, free food, too.

I had my old friends gathered around me and had successfully friend-zoned James. He sent me a text late last night: Second thoughts? Wanna come over?

And I answered: Not on your life, enjoy your left hand.

And he texted me a smiley face and then: Sweet dreams.

I had Hayley. She wasn't always a perfect friend. But she had been constant.

And I had my new friendship with Magnus. He was interesting, a bit lost, but also so competent, strong and sure at the same time. I couldn't figure out how he seemed so powerful even though he didn't know how to drive. For one thing, though he was completely incompetent, he wasn't defensive about it. That was a relief. It was really sweet how he asked to see my video because he wanted me to explain it.

I liked it when he said my—

"Mistress Kaitlyn!" My name was yelled outside. Also, there were hoof steps on the pavement.

I rushed to the front window. Magnus was on a horse riding up and down the road outside my parents' house. He called again, "Mistress Kaitlyn!"

I stepped out to the front stoop and called to him thirty feet down the street. "Magnus Campbell, what are you doing here?"

He turned his horse, a breeze through his hair, muscles taut on his forearm, a beaming smile, and cantered to my front yard. And yes, this made me a little breathless. "I have come tae ask ye tae shew me the fort. Chef Zach says tis verra historical."

"Fort Clinch, by horse?"

"Aye, by horse. I canna park Sunny here."

I patted the side of my hair. I had slept in a braid. Now fuzzy. My pajama pants were covered in little kittens chasing balls of yarn, which was ironic because I have never knitted or enjoyed kittens much, having a pretty strong cat allergy. My tank top had a smear from a dollop of Nutella I dropped that morning while eating waffles for breakfast. I hadn't cared because television watching was the only thing on my agenda. And just a couple minutes ago I thought I had mojo.

"Okay, but I have to get ready."

"I will wait for ye."

I rushed into the house, threw clothes all over the floor trying to find the right pair of pants, then the perfect crop-top, and rushed to the bathroom. I sniffed my pits, rubbed a razor over them, splashed them with water, patted them dry, swiped on deodorant, untwisted my hair from the braids, and finger combed the curls with frizz-stop oil.

I peeked through the blind. Magnus was standing beside his horse, looking up and down the street in a white linen shirt and a kilt that draped and hugged in all the right ways — I brushed my teeth, splashed water on my face, and arched my eyebrows and darkened my lashes for a 'natural look.' Finally, I got dressed.

Final check. I looked pretty gosh darn good considering twenty minutes before I was curled on the couch with no plans but TV.

I met Magnus outside.

Magnus easily pulled himself up and onto the horse. He held down a hand. "Have ye ever ridden?"

I shook my head. I was a little awestruck now that I was looking up at this great big horse. Magnus was up there, looking down. What was I supposed to do, somehow scale the side of this living beast? It was like climbing those rope ladders into tree-houses while all your friends waited for you at the top, never as easy as you wanted it to be. I put my hand in his and he raised me enough to get a foothold. He directed my right leg across in front of him, firmly held my left thigh as I balanced, and once I landed, pulled my hips close.

He held the reins in front of me, his arms around, and the

horse broke into a trot. My parents' house was only two blocks off the beach, so we quickly made it to the sand and turned north.

The temperature was uncomfortable, the hot sun beating down. Sweat pooled on my upper lip. The horse had a nice rock and roll between my legs, but the pitch and rhythm caused me to be hyperaware of Magnus's chest, almost, not quite, pressed to my back, his thighs pressed alongside my thighs, his hands just between my —

His breath was so close, and the horse's movement so hypnotizing that I was lulled into fantasizing. I considered collapsing into a feigned faint so he could carry me off and do whatever. My excuse would be: horseback was pretty hot. Very hot.

It took about forty-five minutes to reach the beach access for Fort Clinch. We tied the horse along a railing in a shady spot in the campground, gave it water, and paid the ranger to keep an eye on it for us. Then Magnus opened a saddlebag and pulled out a package of waxed paper wrapped around a hunk of aged cheddar and a loaf of bread. We made a few rudimentary, but delicious, sandwiches, and followed it with swigs from a glass bottle of water.

And then we walked up the path to the fort. When we pulled into view, Magnus stood still and looked down the outer walls, up at the cannons, and around the base. I waited until he was done inspecting. We reached the front gate and Magnus pressed a hand to the stone.

I said, "It was built around 1850. It's very, very old."

He started, surprised. "Oh, and how many years...?"

"A hundred and seventy years, give or take."

His brow furrowed as we walked through the tunnel to the interior of the fort. We explored the entire building, the hallways, turrets, and up on the cannonades. Magnus barely spoke. He ran his hand along the bricks and on the cannons. In the areas that were made to look like civil war bunk houses he stood for a very long time.

Whenever he was quiet staring, I found myself explaining. "This room looks like a bunkhouse from the Civil War," and, "this is a pump for water, just like they used back then."

He listened, nodded, and then we walked to the next place. We did this for a long time, from tunnel and wall to the next tunnel and wall. "Sometimes there are re-enactors here."

He asked vaguely, "Re-enactors?"

"They wear costumes and pretend to live during the Civil War."

He said, "Och aye, because twas so long ago. I see..."

Finally, after seeing everything, we walked back to his horse and led it out to the sand. The beach was wide here, the sand white and glistening in the sun, powdery, covered in shells.

"Have you ever seen anything as beautiful as this beach, Magnus?"

He looked at me sidelong. "Nae, I have never seen such beauty."

We took off our shoes and took a few steps. "I love the feel on my feet. It makes a noise when I step in it, like a faint vibration — a crunch in my head, not my ears. Do you hear that — listen, the sand?"

"Aye, tis verra loud."

"That's right, I forgot how sensitive your ears are." We stood for a moment, digging our toes in the sand, staring out at the water, Magnus's horse standing calmly beside him. I said, "Here's the last thing I'm going to show you today, unless I think of something else of course — when you come to the beach you have to dip your toes in the water. It's tradition."

We walked to the edge of the ocean and squished our toes into the wet sand. The warm water lapped around our ankles. "If you walk on the beach, you have to have sand from mid-calf-down; it's like a rule." I splashed water and sand on my feet. "And now you have to look for seashells and shark teeth."

"Shark teeth?"

"I'll show you." I found an area of shells that looked promising. I crouched and sifted through the tiny shells and sand. "There!" I held up a small black triangle. "The tooth of a shark. They're everywhere on these beaches because we dredge out the channel and put the sand on the shoreline to keep the beach from shifting away."

Magnus turned the shark tooth in his fingers. "Tis marvelous. I have seen sharks afore, but nae their teeth."

"When did you see a shark?"

"When I crossed tae France."

"Wait — what? You've been to France? They're definitely part of the EU, and you've never seen a McDonalds?"

He grinned. "I consider m'self quite fortunate. If I had already seen a McDonalds, ye couldna introduce me tae it. From what I see ye are verra happy while providing instructions." The edge of his lips turned up in a smile. "I am afraid ye would find me verra bland and ill-suited if I had seen much of this already."

I laughed. "I do really really love to show things to people. I hope I'm not making you crazy."

"Nae, tis as it should be, I know nocht about this place."

I returned to crouching and sifting around in the shells for another tooth. My chin on my knee, thinking. After a few minutes I wondered aloud, "I mean, I thought the world was a lot of the same thing everywhere. That France would have junk food. I guess I should go travel, huh? Is Scotland beautiful?"

"Aye, tis a braw place."

"Braw?"

"Tis grand, braw."

I repeated, "Braw," then dropped to sitting, splaying my legs out in front of me. I gave up on shark tooth hunting because the sun was heading down. The sunset cast shadows on the shells and dips and hills of the beach making it impossible to spot the tiny little triangles. Magnus crouched beside me, holding the reins, watching the waves.

I asked, "Do you miss Scotland? Will you go home soon?"

"Aye, I miss it verra much. This place tis fair full of bonnie maidens," he cast a smile at me, "but tis verra foreign. I will be reliev'd when I return. Soon I think, much there needs be done." He looked down at the shark tooth in his palm. "Might I keep this?"

I nodded, so he placed it in the bag he wore at his hip. He stood and offered a hand to help me up. "Tis growing dark, we should return. Will ye stay tae dinner?"

"I have plans tonight with Hayley, our weekly meet-up at a little restaurant off Centre Street. Would you like to come?"

"Will ye drive the Mustang?"

I said, "Definitely. I'm really cool when I drive it, have you seen how cool I am?"

"Cool?"

I chuckled. "Like grand."

"Och aye, ye are braw when ye drive my car." He swung up onto the horse and held down his hand. It took me two tries. I was tired and missed when he pulled, falling back and off.

Magnus laughed. "You ought tae go up, not down."

"I know, but my legs are wiggly." The next time I was able to swing up in front of him again. Something about the long day together, the close proximity, the long pauses — I began to suspect he was going to kiss me. Like *really* kiss me.

And that I really, really wanted him to.

The day was still warm, the ocean sparkling in the long afternoon sun. The tide was low. Shells crunched under the horse's hooves. Our bodies rocked together as we rode, again in silence, but a comfortable one. It was also uncomfortable, charged and expectant, those two things existed in the space. His forearms rested on my thighs and I let myself relax a bit, leaning back, closing the space between us.

With his arms and shoulders curved around me, I could smell him — musk and spice and leather and wool. I closed my eyes, the movement rocking me. Could I be this silly; was I falling for the rich Scotsman?

Hayley knew I was a sucker for a prince on a horse. I lived in the real world though, I never thought I would actually meet one. What did I know about this guy, anyway?

He was running from something. Dangerous. He carried a sword. That was truly all I knew.

He shifted slightly, took the reins in one hand, and twisted to look behind us. I missed his arms around me. I had gone untethered.

Then he shifted again. His arms enclosed me, white linen sleeves brushing my bare arms, the reins went back into both his hands equally, and I could have sworn he inhaled deeply, just near the back of my head.

Quietly, in his rumbling baritone of a voice, he said, "Tha thu a 'fàileadh mar ghaoith."

"What does that mean?"

"You have the scent of a breeze, or perhaps, osna, a sigh."

My breath caught. "I do — I mean, that's a compliment?"

He said simply, "Aye."

And I wondered if I really truly might swoon into his arms. Except I was already there, in his arms, collapsing would just be extra.

CHAPTER 18

Finally home, Magnus dropped me at the closest beach access. The walk was easy for me, but a horse traipsing up and down the subdivision's roads might cause a problem.

I sort of hoped there would be some kind of kiss goodbye. Possibly like that scene from the movie where the couple collapses into the surf. We could kiss in the water with the waves washing around us, or not. That might be weird. But anyway, our goodbye was far more ordinary. Magnus helped me slide down to the sand and then he looked down at me, the horse stepping side to side. I supposed it was happy to have me off, lighter now, wanting to run.

I said, a little awkwardly, "I'll pick you and the Mustang up at seven?"

Magnus nodded. "I look forward tae seeing ye." And then he rode away.

On the walk back home I considered the day. Was I starting something with the Scotsman and was that okay?

I had been mooning over Braden. Now I hadn't thought

about him at all since yesterday, except to lament the time I wasted thinking about him. He sucked. And Magnus didn't. That was nice. I actually liked Magnus a lot. Like a lot a lot.

At home I got dressed for the night. A cute sundress — a little slip of a piece along with strappy sandals. I put my hair up into a messy bun. I had a little pink from the sun across my nose and hoped it made me look cute and sunshiny.

I drove to Magnus's after eating a quick dinner with my parents.

They were irritated that I was partying so often and not focusing on my next plan. I tried to tell them I was still sad about Braden, but I don't think the sun-kissed nose and the cute little dress really sold: depression.

Mom squinted her eyes. "Are you seeing James tonight?"

"Just meeting friends."

She met my father's eyes. "The gossip on the island is that you're spending a lot of time with Magnus Campbell. I need to tell you that does not seem like a good idea."

I scowled. "I'm not spending a lot of time with him. I — we're friends."

She said, "Good, keep it that way. Your father is his money manager. I'm making a tidy sum off his lease, plus I plan to speak to him about some real estate investments. If you're playing footsie with him under the table, it might complicate things. So don't." She ended firmly.

"Don't complicate things or play footsie?"

"Don't be a smart ass Katie, you know what I mean. A big part of our income this month and possibly into the foreseeable future is dependent on the estate of Magnus Campbell. It won't be a good idea if you go messing it up with him."

"I'm not going to mess anything up."

"Well, you know how you get dear," said Dad.

"How I get? Man, I'm so sick and tired of people saying that to me. I don't *get* any way. I react when people treat me badly. That's all. I just happened to be on camera when it happened. I'll admit it wasn't a good look for me, but Braden is the asshole in this situation. He's the one who gets..." I trailed off because I had stopped making sense and sounded like a petulant kid.

Was that a side effect of being in my twenties and living with my parents — every interaction turned me into their child?

Mom said, "Well dear, you brought it up. Your dad and I spoke about it and unless we see real improvements in your life, a job, money coming in, something besides sunbathing all day, you'll need to find a new place to live."

"You're going to kick me out? My fiancé broke my heart a month ago, and you're punishing me?"

"No, see, this is what you do. I explain what will happen if you don't do something and all you hear is what will happen. You completely ignore what actions you can take to make it not happen. You've always done that since you were little. I would say put your toys away or I'll take them all and donate them to poor kids who will be grateful for them, and you'd burst into tears completely ignoring the part where you need to put your toys away."

"So you're saying I don't accept your threats in the manner you intend them, and that's my problem? Maybe I simply don't respond well to threats?"

Dad chuckled. "Now now, don't go flying across the table."

"Jesus Christ Dad, are you serious about this?"

Mom said, "You've been here for a week, we're just wondering how long you'll be staying."

I sighed, deeply. "Fine, I'll move out."

"That's not what we're saying at all."

"It's what I'm hearing. I'll see if I can stay with Hayley for a bit while I figure out what to do next. Maybe a hotel. I can probably afford that for a few weeks."

Dad said, "If you invested what little money you have left it would grow."

"When new money was coming in, it might have been good for investing, but right now I need it for living."

"You could be a YouTuber again."

I pushed food around on my plate. "I've been disgraced. I'm not going to be able to start over, not without some serious PR, and I don't really have it in me. I would like to go to school…"

"You quit school to start your business. Now you quit your business and want to go back to school. Maybe you should consider real estate. Sell houses that's where the future is."

Dad said, "Or plumbing. There's great money in plumbing, or risk management in the financial sectors."

They both cleared their plates as if the matter had been well-discussed.

I SnapChatted Hayley a selfie with crossed eyes.

I wrote: Parents suck, can I crash at your place for a week?

Her reply was a selfie with a grin. She wrote back: Yes. Pay rent and you can stay as long as you want.

I took a photo of myself frowning: How much is rent?

She smiled in her picture: $200 a month.

I wrote back: Done.

CHAPTER 19

I drove to Magnus's to pick him up. He was waiting
downstairs again, a knife at his hip, sword on his back.
A little pink on his nose too, but his came across as rugged and
handsome. He seemed happy to see me and I caught him
checking out my legs, which was entirely the point of the dress.
Nicely done, self.

I loved driving the Mustang. It was fast, with a purr, and
when I was driving, it made me feel sexy.

I looked over my arm at other drivers imagining them thinking, *Who's that sexy girl?* Because I looked amazing and beside
me? Magnus. Handsome. Hair blowing in the warm breeze. And
we were going out together. His shoulder near mine, my thoughts
on him. His leg draped in his kilt, so close to my leg, mere inches.
Farther away than today on the horse, but still...

"What did Chef Zach make you for dinner tonight?"

"A dish I believe he called fettochina alfredric. Verra delicious, but all Chef Zach's recipes are good. This evenin' he had
me listenin' tae Grand Band. He and Emma danced on the deck.
Twas a braw evening. I would have liked ye tae be there."

I glanced over my driving arm trying to read his face. "I wish I had been. My dinner was frozen broccoli and rice with leftover chicken. The entertainment was my mom and dad telling me to get on with my life. I'll be moving in with Hayley this weekend."

"You have been punish'd, for what offense?"

"It's more like a threat of punishment to force me to get a job, but I don't like threats. I never have. So I went ahead and told them I would move away." It dawned on me right then that this was a sad, sad story. Not a principled reaction, but a depressing turn, further downward, of my life to a very bleak rock bottom. "I guess after I lost my fiancé, my career, my apartment and money, losing my parents is the next glorious step in my epic, awesome life."

He watched me from the corner of his eye. "I was sent from my home when I was but eleven years auld. I lived under the guardianship of my uncle, in London, verra far from my kinsmen and my Highland home. So I understand what ye are goin' through. Tis difficult when your life is a trial tae your parents."

"But you're living with your mother now, protecting her. It's better, right?"

"Nae, tis nae better. I must do as she commands, but my plans are verra different from Lady Mairead's plans. Soon enough our paths will diverge."

I turned the car up Sadler Avenue toward the restaurant. Parking was easy, just down the street. We walked together past quaint little historic buildings, keeping an easy stride that matched well. When we walked into the small bar all eyes turned to us. I was decent height for a girl, but he was tall and big shouldered and still had that smoldering darkness. I could never reconcile it with his actual coloring. It seemed as though he was unlit.

It made me believe in auras actually; I never had before. Seeing his shadows were darker, his light dimmer, made me understand what people meant when they used that word.

But also, he wasn't frightening. I had dropped my guard days and days ago and trusted him completely. He seemed so competent and true. I pushed through the crowd toward Hayley, Michael, Quentin, and James sitting in the back in the courtyard. Sarah was sitting beside Hayley and there was an empty chair beside James with a girl's pastel sweater thrown over the back.

For a testy second I thought, *really jerk, a date already?*

But then Magnus pulled two chairs away from the table for us. And I forgot everything else but being there with him.

He yelled, "Tis verra loud."

"It is." I took a cocktail napkin, tore some strips, wadded them up, and gestured for him to lean forward. I pressed the paper into his ears, my hands resting on his jawline, his eyes closed, trusting. Then he opened his eyes and they lingered on mine.

I collected enough air to ask, "Better?"

"Verra much."

Tom, the bartender, tapped him on the shoulder. "Hey man, you aren't allowed to have that weapon in here."

Magnus joked, his smile wide. "Oh? But what would happen if the MacDonalds attack?"

"The McDonalds — what are you talking about? This is Fernandina Beach — there better not be *any* attacks."

I said, "Weapons aren't usually allowed in bars. He has a point."

Magnus laughed. "I have a point as well. Where I hail from a man of any sense winna enter an establishment without his sharpest point in hand."

"Well, I'm gonna have to ask you to leave or put it in your car."

I asked, "Tom, could you keep it behind the bar for him?"

"I suppose, but there better not be any trouble."

Magnus stood and removed the big sword and the smaller

sword and passed them both to the bartender. He smiled sheep-ishly. "I feel rather bare to the world."

Tom chuckled, "I think you'll survive."

My group ordered another pitcher and everyone drank heartily and talked and laughed happily. Hayley raised her glass and slurred. "To Katie, my new roomie, we'll be the bestest sharers of rooms ever."

I said, "Hear hear!" And then asked, "How long have you been drinking, Dearie?"

She said, "Since early. You can be my designated driver."

"Sure, I can give you a ride home when I take Magnus home."

Hayley acted like she just noticed him. "Magnus! You better be nice to our Katie." She wobbled on her feet. "She is a sweet girl and she doesn't deserve any more assholes." She giggled, and pretend whispered, "Not like that last guy, James. He was a *total* loser."

James said, "I'm sitting right here."

Magnus seemed jovial and not embarrassed at all. "Your Kaitlyn does deserve better, you are exactly right Mistress Hayley."

James was in a conversation with his date and missed the comment.

Hayley energetically fanned herself. "Jeez did you hear him say my name? That is so hot."

She wobbled to look over at Michael, sitting on a barstool, bleary-eyed and wobbly headed. "Did you hear how hot he was Michael?"

Michael chuckled. "Glad he's not my type. I mean your type."

"Oh yeah, what's my type?"

I said, "Drunk guys you've been in love with since high school."

She giggled. "Right! Just be nice to her, don't break her heart, don't leave her, and always tell her the truth." As she said it she leaned so far over the table that she was very much in Magnus's space. And saying things to him that were way past our point-in-time reference. If he wasn't afraid of my baggage yet, she was probably filling him full of fear now. She raised up and said, "Let's dance!"

She grabbed me by the hand and pulled me to the crowded dance floor and we bopped around to the beat. I was trying to look sexy for Magnus but James started a conversation with him. Then they were all laughing and talking and the song was almost over and he hadn't looked up at me once.

I was about to give up because what was the point of dancing with Hayley who was stumbling drunk, to a song I didn't even like much, if not to get the attention of —

He turned.

He brought his gaze up and across the dance floor and watched me dance, focused and intent and interested. My breath caught in my throat. There was something in his eyes, a longing that I had never — had never been directed at me.

For a moment it was as if I owned him. With one gesture I could compel him toward me. I could lift my hair and he would come kiss my neck. I could smile and he would — but then he dropped his eyes and pulled himself away.

I kept the beat a moment longer with Hayley swinging her head back and forth not quite to the beat. "I'm going to sit down!"

We both went back to the table and joined the others. The boys were all talking about the video playing on the wall, a montage of surfing wipeouts. James was doing a comedic narration since there was no sound over the loud, loud music. And Magnus was laughing at James's dialogue.

His big booming laugh made me laugh until I snorted. Then Magnus laughed harder and James became funnier and funnier. James's date for the night was acting kind of bored and yeah, that was cool too. Because me, I was the life of the party and kind of loving my vibe a lot.

~

At the end of the night, Michael picked Hayley up and slung her over his shoulder because she really couldn't walk, and it was definitely time to go home. Somehow he deposited her into the back seat of Magnus's car and jumped in beside her. "Don't let her throw up, Michael, this is Magnus's new car."

"Yeah, yeah." Michael's head lolled like he was about to spew too. So I drove them fast to Hayley's small townhouse, and Magnus and I helped Michael get Hayley to the front door. She called, "Don't do anything I wouldn't do," as she was pushed up the steps.

Magnus laughed as we returned to his car. "I daena think that leaves much."

"That's what I always say."

I loved it that our thoughts jibed. And actually, now that the night had been so good, plus the day, what I was hoping was somehow it would lead to me spending the night. I mean, why not? He clearly favored me. I had to drive him home. I would get out of his car and he could invite me upstairs. He lived with his mother, but not in the traditional way. It was more like she lived with him. She was very formal; she might disapprove, but then again, she seemed to like me.

My breathing was a little faster than usual, and our silences were deep and uncomfortable, like he was trying to figure out how to speak, what to say. Finally I pulled his car into his driveway and into the garage. I stepped out of the car and jiggled the keys back and forth in my hands nervously.

"That was fun," I said for the fourth time. *Dumbass.*

"Aye," he said vaguely. He squinted because the lights of the garage blared on when we drove in. He strode to the wall and flicked them off, overriding their insistence that we be able to see.

He returned to the back of the car and leaned against it. So we were going to stay in the garage?

"There's something I must say to ye, Mistress Kaitlyn."

I leaned beside him on the back of the car. Our view was out the garage door, the driveway, the back end of my Prius, and the road out front lined by low sand, shrubs, and a mailbox.

"Yes?"

Our arms were close enough to touch again. We had been so close like this all day, and I was so aware of our edges — the tiny distance between us, full of intrigue and electric interest.

"I haena known ye long but you art a bonnie lass, and I like ye and..."

His words were so lovely, formal plus old fashioned; I couldn't wait to hear him say something really romantic.

He stopped and looking out the garage door his eyes went far away. "I wish ye the best, I do. But I have tae leave. Tis important that ye know I dinna mean tae leave ye, tis nae about ye. I just have tae go."

My heart sank to my strappy sandals. The sandals that had been digging into my toes for the last hour because they weren't made for dancing but I wore them anyway because they made me look amazing. My calves were freaking perfect even though they hurt like hell, and what the hell was he talking about? "You're leaving? You didn't mention you were leaving. I mean, you did, but..."

"Aye, I dinna intend tae, but I know now I must."

I scowled at the floor. "I thought..."

"I am pleased tae have met ye, the maiden with the fiery temper. The ruler of the North Wind. I appreciate ye knowin' how the New World works and shewin' it tae me."

I scowled. "I don't know how the world works. I'm apparently the most clueless person in the world."

He shook his head.

I stood straight and smoothed down the skirt of my dress and tried to be the kind of person who wasn't about to cry. "When do you leave?"

"The Buck moon."

I was incredulous. "What even is that, Magnus, who says that kind of thing? The Buck moon? When the hell is the Buck moon?"

He said, "The next full moon, eleven days on."

"Great, just great." I crossed my arms and looked down at my tired feet.

"I wanted ye tae know, so you wouldna think—"

"You know, you don't owe me an explanation, Magnus. You don't owe me anything. Who am I, the first girl you met in Florida? I gave you a ride. That's it. don't worry about it." I grabbed my purse from the back seat of the car and fished my keys from inside.

He said, almost to himself, "I wish I would have taught ye tae fight."

My hands were shaking and my voice wavered. "Whatever, right? Maybe I'll see you around."

I stalked to my car, ripped open the door and climbed in, started it, and whipped the car out of the driveway. I checked the rearview because I kind of hoped he would be standing there, dejected, watching me go, second-thoughting. But no, he had gone inside. The garage door automatically slid down, closing me outside.

Hayley was too drunk for visiting. I went by a convenience store and bought a six pack and a red cup, parked at the end of my street, and walked out on the beach. I popped open a beer and like a poorly built dam during a hurricane, all the tears I had been swallowing down for the past twenty minutes spilled over. I drew my knees up, wrapped my arms around, and cried into my kneecaps. I cried because I was lonely. And unloved. I feared I might be unlovable. But also worst of all that I was a joke. The kind of girl that people suffered. A good portion of my tears were about Braden and my whole lost life, and a lot were about self-pity and despair — *would my life never be better than this?*

But a surprising lot of my tears weren't just about the rejection, they were about Magnus. Because I really liked him.

He had been so exactly right, so easy. Uncomplicated. As if he had been my guy since the first time I laid eyes on him. Mine.

And I know there were issues. He wore a freaking sword. He was from some podunk town in Scotland, practically Amish, possibly a cult or something. And Lady Mairead had scars on her cheeks. There hadn't been an explanation about that, not a good one. But Magnus didn't scare me. I felt safe with him. All my worries fell away when we talked.

I cried for a long time, remembering Magnus whispering, *you smell like the wind.*

And now, this. Stupid ass. He was leaving. He announced it like I was going to be hurt by the news. How asinine, how overly full of himself. I chugged a beer and opened the second. The breeze was a little strong tonight, still warm, but blustering a bit. The tide was coming up.

It was almost chilly actually.

I stood and picked up the rest of the six pack and walked it back to my car and drove it the two blocks to my home. The lights were out, which was good; it was late, and I didn't want my parents interrupting my pity wallow. I would be eating ice cream and drinking beer in my pajamas tonight.

CHAPTER 20

The next day I woke up at noon because I was unemployed, unmotivated, unwanted.

I ate lunch and texted Hayley: What time will you be home today? I'll meet you there with my stuff.

She texted back: Girlfriend that was some serious partying, hung-over! I called in sick. Come on over.

So I loaded my two boxes of clothes, my toiletries, and my bedding in the backseat of my car and drove to Hayley's townhouse.

She had a guest room. She was ecstatic that I was there but also hung-over, so I made us some grilled cheese sandwiches, with cokes and chips, and we ate lunch on the couch with the AC on full blast. Hayley lamented how terribly she felt, and me too; I told her the whole story.

"You like him, huh?"

"I did, he was — I liked him. I haven't felt like that in a long time because Braden was different. We were getting married. It was all boring, planning, and scheming over more subscribers for our channel, marketing."

"What about James?"

"It was a long time ago that I had any real feelings for him. I just thought he was a good idea." I dropped the plate to the coffee table and leaned all the way back on the couch and pulled the comforter on me. We had the AC so cold we needed blankets.

"Come to find out, I'm super stupid. I thought James was a good idea, coming this close," I pinched my fingers together, "to getting some kind of special disease with a name like the clamp or the hat rack or something. I would have been on the cover of People magazine: Unemployed young woman gets a case of 'hat rack' from rubbing her thonged crotch on the pants of her philandering ex-boyfriend because she thought it was a Good Idea."

Hayley giggled. "Remember when you thought it was a good idea to sneak into the fort at night? We walked all the way there, miles, snuck in a window, got lost inside in the dark, totally freaked ourselves out, and missed curfew?"

"We climbed through the one window wide enough to fit through, and then every window we tried was too small. We were racing up and down the tunnels looking for the right window in a complete panic. I actually believed that maybe the wide window was gone, like in The Maze Runner, the fort was a puzzle and had shifted in a circle and we were stuck there until the window shifted back or something."

"Funny how the dark can get so freaky. Like this house. I hang out here all day, but then night comes and it's a little scary. You'll see. That's why Michael spends the night every night."

"Why doesn't he just move in?"

"Have you smelled his feet, Katie, seriously? That boy can move in when he finds odor-eaters that work." She giggled so hard, she had to wipe her eyes. "Nah, he wants to move in. We just have two houses and can't decide what to do about them. He also has a roommate and likes his place; it has a dock. His boat is right there, ready to go. I love my townhouse. Right now we're like those rich people who live separated."

"They usually hate each other. They do it because it's easier than a divorce. You and Michael really like each other. Are you saying that living apart is easier than marriage?"

"Yep. And I've always loved him, and he's always loved me. We'll figure it out someday."

She looked at me for a second. "I thought Magnus really liked you too. He had a way of looking at you that was... Crap, I can't figure out the word. I'm way hung-over. Like he wanted to eat you for dessert."

I pulled the blanket up to my chin. "I thought so too. And I thought he was going to kiss me. And I thought he would invite me upstairs to spend the night. I was wrong on all counts. Just like I was wrong about James being a good idea. Just like I was wrong about Braden loving me. It's hard to be that wrong, so often, without there being a real issue on a systemic level. And six weeks ago I thought I was amazing." I burst into tears.

"Oh baby, poor baby." Hayley sat up on her end of the couch and held onto my knees. "You are amazing. Maybe the dickhead YouTuber, and the dumbass contractor, and the weird ass Highlander aren't the best choices for ye."

"Ye... God, when he calls me 'ye' I just want to crawl into his arms. Isn't it piping, smoking, hella hawt?"

Hayley said, "When he says, 'Aye,' it has like four syllables, and all of them sound sexy. Michael turns you'all into a four syllable word, but he just sounds like a redneck." She smiled. "My redneck though. All mine."

"What is up with him wearing that kilt, anyway?"

"What is up with him carrying a sword everywhere he goes? Maybe you're just turned on by mystery and danger."

"Exactly. I can't be trusted with choices or men or life decisions or really anything."

"As James would say, 'You just have to be smarter than the tool you're trying to operate.'" She leaned back on her arm on the couch. "My head hurts too bad to know if that applies."

"It does. He's got one of those quips for every situation. Maybe he would be a good idea?"

Hayley sighed. "Stop with James already. I can't keep getting my hopes up. I think what you need to do is the exact opposite of what you think you should do."

"The opposite? Like instead of crying I should..?"

"Go to a club, meet a guy, take him home."

"You forget that's what I was doing the other day with James. Trying for meaningless sex to get over Braden. Maybe I need to become a lesbian." I peeked over the comforter, with my eyes crossed.

"I don't think you choose that. You were the most boy-crazy girl I knew through school, so yeah, I think you're stuck dealing with men. Or toys. My head hurts; this has been a hell of a hang-over. My point is, what you're doing right now, not working. If opportunities come, take them, make something new happen. Meantime, let's watch a good movie. What about Clueless?"

"Yum, Paul Rudd."

"See, not a lesbian."

CHAPTER 21

For dinner that night we had pizza and a couple of beers. Pizza because we were still lying around like invalids. Michael had worked, although as he put it, "not well." Everyone had to work the next morning, and it was Friday, so there was no skipping.

We turned in fairly early, but then Hayley and Michael had noisy sex for a while with paper-thin walls, which sucked. I wrapped the pillow around my head. Then I used earbuds and Spotify, listening to Ed Sheeran. Magnus would probably like Ed, and yet, it wasn't up to me to show him.

Hayley and Michael went to work early. I slept in and promised to do laundry. Then Hayley and Michael came home and Michael reported that Zach told him Magnus had gone to the dentist and the doctor because Lady Mairead's nurse, Beth, made him because he had never gone before. Hayley quickly changed the subject, but I was left with a pang of sadness. Too much information about someone I wasn't supposed to care about anymore.

I stayed in, while they went out for the night, feeling terrifically sorry for myself. I was alone and unnecessary. Not one person in the world needed me. I watched TV.

Saturday was Hayley's day off and we lazed around all morning. Then we went shopping and met up with Michael and James for dinner. They told us Magnus had gone with Quentin to Jax Beach to check out the military base there. Again, not enough information and too much at once.

Hayley asked, "Is he going to come out tonight?"

James said, "Who, Magnus? Nah, Quentin is dropping him off before he comes." I could have sworn he flicked his eyes toward me.

Everybody showed up, Sarah, Quentin, more friends from James's work, some from Michael's work. We filled four tables and the band was loud and good. We danced and talked and finally Uber-ed home.

I tried to be fun through this whole thing. I mean, I only knew Magnus for a couple of weeks. It was ridiculous to pine for a man I barely knew. But it was a small island. I had forgotten how hard it is to break up with someone in a small town. Not that we broke up. We hadn't been anything at all. Just friends. And now he didn't want to be around me at all.

What had I done?

That was the phase I was in now—what did I do? Did I come on too strong? When I was alone with my thoughts they always came back to one thing, I was unlovable. It's not an easy thing to come to terms with at the ripe age of twenty-three.

Sunday, James, Michael, and Hayley arranged to have a cookout at James's house. During it I heard about how James was planning to take Magnus to work with him Monday because Magnus wanted to see houses being built. My friends mentioned this stuff because they didn't want to be accused of hiding it but it all came out like a confession, with shifty eyes and apologetic glances, which, quite frankly, hurt my feelings even more than before. I didn't know what I would do if I saw him, but also, ouch. He had cut me from his life completely, and it stung.

And that's why I decided that if nothing changed by the next weekend I would do something drastic. Like Tinder. Maybe, especially, because Hayley and Michael were noisy as hell and I needed to spend the night somewhere else but she wanted me to extend my visit. She loved having me here, the one person in my life who actually liked me.

One night, home with Hayley, having a beer, talking over her day, she said, "Let me get you a job."

"A job? Like temp work?"

"I need someone to do a call center for credit card billing. It's the bottom of the pile, but it would get you out of the house."

I feigned horror. "But I like the house. I want to stay in the house. Maybe I could be a bartender. Then I would see you more often."

"Yes! There's an idea. I would love to be best friends with a bartender. Do that."

"How do I do that?"

"I think a class. I'll research it tomorrow." She swigged from her beer.

"Good, because ever since I was a little girl I wanted to grow up and serve alcohol to people."

"You joke, but it's a good idea. It's the opposite of what you've been doing. Lying around here, being a super sad, cautionary tale."

"Yeah." I stared off into space. "Does Magnus still live here?"

"He's still in town. Zach still loves working there. He told Michael that Magnus's favorite band now is Foo Fighters. Also that he's teaching them self-defense with swords. Which is so cool. I'm the best temp company owner in the world that I got him that job."

"You know I kind of got you the job."

"Yeah, true, but not as cool. I wish we knew what happened — you were his main go-to person for everything. It was clear he liked you. I wish I understood what happened there."

"Is he dating someone?" I tried to make it sound casual, like whatevs.

"No, definitely not. Emma told me he acts like he's leaving. He's getting everyone ready to run the house while he's not there."

"That's why. He said he couldn't go out with me because he was leaving."

"At least it was true. Not much comfort, but he wasn't lying at least. That's an improvement for you."

"Yeah, but why won't he see me until he goes? Am I repulsive?"

"You know that's not what it is. It's more likely he liked you too much. That he was worried he would—"

"Oh god, are you going to be one of *those* kinds of friends? A guy doesn't want to be with me, tells me, goes out of his way to avoid me, and you're going to tell me it's because he liked me too much? By that logic Braden must love me so, so very much."

"What's your theory then?"

"That I'm repulsive. And that you're right, from now on I need to do everything the opposite."

CHAPTER 22

The following morning I was laying in bed, trying to decide between getting up and putting on yoga pants and exercising for an hour, possibly topping it off with a run on the beach because I used to run all the time and hadn't exercised in weeks and weeks. Or start drinking.

I was only joking about the start drinking. But was I? Maybe it was the opposite thing. Or maybe because I thought of it the opposite was not drinking, and exercising was the opposite of that. But then again I used to exercise all the time. So was drinking all day the best idea?

My phone rang. Mom. "Hey."

"Hello dear. Two things, your father and I want to see you Saturday for dinner."

"Okay."

"Are you still in bed?"

"How can you tell?"

"Your voice." She sighed deep and loud.

"I'm thinking about going for a run."

"Good. Do that. Also, look for a job. But the main reason I'm calling is Lady Mairead Delapointe wants to see you. I was just there, talking to her about their lease. They intend to continue living here, which is fabulous. And she asked if you would come see her this afternoon. Do you have any idea why?"

"No idea. Did it sound like a visit or a meeting?

"I couldn't tell. I tried to get clues, but she said she had something to discuss with you. Is it about her son? I told you to leave him alone — did you break his heart?"

"Nope, we're not even speaking right now."

"Well, go see her at three o'clock today. And call me after, to tell me what it was about; I'm dying to know. Talk to you later."

I hung up and lay there wondering, *would Magnus be there?* Why would Lady Mairead want to speak to me? I stressed about it for so long that I couldn't possibly exercise. It was about time to shower and get ready. Plus, I supposed drinking was out of the question. I imagined I might need my wits about me to have a 'discussion' with Lady Mairead because the only thing it could possibly be about was Magnus Campbell and I needed to be ready.

CHAPTER 23

I drove up and parked in their driveway. I glanced in the garage, open, but the horse was gone. Magnus wasn't home. I had gotten all dolled up: Makeup. Hair done. Cute outfit. I chose pants because Lady Mairead struck me as someone who would be judgy about bare legs. Her own clothes looked like they had been designed centuries ago.

Emma let me in when I knocked and told me Lady Mairead was expecting me upstairs in her office. She gestured that it was to the left of the stairs. Zach called from the kitchen, "Katie, you want a coke to take up?"

"Sure." He zipped around the counter island with a glass, an expression on his face that came across as curious and a little worried. I carried the glass up with me and knocked on the office's closed door. By this point I was thoroughly intimidated by the moment.

"Come in."

I entered and Lady Mairead graciously told me how much it meant to her that I had come. She directed me to a comfortable stuffed chair and had me place my glass on the table.

Her clothing had changed. She was wearing a blouse, slacks, and high heels. She looked less formal but still dignified like one of the 'blue hairs' that ran the local clubs where the rich residents gathered to socialize, show off their gardens, and decide who would govern the Island. Even with the scars on her cheeks. She coughed, a thick hacking cough into a handkerchief. "I haena been able tae recover my health since I arrived."

I said, "Coughs sometimes take a long time. Have they given you antibiotics?"

"Yes. The healers say my immune system is nae good, so while I remain in the New World I will likely remain ill. I must return tae Scotland soon." She sat and smoothed the fabric of her pants.

I said, "Oh, you're leaving too?"

Her eyes narrowed. "Magnus has told ye he is leaving?"

I instantly regretted saying it and racked my brain trying to remember if he ever asked me to keep it secret. But no. Plus, why should I help him? I didn't have a clue why his mother shouldn't know his plans, except for the argument I overheard. And that wasn't information for me to know.

I made a split second decision that it was okay for me to speak freely. "Yes, he told me he was going back home."

She asked, "Why haena ye been here tae see Magnus?"

I chewed my lip. Was I getting him in trouble? Where was the line of questioning going? "He asked me not to come anymore. He didn't want to see me because he was leaving or something."

She said, "I see."

A clock ticked in the corner of the room. The AC hummed. The large windows overlooked the beach, the ocean, most of the whole sky, and the sea grass waving. I did love sea grass. It gave our beaches such a unique look. There was nowhere else in the world with beaches so white, dunes so undulating, with the white crunchy sand plus the sea shells. It was a paradise and still so unspoiled.

"I asked ye here, Mistress Sheffield, because I have a business proposition. Tis complicated, but I trust ye will see the merits of it if ye will allow me tae explain."

"I don't know if Magnus would want you to—"

She squinted her eyes. "You have a great many misconceptions where Magnus is concerned. Trust me." She coughed again.

What the heck did that mean? So I took a deep breath and told her to go ahead.

"I have a number of problems here in the United States of the Americas. One, I daena have adequate paperwork tae protect our fortune. Master Sheffield, your father, is holding our accounts open, but tae release our money requires proof of our birth. Also, there is a tax burden. Tis all verra complicated. I, as ye know, left my home in a hurry and dinna bring my papers along. Getting them will be verra difficult. That is problem number one."

She almost sounded like one of those Nigerian princes that emailed me every so often: *I have millions of dollars and no way to get it, please help me.*

"Another problem is my son, Magnus, is a hot-headed fool. He intends tae return tae Scotland and fight my husband. His uncle, the Earl, will raise an army. His cousins will fight alongside him." She coughed long and hard into her tissue. When she recovered, she continued, "He is greatly underestimating my husband's strength. And severely misconceived about how much he is hated. My husband intends to kill Magnus—"

I was shocked. "Aren't there laws? You could go to the police? This is murder. You're talking about murder."

She waved my words away. "I will stop my husband from killing Magnus. I made an arrangement with Magnus's father I would protect him. And I have gone tae great lengths tae that end. Tis why I have brought him here tae the New World." She looked at me for a moment. "I intend to leave him here while I return tae Scotland tae end my husband's thirst for Magnus's blood."

"So saving Magnus's life is why you're here? Is he what you stole?"

She leveled her gaze. "He is in great danger. There has been a large amount of intrigue and mischief tae get him here tae safety. Tae keep him alive requires a tremendous amount of strategy and fortitude." She coughed into her handkerchief. "I have a plan in place. Tis a delicate matter but Magnus is in no mood for delicacies and strategies."

She shook her head. "He is battle-planning. Drawing his broadsword, marching around here as if I canna see he is headed tae battle." She scoffed and shook her head.

Then she raised her eyes to me expectantly.

"I'm not sure I understand how I can help?"

"Nae? You daena see the issue?"

I shook my head and remembered my cold coke with the melting ice. It would be watered down now, sadly. I took a swig, dripping condensation on my lap. Watery, without a bit of fizz.

That's why my attention wasn't completely on Lady Mairead, when it should have been. That's why when she said what she said next I missed it, or thought I did because it couldn't register, so I just looked at her blankly while wiping my pants with the cocktail napkin. "Excuse me, what did you just say?"

"I want ye tae marry Magnus Campbell."

Oh.

Crap.

What?

She appraised me for a moment. "It solves all of my problems verra tidily, actually."

I froze damp napkin in hand. "No, that — no... What? That's not going to — wait, Magnus doesn't want to see me — he's not going to marry me. That's not how this works. You can't ... Mothers don't ask girls to marry boys, boys ask girls to marry them. That's how it works. It's not a business arrangement, plus — what?"

She raised her brows watching me fumble and grasp for some sense in this ridiculous notion.

I finished, "So yeah, no."

"Nae? To the business proposal ye haena heard yet? I have only explained the reasons, nae the facts."

"Okay fine, my answer is no because that's not how marriage works, but if you want to tell me what the deal is first, fine."

"Mistress Sheffield, this is *exactly* how marriage works. Across all time marriage is an oath before God, but tis foremost a contract between families. Whether tis mutually beneficial or nae depends upon how well the contract is argued and formed."

"Lady Mairead, Magnus and I aren't even speaking to each other. This whole discussion is really odd. I don't know what to make of it."

"Allow me to explain. I am proposing that ye marry Magnus Campbell before the next full moon."

Was she kidding—

"In exchange I would have all our wealth transferred into your name. As the wife of Magnus Campbell, you would be part of the great and powerful Clan Campbell. Your children would carry his royal bloodline."

"Magnus is a royal?"

"Yes, his father is a king." She dismissed this with a hand. "But you winna worry about the accompanying danger and intrigue because ye would remain here in the New World until a future time in which Magnus is asked to ascend his throne. You would be a very wealthy woman, and, as I said the other day, ye could forget trying tae find a man that suits ye and begin your life as a married woman. You would have the running of the estate tae deal with; your mother has been selling me investment properties."

My eyes were wide. "It would all be mine?"

"Technically. It would belong to Magnus Campbell and his first-born son, of course. But as his wife, a citizen of the United States, and a young woman who understands economical realities, you would be the real seat of power. In the event of his death though, twould all belong to you outright. And your children."

"Whoa, now there are children?"

"Tis a marriage, of course there will be children."

"We haven't even had a date. He never even kissed me."

She shrugged.

"I've only known him for three weeks."

"In my family we art oft introduced tae our husbands on or just before our wedding day. It daena change the fact. Hae ye considered it might be easier? Tae be bound tae someone without so much deliberating and planning?"

"No, never, I've always wanted a very romantic wedding, to be in love."

Lady Mairead shook her head. "Mistress Sheffield, Magnus will die. If he goes back tae Scotland, my husband will find him and Magnus will be put tae death. I say this as if the death would be immediate, but twould be protracted. With a great deal of pain." She gestured toward her ugly jagged scars. "You can see by my face that he is bound tae be cruel. If my husband daena find him first, and Magnus rides into battle against him, Magnus will die. If Magnus daena lose his life on the battlefield, he will be found, and he will be murdered. This is his fate. I need ye tae save him from his fate. If you married him, you would convince him tae remain here."

"Why would he stay here? Men leave their wives to go off to war all the time."

"True. Tis nae a perfect impediment, but he would think first and not be so brazen. He would see and understand the limitations of his plan. You would be someone tae live for and that is often enough. His father was verra dutiful tae me, and if I told him nae tae do something he would think on it verra deliberately. I would expect ye to make a strong case and be compelling. Keeping him here would be your first priority."

"Magnus's father must have been very different from your current husband."

"Like night and day. But I married Lord Delapointe tae broaden my land holdings and for the protection. I may be at his mercy, but I also have strategies."

"So you think that if I married Magnus I would save his life, plus I would be rich? What is the downside?"

"There art downsides tae every partnership. Magnus is young, impetuous, and believes he is invincible. That might grow old in time."

The truth was, I was so blown away by this conversation I couldn't think. My autopilot had kicked in as if music was playing and my feet were tapping though my brain was saying, *what the hell are you doing, I don't want to dance* — "How would you make him marry me?"

"I would tell him tae."

"You must have a great deal of power over him."

"Ah, but tis nae me that holds the power."

"Oh." I stared at my hands considering. "Wait, are you saying I have power over him?"

"Verra much. You art a woman, ye must see how he looks at you. He speaks of ye a great deal and worries about ye. I will tell him he must marry ye tae secure our fortune. He will nae object. When I tell him he canna return to Scotland, he will be verra angry, but ye can calm him. I will expect ye tae."

"I just — none of this is what I expected. I don't know if—"

"How old are ye Mistress Sheffield?"

"I'm twenty-three."

"Magnus is turned twenty-one. Tis time for ye both tae marry. The alliance would bind you in mutual protection and responsibility. Are you Catholic?"

"No, Episcopalian."

"Ah good. Your priest came tae me while I was in hospital. We have become quite close. I will discuss this with your parents as well, I simply wanted to have your agreement first."

Her mention of my parents brought a little sense to my brain. "You don't need to discuss this with my parents, it's my decision. They don't — that's not how it works with us. When Braden asked me to marry him I was twenty-one. I said 'yes' and told my parents. They said, 'great.' I get to make my own decisions, part of being a grown woman."

She nodded and quietly continued to sit.

"I don't know if I can say yes, I need to think about this?"

"Would it help if I sent Magnus tae speak tae ye?"

"Yes, probably, but I don't think he will — he—"

"Magnus will speak with ye by the end of the day. I daena want tae send him though unless ye are amenable tae the idea. If you turn him away, I daena believe there is anything I can do tae keep him here. I am afraid for his life. I need ye tae understand that."

I sat thinking this through, but how do you think through something so outlandish, so bizarre? I met Magnus just a few weeks ago — give or take a few days. We had become friends, but then he didn't want to see me anymore. Now his mother was proposing to me. Had I dropped through the floor into another century? I again wondered if I might be being pranked.

She said, "I need tae know your answer, Mistress Kaitlyn."

It made me feel a little panicky that I used up most of my deliberating time thinking about how weird it was. I really wasn't the kind of person who could make these kinds of decisions.

I usually went for romance, love, the romantic gesture. Braden had asked me to marry him during a video, live of course. He invited four other YouTubers to make guest appearances during a holiday cookie episode. They each brought a recipe and made a cookie. What I didn't know was when they displayed their finished cookies, the first cookie had the word 'will' frosted onto it. The next was frosted with 'you' and then 'marry' and 'me' and finally Braden's cookie 'Katie.' Everyone agreed it was incredibly romantic. Our viewership numbers exploded. I threw my arms around Braden's neck and cried, "Yes!"

That worked out terribly.

How in the heck was I supposed to make this decision?

Was the opposite of myself to say no? Or yes?

I desperately wanted to talk to my grandmother. Growing up I spoke to her about any life crisis, but now she wasn't as helpful anymore. And so I had been vague about Braden. I told her he had broken up with me but left it at that, and she didn't press. But she didn't press about much these days. I remembered one of her favorite platitudes though, "Do what makes the best story."

A no meant living with Hayley, or my parents, trying to come up with a next plan. Living in what ifs. Wondering, "What should I do?"

Yes meant, what did it mean — God, getting married? To a stranger? Yes meant a whole lot more.

It was a terrible idea.

Though Magnus was very easy on the eyes.

And I missed him.

I was sad about him all week. Feeling sorry for myself.

What I needed to do was the opposite. Hayley had said to and normally I wouldn't listen to Hayley, but hey, do the opposite. The opposite.

And suddenly without my brain deciding to, I said, "Yes, I mean, okay. Sure, I'll marry Magnus. I mean, if he wants me to." I literally couldn't believe those words came out of my mouth. *Marry him?* What the fuck, Katie. The only thing that would save my ass now was that he wouldn't want to. Another total and complete rejection. The biggest kind. So there was that. Better pull up my big girl undies and get ready.

Lady Mairead beamed. "Ah Kaitlyn, tis excellent, thank ye." She went to her desk and pulled a legal pad from a desk drawer. She gestured for me to come beside her and with a pen in long, looping, calligraphic handwriting, wrote across and down the whole page. At the bottom she signed her name.

"Oh, you want me to sign something?"

"I told ye I am nae interested in commanding Magnus tae comply and have ye change your mind at the last hour. I needs be assured of your agreement." She turned the paper toward me and I read her ornate writing. "Lady Mairead Delapointe of the Clan Campbell in the lands of Argyll and the country of Scotland, and Kaitlyn Sheffield of Amelia Island, Florida of the New World, the United States of America, have entered into a marital agreement, One to bind Magnus Campbell and Kaitlyn Sheffield in matrimony, on this day, June 30, the Year of our Lord, two thousand seventeen.

I said, "Just to be clear, I'm agreeing — as long as Magnus agrees, and I need to speak to him about it — before."

"He will see ye this evening." She handed me her pen.

Her signature had a flourish that swooped under her name four times back and forth. Mine in comparison looked simple and immature as if I was a child, signing a contract with a queen.

I handed the pen back and pushed the paper pad away. My phone beeped. I fished it from my pocket. It was a notification of a text from Hayley: Hey girl. Michael has invited the usuals over for a cookout this evening because Friday!!!! He won't be off until six. I have a meeting, can you pick up stuff? I'll send a list.

Lady Mairead asked, "What are your plans this evening?"

I looked up. "Looks like I'll be at home, I mean, my friend Hayley's house." I stood to go.

"Farewell, Mistress Sheffield, and thank ye again. I will see ye later in the week."

I glanced through the window. Magnus was riding his horse over the dunes toward the house.

"He's home."

Lady Mairead followed my gaze. "That he is. If ye pass him please daena speak of this matter."

"I wouldn't dream of it." I jogged down the steps wanting to get to my car before he came across the dunes, mortified he might find out I was here.

Dread filled my stomach. The familiar feeling of embarrassment and shame that I had been carrying with me for weeks had deepened. Not only was I unlovable, but now I was conspiring. Stalking. I had agreed to marry someone against their wishes, was this a new low? What if he hated me?

She had used the word, 'command.' She would 'command him.' Is that how I wanted to get a husband?

I made it to my car without seeing him. I pulled the Prius out of the driveway to the main road, kicking up a sand cloud, and looking behind in the rearview mirror. He had ridden around the corner and was watching the tail lights of my car as I drove away.

He was in for a surprise.

I was so freaking embarrassed. Mortified.

Was I really this desperate for love and attention — an arranged marriage?

CHAPTER 24

I drove halfway to the grocery store before, shaking and unable to concentrate, I pulled over in a parking lot to sit with my eyes closed trying to calm down.

Lady Mairead had made the marriage seem necessary and normal, but that was not normal. I had never met anyone who married someone who didn't like them, and—

Another text from Hayley: Beer (Lots, sounds like at least twelve of us.)

Hamburgers, buns, ketchup, mustard, nope, I have mustard. Pickles, lettuce, cheese. Also chips. Am I forgetting anything? I'll pay you back tonight. Thanks!

I wanted to say, "Girl, wait until you hear what just happened." But it was too — too — I couldn't put it into words that she would understand. There was no way I could explain it so that she would say, hey you did great that's an excellent decision. Well done. Glad you signed that paper. God, was that paper binding? Would I need a lawyer? I decided to pretend like it never happened.

It probably didn't, anyway.

For sure that was a hallucination. Last I remembered I was trying to decide whether to drink or exercise. That must have been a crazy jog. Or else I was very drunk. And if I drunk-hallucinated that conversation I might have a serious drinking problem.

I called my grandma in Maine. Her phone rang and rang and rang until finally her nurse answered. "She can't come to the phone right now, she's napping. And I'm sorry Katie but today's been a bad day for her. She doesn't remember anything. I can tell her you called but she might not know who you are."

I told her I would call back later. Then I hung up and put my head on my steering wheel and talked to myself. "Hey Grandma, I met someone. I really like him, but — it's super complicated. I'm trying to take your advice and live the best story, but I think I might have screwed up, made a bad decision, and... Did you love Grandpa?"

When I raised my head, my cheeks were wet.

I scrambled through my purse for a piece of paper and a pen and scrawled a note to myself. *Call Grandma back.*

Magnus was probably buying tickets to fly back to Scotland right now. Because he was a grown man. He didn't have to do whatever his mom told him to do. He definitely didn't need to marry a girl he didn't like.

It was kind of a green card thing though. Maybe that would be enough of a reason? A business reason? Would we get married in a courthouse? And how long would we have to stay married in order for him to get his green card?

I could investigate with my phone but looking up that information meant possibly checking Braden's YouTube account, and there was no way I could handle that right now.

What if Magnus did show up tonight? I couldn't even wrap my head around the possibility. What if the man I was going to marry — without ever even kissing him — what if he showed up tonight and wanted to talk to me?

I needed a new outfit. It was almost four. I needed an outfit and the food for the party and beer, so I drove off the island to Target and headed straight for the women's clothing section. Trouble was there was a lot of red white and blue clothing for the Fourth of July or dresses that looked like the ones I already owned.

I bought a little sundress in blue. But I needed a new bra to wear under it. And what about panties? Gasp. Would he see my panties? Was I going all the way with the Scotsman when — I kind of needed to sit down.

I threw a bra and a pair of panties in my cart and headed to the makeup section. New mascara and an eyebrow pencil, not because I needed it but because I was flailing. Did I need new shampoo? Hairspray? I hadn't used it since 2009. What about a new curling iron, should I curl my hair? I checked the time, I had literally been there for almost an hour. I picked out a pair of flip flops that were metallic and would look excellent with the dress and especially if I shaved my legs but now it was looking like I might not have time — I needed to get home, quick.

I raced to the food section and grabbed hamburger patties, buns, ketchup, chips, and beer. And got in the line almost to the counter and remembered ice. I begged someone to hold my place while I went to grab it and so by the time I was headed to the car I was harried and worried.

Had she said tonight? Or this afternoon? What if I missed him? What if I blew it, and did I care?

Why would I care?

I had entered a contract and what was it even, marriage? What the hell had I been thinking?

I drove back to the island and Hayley's townhouse. I frantically packed the ice into the coolers and flung beer cans onto the ice and wished I had done that in reverse. I tried to paw aside the ice and dig the beer further into the ice cubes, but I had botched the most important step to a successful party: cold, perfectly iced beer.

I checked my phone. It was after five. Should I shower — what if someone arrived? Anyone, like someone else. Michael was coming first, right? I was having trouble thinking and remembering Hayley's instructions. I left Michael a note:

Hey! In the shower, make yourself at home. Beer in the cooler.

XOX, Katie.

I hurried up the stairs to shower, shave, beautify, tearing tags off clothes as I went.

CHAPTER 25

I was freshly washed and beautiful. And I had done it fast. When I sauntered downstairs Michael and Quentin were out on the porch. Hayley had just arrived. "You look beautiful, a new dress? Do I have to look that good?"

I said, "This? I just threw it on. And you know, life of leisure." I laughed awkwardly because somehow now I could not get my face to work. Or my lungs. Or my words.

"Still, I should get out of my work suit, back in a jif." Hayley bustled away.

Hayley's townhouse butted up onto a hill. You couldn't see the ocean from here, as it was lower than the beach, but it was only a block away. She had no yard, but a big, very big deck with a table and chairs, a beer-pong table, a large gas grill, a bar, and lots of railing to lean and perch on.

I sat on the railing and watched Michael and Quentin play beer-pong for a few moments until Hayley returned and corralled me into helping shape the hamburger patties. While we were in the kitchen more and more people showed up, heading directly around the house, filling coolers, and joining the game.

To call me nervous was an understatement.

I was back in eighth grade with Maisy Johnson telling me she was going to kick my ass after school, and then waiting those excruciatingly long four and a half hours. It never happened. She lost interest or whatever.

Maybe, probably that's how this would work too. Just nothing.

That would be nice.

I was having serious doubts whether my conversation with Lady Mairead was even legal. Was it legal to marry someone to help them get citizenship, to establish access to their fortune? Weren't there rules?

I needed to get a grip.

I played a round of beer-pong and was very good. Also getting a little buzzed. I needed food. James and Michael were flipping patties on the grill. Hayley opened bags of chips and piled napkins, forks, and plates near the grill. Dinner was about to happen, a perfect ending to a perfectly weird day. Nothing. At least I got a good dress.

The music was loud Green Day. I was perched on the railing beside Hayley, who was flirting with Michael, while I teased James about his incompetence as a grill chef.

And then there was the unmistakable sound of hooves coming up the street.

My stomach dropped.

No one else seemed to notice. I tried to pretend like I didn't hear. Did he actually come? Hayley's front door bell rang.

"Weird," she said, and traipsed through the house to get the door.

I took a large swig of beer and tried to act natural.

A moment later Hayley returned, followed by Magnus.

He looked amazing, handsome, powerful, strong, his eyes swept the deck and landed on me. Hayley announced in her loud voice, "Everyone, this is Magnus, Magnus, everyone." Most of the party said some form of, "Hi Magnus," but he was focused on me, walking directly for me.

James intercepted him with a hearty handshake. Then Michael had to say something. But finally he turned to me, still sitting on the railing, as if I had no idea he was there to see me. Hayley looked from his face to mine.

He asked, "Mistress Kaitlyn, might we go for a walk?"

I said, "Yes."

CHAPTER 26

*H*e checked on his horse, tied up on a low railing beside the driveway. I asked, "Do you want to go to the beach?"

"Aye, I would like tae."

We walked the block and a half in the heat and sunset light of 7:45 pm in July in Florida. We were both totally quiet. I chewed my lip.

Magnus's face was clouded over. He seemed very upset. I stole glances and tried to calm my nerves.

His boots thudded on the boardwalk to the beach. I walked a half step ahead so we weren't directly side by side, bumping elbows. The whole time felt a lot like being called to the principal's office. I was trying to get my story straight. *I didn't mean to sign a contract with your mom forcing you to marry me, it just kind of happened.*

We got to the end of the walkway and the steps to the sand.

"Wait, Mistress Kaitlyn." He leaned against the railing. "Might I speak tae ye here?"

"Of course." I was having trouble meeting his eyes. A very

warm breeze rose and whipped some of my hair across my face. I tucked it behind my ear. He didn't speak, but I could feel his eyes on me, watching me, intently.

It was too much pressure. I blurted out, "I'm so sorry Magnus, about today. I'm sorry I got in the middle of this with Lady Mairead. I didn't know what to do. I didn't plan it, I promise, I just — I'll go back to you not seeing me. I can do that. Can we just forget this happened?"

"Kaitlyn..." He didn't finish and seemed to not know what he wanted to say.

I stared down dumbly at my hands.

"Kaitlyn," he said again simply. "Tis nae..." He shook his head and shifted his feet. Then he took a deep breath. "Lady Mairead and I have a strong disagreement about which of us ought tae return tae Scotland. We left somethin' there, somethin' verra valuable, and she wants tae retrieve it. I believe I am better suited tae the task. We have been arguin' about it for weeks and now she has involved ye, Kaitlyn. I'm deeply sorry for that."

He was saying my name without the 'mistress.' It threw me for a second, and I didn't know what to do. "Oh. It's okay, I mean, you made yourself very clear the other night; you don't want anything to do with me. I just felt terrible all day about this and so worried about — what I'm saying is you can un-involve me."

"Nae, I canna." He shuffled his boot on the sandy boards. "I thought I could. I planned I could away tae Scotland without seeing ye. I told myself I would see ye if I returned someday. But now..." He shook his head. "I have been overturned."

"That's what I mean Magnus, consider me gone. I can't even believe this was — look, Lady Mairead took me by surprise, in retrospect I should have refused to sign it. I'm sorry I put this pressure on you and—" I turned to walk back to Hayley's.

Magnus said, "Kaitlyn, please, stop."

I turned to him. "Let's just consider the matter closed. It's giving me a stomachache, and I feel really, really foolish about it. I just — I can't figure out what's wrong with me that I do this..."

"Ye do what?"

"I don't know, like get my hopes up. Not that I hoped to marry you that's not it but just hoped someday someone might want to, um marry me — it's stupid and doesn't involve you, not really."

Magnus nodded and stared out at the ocean. "I was verra upset when Lady Mairead told me about your meeting. I was furious she involved ye. Our argument this day has been long ranging. But she has shewed me your signature and I — I canna — she is a formidable adversary — she knew what would make it impossible for me tae leave."

"What would?"

"You, Kaitlyn." He leaned on one side of the walkway. His eyes met mine across the space.

"But you didn't want to see me anymore." I leaned on the railing across from him.

"Tis nae that I dinna want tae see ye, tis that I canna. Because I am a dead man, Kaitlyn. There is nae alterin' that fact. And when I look at ye, I want tae live."

"Oh."

He took another deep breath and finished. "Without ye I can do what I need tae do; go tae Scotland, retrieve what we lost, and I will die there. Tis the natural order of it."

"Don't say that Magnus."

"What, that Lady Mairead wants tae save my life? That she has dragged ye in on it? You will save me Kaitlyn? You winna allow me tae die?" His eyes were intense.

"I won't. I signed it because I didn't want you to die."

He nodded. "Aye." He stared off at the ocean again for a long while.

Then he said, his voice low and rumbling, "Ye mean tae marry me tae keep me alive?"

"I mean, I signed the paper, but I told Lady Mairead I needed to speak to you first. If you don't want to, we can not."

"She means tae hold ye tae it, Kaitlyn. I mean tae."

This was all very irritating and round about.

"You mean to... what, hold me to it?"

"Aye."

"This isn't how it works — we can choose to get married or not. Lady Mairead gave me a lot of reasons, but we can probably figure something else out. We don't need to—"

"We do."

"But you barely know me."

"I know ye. Tis enough."

I huffed.

"I have spoken tae the priest, we will see him two days on."

"Oh, so soon?"

"I will still need tae return tae Scotland even though we are married. Lady Mairead means tae go soon; I will go before she has a chance. I must. It will be good for ye though; ye would keep the estate if I daena return."

"Good for me? No it wouldn't be, Magnus. Don't be so dark and dramatic. If it's this dangerous, you shouldn't go. Nothing is worth that." I huffed. "And I'm not in it for the money. I mean, I just want that to be — that's not *why*. I just want to help, and I couldn't think of any reason not to."

"I can think of a thousand reasons, but I still want tae marry ye, Kaitlyn."

My eyes met his. "Really?"

"Aye."

"This isn't how this is normally done."

"Explain it tae me."

"We're supposed to have loved each other for a long time.

We're supposed to plan a big wedding, invite too many people. You're supposed to make a grand gesture, declare your undying love. Plus there is supposed to be a ring."

"I have made an appalling mess of it, but I would wish my meaning tae be clear — I will marry ye, Kaitlyn, and I will become better as time goes on."

I arched my brow. "I'm supposed to just trust you that you'll get better in time?"

"You will be there tae guide me, rionnag, I will follow you."

"What does ru-nak mean?"

"Star."

"That's better."

"You have become mo reul-iuil, my North Star."

"That's a lot better."

"I will give ye a ring when we marry, two days on."

"We're really going to do this?"

He nodded slowly, watching my eyes. "And when ye art my wife, twill be verra hard tae leave ye. Mairead is verra wise in this. For you are sollier, 'bright', the sun, 'ghrian', mo ghradh."

"What does 'mo gra' mean?"

"I'll tell ye one day."

"See, that's not the way to teach people things you have to tell them when they ask, no judgement."

"'Mo ghradh' means my own love."

"Oh. That's a lot, lot better."

We stood there awkwardly because this was the moment for him to sweep me into his arms but he didn't seem to intend to.

He straightened. "We are decided?"

I said "Yes," and we walked back to Hayley's house.

CHAPTER 27

*W*e returned to the deck. It was pretty obvious we left the party to be alone to talk, but when we returned Magnus stood with the boys on one side of the deck, and I rejoined Hayley on the other. She whispered, "You okay?"

"Yes, I'll tell you about it later."

People were watching me, watching Magnus, curious, but he sent no signals that we were together. Instead, he jovially laughed and talked with the boys. So I laughed and talked too, and soon everyone seemed to forget that I had gone off with him. Clearly there was nothing going on with us.

And I began to doubt that anything was really going on. I wasn't in a relationship with him. Not publicly. Maybe he meant it to be a secret? I had forgotten to ask. He had spoken very romantically, but only after I asked him to. Perhaps this was simply a green card marriage and we were going to keep it strictly legal, business-like, secret.

Which was fine. Because now I needed to actually tell people, it sounded freaking crazy. Like maybe Katie-needs-to-go-away-for-a-while crazy, for a rest, at like a Lindsey or Britney kind of spa.

I piled a plate with a burger and chips and ate at the railing beside Hayley. Michael across the deck teased Magnus about eating his burger the wrong way. He glanced at me and I pantomimed turning mine over. He turned his burger right side up and grinned at me. As if we had inside jokes. Like flirting. I laughed and swigged more beer.

James said, "Katie, when you're done, a round of beer-pong?"

"Definitely!"

Playing beer-pong was fun. The whole party was fun. I was relieved to have the confrontation behind me, plus I had a secret. An admirer. A husband. Was I crazy?

He couldn't take his eyes off me.

I got kind of wild with power laughing and joking with my friends. James dropped another ball in my cup and I chugged. He laughed. "If I get you drunk enough Katie, maybe you'll go for another skinny dip later?"

I scoffed. "You trying to get my clothes off James? Because that's not going to happen."

"I don't know, sober Katie told me off the other night, but I'm thinking drunk Katie might want a welcome back gift." He was totally joking and this was what we did, normal Katie-James banter. Most everyone at the party was watching and laughing, but the moment was also electric-charged because of the situation. The secret situation.

I joked, "Sober Katie is a smart lady, but that doesn't mean Drunk Katie is stupid. Both wouldn't touch you with a ten-foot pole—" I stretched my arms wide. "I mean," I brought my arms slowly together, closer and closer, "a ten inch, I mean," with my fingers right in front of his crotch I said, "a ten centimeter pole."

James laughed. Magnus laughed appreciatively, his eyes twinkling. He chugged from his beer.

James said, "Truth is, Katie, you have the ability to make it grow, if that's what you want."

"Don't want."

"Suit yourself but seems like you're probably in a bit of a dry spell. I'm just offering to give you a little something to see you through."

"The key words being little something."

More laughter from the group. The music was loud, the spirit high, the mood jovial. Magnus's eyes following me. James joking with me and me joking back. Yes, I was vibing.

James said sarcastically, "See, this is why you're so universally adored, Katie, because you're such a nice girl."

Sarah added, "With claws."

Hayley said, "Sarah, I swear to god, stop bringing that up. A hundred percent you would have done it too."

"That's okay Hayley, no worries, everyone's seen the video, right Sarah? But hey, I trimmed my nails tonight. I won't damage James's pretty face." I put down my beer and wiggled my fingertips toward Sarah. She smirked.

James joked, "See, you said 'pretty face.' I'm working my magic on you."

"I meant that in the loosest sense of the term. Your face is pretty like the moon is beautiful and flat and overly round and full of gaping craters."

Quentin fell on the floor he was laughing so hard.

James said, "I missed you, Katie. So glad you're back."

I smiled and met Magnus's eyes.

James said, "Magnus, beer-pong table is open, you can try it out."

"I have never played. Kaitlyn, will ye show me the game?"

Hayley looked from him to me again.

"Sure." I explained the rules and showed him how to make the shot. We played. He was a fast learner, but I was far more skilled. When I made him drink, I yelled, "Suck it, Magnus," just like I would have with one of my buddies.

James said, "Watch out Magnus that there is Katie's mating call. But if you're thinking her ass looks great in that dress, I have to warn you, our Katie is a handful. You're new to the island, find yourself a nice girl without this much attitude." He chuckled, happy with himself.

Magnus chucked the ball into a cup. "I believe I am able tae handle whatever Kaitlyn offers."

James, Michael, and Quentin all fell about riotously laughing. James boomed, "Challenge accepted! What do you think Katie, are you willing to welcome Magnus to our shores? I hear he's leaving, maybe a goodbye gift?"

I raised my brows at Magnus, across the table. He didn't seem on the verge of announcing anything.

I said, "James, I know you are a straight man and completely inept at seeing what's attractive in other men, hence the pink shirt, but if you had an ounce of sense you'd see that if Magnus wanted a goodbye gift, every woman on the deck would give it to him."

James chuckled and feigned incredulousness. "What about you Hayley, do you have any idea what she's talking about?"

Hayley grinned. "No idea."

Michael laughed. "I'm a dude, and I know Magnus is totally hot."

Magnus smiled mischievously. "Thank ye Michael, I think ye are mighty bonnie as well."

We all cracked up.

Michael held up a glass. "I'm spoken for though."

Hayley, tipsy, leaned over and kissed him on the cheek.

"Ah then Magnus, I know you're disappointed, and by my recollection you've been a month here. It's time for an American girl to throw a little action your way. We already discussed the merits, or lack of, of our Katie—"

"She is spoken for, as am I."

James said, "What?"

Magnus placed his paddle and ball on the table. The rest of the party, everyone within hearing distance, the core group, and the spectators, all went quiet.

Hayley said, "Katie, what is he talking about?"

James said, "Katie is spoken for — you know something we don't?"

Our eyes met. He said, "Aye, by me."

Everyone looked around awkwardly.

James laughed heartily. "Magnus, my man, despite the presence of your horse parked outside and the sword on your back, this is the 21st century. You don't get to just claim girls without a lot of hassle first."

Hayley said, "I'm sure Katie would need a bit of dating or some—" She paused watching me smile at Magnus. "Katie, what's going on? I left for work this morning and you were still in your pajamas heart-broken because of this dude."

"A lot has changed today."

James said, "Okay, so Katie is dating the Scotsman? That makes my whole conversation earlier pretty awkward. Sorry man, with a little heads up I would have kept my hands off your girl." He sized Magnus up. "Y'all aren't even touching each other though, how's a man to know you're together? You know, if you don't want other men flirting with your girl you need to send some clear signals." He took a swig from his beer.

Magnus smiled. "See though, Master Cook, watching Kaitlyn spar is one of my great joys. Stopping ye, would have meant stopping her."

"True that. She has a way with belittling a man's manhood. You sure you can handle her?"

"Aye, I am sure." Magnus stood. "Kaitlyn, with all the preparations for the day, I must away. I winna see ye tomorrow unless... Would ye want me tae speak tae your father?"

Every person at the party watched us converse across the deck, across the ping pong table, back and forth, as if we were volleying at a tennis game. The conversation was captivating because it was frankly so mysteriously unusual — the way Magnus was stiff and formal and speaking about something that probably sounded suspiciously like much more than a date.

"I think it's okay, I'll talk to him about it. That will be best."

Hayley muttered, "Your father, what on earth for?"

Magnus said, "The time for the following day is nae set, I think it would be past noon — I will speak with the priest and have Emma call ye."

Eyes were boring into the side of my face but I ignored them. "I'll need a dress?"

"Aye."

Hayley's eyes were wide. "This better be for a date, Katie."

"I will see ye in two days, Kaitlyn Sheffield."

"I'll see you in two days, Magnus Campbell." And he turned to go around the house to his waiting horse.

In hindsight, if I had followed him, would I have kissed my future husband? But he acted as if he wasn't planning to touch me, not until we were married. Which seemed excessively formal but also very, very hot.

Because by now, this point in our relationship, I was falling. From his rumbling voice saying, Kaitlyn, to his care and attention, and of course those shoulders. I was falling hard. And sinking because my knees were weak.

I turned around, and Hayley said, "What the fuck, Katie, are you marrying him?"

In answer I shrugged. "Yes?"

Everyone started talking at once, or laughing, asking me to

explain myself, making loud obnoxious observations about my sanity.

Hayley commanded, "In the house, now. We need to talk."

As she dragged me by the arm, Quentin said, "Uh oh, Katie's in trouble."

She led me into the kitchen. Then stood, arms crossed, tapping her foot, a caricature of 'pissed off girlfriend.' "Explain yourself."

"So while you were at work today, I decided to get married to Magnus Campbell."

"The Scotsman with the sword? Have you lost your mind?"

"No, I'm perfectly—"

"Because you don't even know him, is it a green card thing?"

"Kind of. Sort of. A little. His mother said—"

"His mom? Look, I'm worried about you, this is like not just crazy, this is Dateline crazy. The kind of crazy that gets a cover on People magazine,"

"I'm aware how it sounds."

"So his mother arranged it?"

"Yes, today. I told her I wasn't agreeing until he came to speak to me, and he did, tonight."

"And that was enough? What did he say? You don't even know him. What if he beats you? What if he's part of some weird sister cult that lives on a mountain top and no one notices until one day the town's puppies begin to disappear and then they send out a private-eye and there you are chained to the chicken coop?"

"That is a highly specific 'what if.'"

"What *if*?"

"I trust him."

"How?"

I considered it for a second. "You know how me and James are always bantering back and forth? He was listening tonight, not minutes after we decided to get married, and he didn't even bat an eye. He thinks it's funny. That means he's not jealous, or crazy, or defensive, or an ass. He's got a sense of humor plus he's not possessive. Okay next."

"You want me to keep asking questions?

"Yes, I need to work this out."

"You, my dear friend, have always said, 'sleep with the guy, first date. If it sucks, you won't have to disentangle yourself later.' That was your motto. You haven't even kissed him yet. What if he's got one of those tongues that flops around in your mouth like a flounder. Or, oh my god Katie, what if he's got a micro-penis?"

I blinked. Okay that would suck. And yes that had been my motto. I was strictly in the 'sex might not fix a problem but it sure is fun' camp. And I was very hot for him, someone, anyone right now. Especially him which was a good sign I figured, since marriage was forever and all.

"Earlier when I made that crack about James's tiny penis, if Magnus's had been of the micro variety I don't think he would have found it funny. He would have been offended. Right? So yeah, he's fine. Next question."

"What about the sword, the weird storm-omen business, the way he showed up on the beach, all that? What if he's dangerous?"

I screwed my lips to the side and thought.

Hayley got tired of waiting, swung open the refrigerator, got out two beers, popped open the tops, and handed me one. She took a swig and raised her brows, waiting.

"I'm not sure. There is danger — apparently his stepfather is a brutal ass. He beat Lady Mairead. But that's in Scotland. We're in Florida. And he told me," I lowered my voice and mimicked him, "I dinna mean tae let anythin' happen tae ye." I grinned. "He'll keep me safe. He carries a sword."

Hayley shook her head. "Let me think of another one." She paused. "What if you find out you just don't like him?"

"I don't know, what if I found out that Braden was cheating on me a month before our wedding? What if I found out that James liked to sleep with a lot of different women? What if I end up like my parents who are only united in one thing, their disappointment over me?"

"What are they going to say?"

"A crap ton of critical bullshit but they'll come around because I'll be richer than them."

Hayley's eyes went wide. "I must be drunk, I totally forgot about the money. Whoa, you're going to be rich."

"I will be."

"Last one, he drives a horse."

"I'll drive his Mustang. I look prettier in it than my Prius, anyway. You know you told me just yesterday that I should do the opposite of what I usually do. This is that. As a matter of fact, your advice is most of why I'm in this situation."

"I meant date a guy with a beard, or maybe go on a cruise to Jamaica and have a fling with an island guy. Get a job. Not become a mail-order bride."

I wrinkled my nose. "I'm a mail-order bride?"

"A little bit."

We sat for a second. I drained the beer she literally just handed me. It was hard to think because of the buzz I had going. I needed some sleep. I would think better in the morning.

I said, "Hayley, out on the walkway tonight he said some things in like French or something, if you heard them you wouldn't be asking me these questions, you would be offering to take the day off work tomorrow to go wedding dress shopping with me like a good bridesmaid."

Her mouth turned up in a sad smile. "What kind of things?"

"It was something about how I was his North Star and his one true love. I don't remember the words but it was beautiful."

"You're going to marry him?"

"I am. I think I have to, I signed a contract."

She said, "Oh my god, you're crazy."

Michael came in, "Is there any more beer?" James and Quentin came in a step behind.

James asked, "Did you talk some sense into her, Hayley?"

"I did. She's still going to marry him though, but hey, there's always divorce, right baby?" She turned to Michael who was staring into the refrigerator devoid of beer, trying to wrap his brain around it.

He said, "What honey?"

She tapped her cheek. He leaned in and kissed it. "Me and the boys are going to walk to the seven-eleven for more beer."

They clomped out of the house. Hayley turned to me. "I don't have to take the day off tomorrow, it's Saturday. What time do you want to go shopping?"

CHAPTER 28

$\mathcal{W}$hat kind of dress do you buy for a church wedding that was done in a hurry under contract? I had no idea.

When I picked out my dress for my wedding to Braden, it was a concoction of satin and lace and very, very expensive. The kind of dress that said celebrity wedding but not the real kind of celebrity, the 'viral' kind of celebrity. Whatever. It had been the kind of dress to wear at a church with hundreds of witnesses.

My guess was that this would be small. Me and Magnus, possibly Lady Mairead. My parents, if I figured out a way to tell them. I was putting it off until dinner because that was a whole 'nother can of worms.

Hayley drove me to one of the best bridal shops in Jacksonville and explained to the saleswoman that we needed a dress off the rack that perfectly fit for a wedding the very next day. Also that I had no idea what I wanted, or even what kind of wedding it was going to be. The saleswoman tried to narrow it down. "What is he like?"

I said traditional.

And that's how I ended up with a floor-length, full skirt dress with laces up the back. It was beautiful. Screamed 'wedding dress.' And fit me like a glove. It was $650 but that seemed fair. Plus, though I couldn't wrap my head around it, I would be rich by this time tomorrow.

I decided not to do a veil but we found a small headpiece with pearls. This whole thing took two hours so it was 1:30 by the time we were through, stuffing the shopping bags and the gigantic dress box into the trunk of my car. We were hungry. We went for lunch at a beach restaurant and sat outside on the deck. Hayley said, "So this is your last day as a single woman."

"Oh my god."

"See those boys over there?" I glanced over my shoulder. Three men were at the bar, looking my way. "They've been checking you out since you walked in."

I tossed my hair. "Yeah, whatever."

"I'm just saying, you're doing an epic rebound thing here going from a jilted lover to a married woman in about seven weeks. I think you'll miss being able to flirt with men and maybe there's another one out there in the world. Better suited."

"Better kilted you mean?"

"Exactly."

The waitress delivered our drinks. "But I already bought the dress — no going back now. Even if that one on the right is very cute—" I ducked my head. "Crap, he just raised his glass in my direction."

"You're giving all of that up for what exactly?"

"A prince on a horse, a rich husband, a handsome man who's nice to me and seems to genuinely like me, who needs me for legal reasons, with a beach house."

Hayley sighed. "It's super hard to argue against all of that. Or any of that. Having any one of those things probably makes him a better catch than any other boy."

I blushed as one of the men stood and walked toward us. "Hi, I was wondering if you'd like to join us at our table?"

Hayley said, "Actually my friend and I were just taking a break from her wedding dress shopping."

"Ah my bad, I didn't see a ring so..." He wandered away.

"No ring," said Hayley.

"He said he'd give me one tomorrow."

CHAPTER 29

On the ride home Hayley said, "So are you packing up tonight?"

"Wait, what — I have to pack? What the hell is happening? Have I lost my mind? Crap, this is not good." I fanned myself and pretended to hyperventilate though actually the line between pretending to hyperventilate and actually hyperventilating was a really thin line.

Hayley glanced over her driving arm. "Are you okay girl? Are you — look, just breathe in, breathe out, breathe in, there you go."

I was resting my head back, eyes closed. Images flashed in my head of me driving and Magnus with his eyes closed, complete trust that I would get him where he needed to go.

Someone who trusted me so much had to be trustworthy, right? But why the heck was I marrying him when I was still wondering if I trusted him? "When I was marrying Braden I was just going to go home with him afterward. I already lived there. I was used to sleeping with him. I'm going to move into a strange man's house. Hayley, you have to save me. I don't know what I'm doing."

"I don't know either. Half the reason I'm still with Michael is that he's already seen me with hairy legs. You're going to have to hide your razors."

"You're not helping. At all."

"I've never known or even heard of someone literally moving into their husband's house after the wedding. Does that even happen anymore? Who moves the stuff?"

"It all fits in my Prius. It's just clothes and bedding. And my computer and video equipment." My eyes were still shut tight.

"So sometime between the wedding and the wedding night you're going to shuffle boxes up the stairs into your new house. This is weird."

"Oh no — the wedding night."

"Don't panic, that's the one thing you know how to do."

"But not with him. What the fuck, this is crazy. Please tell me something good."

"Okay, let me think, got it — from where I'm sitting it's likely you'll never have to clean another bathroom."

"There is that. Man, I keep thinking I'm getting pranked. Like I'm going to show up tomorrow and he's going to say, 'You didn't actually believe me did you? Who does that?' And it will be just like with Braden. Maybe there will even be a hidden camera. And I can't even talk to him about it because he doesn't have a phone."

"Zach does. Call him."

I pulled my phone from my bag and called Zach.

"Hi Katie, I was just about to call. Magnus wanted to talk to you, and I was going to hold the phone for him because you remember what happened last time."

Magnus's voice in the background said, "Pray tell Kaitlyn I replaced it."

"He replaced my phone. I tried to buy him one while I was there but he refused it. So I'm handing him my phone, here."

Magnus's voice came on too loud. He was yelling. "Hullo Kaitlyn!" I held the phone away from my ear.

Hayley giggled.

"You don't have to talk so loud, Magnus. Hear my voice? This is my normal speaking voice."

"I will try. Tis all rather odd this machine." His voice was much lower, almost too low, but I decided not to mention it. "Tis so small." His voice was not directed into the microphone anymore. I heard fumbling. "Hullo?"

My future husband didn't know how to work a phone. I sighed. "I'm here."

"I needed tae hear ye." Oh. I smiled to myself.

Hayley was hurling our car down the highway while I talked. Pretending not to listen though she was right there and rightly curious.

"I was worried ye might nae come. That ye might be scared tae be there."

"I was buying a dress and I did get scared. I thought you might not want to get married and maybe it was all a prank."

"A prank?"

"Like a joke, a trick. You wouldn't show up."

"I will be there, at the church at three o'clock."

"The Episcopal church, the one on Atlantic?"

Magnus spoke with Zach off the phone, then Zach called out, "That's the one. Oh also, ask her if she's with Hayley."

I answered, "I am, she's driving."

Zach came on the phone. "Put me on speaker."

He told Hayley that he and Michael could come to her house and pick up my things and bring them to Magnus's house while I was at the church.

Hayley grinned at me. "That sounds great. Good plan. That was one of the million things Katie was worrying about."

Zach said, "You should see Magnus, he won't stop pacing. I'm thinking about feeding him dinner so he can go to bed already and stop driving us crazy." He laughed, then hung up and that was the end of the conversation.

I checked the phone twice to see if somehow Magnus was still on. He wasn't. That had been a lot of discomfort for him, anyway.

Hayley said, "Your boy is nervous. How's that feel?"

I stared out the window at the pine trees gliding by. "Terrifying."

CHAPTER 30

J ate an early dinner with my parents because they had
plans after, which was perfect because I did not want
a lingering conversation. They were going for drinks with friends
and were expected at eight. I sat down to eat a meal a lot like the
one I made for Magnus the first night, roasted chicken off the
rack. Mashed potatoes and mac and cheese from tubs.

About five minutes in I said, "I have news."

Dad was gnawing a drumstick, his fingers covered in grease.
Mom wiped her hands on a napkin. "A job, I hope?"

"More of a fiancé."

I had both of their attentions now. They were staring right at
me though Dad continued to chew with greasy lips. Mom
glanced at my hand, my ring finger, then squinted her eyes. "Is
this Braden we're talking about because you know how I feel
about him."

"No, this is someone new, Magnus Campbell."

"He's asked you to marry him?"

"Tomorrow."

Mom said, "He's going to ask you to marry him tomorrow?"

"No, he asked me to marry him yesterday. We're going to get married tomorrow. I have a dress." I grinned, a bit maniacally.

Possibly it was the unstable nature of my grin that made my parents stare at me for longer. Then they began to ask confused backstory questions, like: How long have you been dating him? How long has it been serious? Do you know him, *really*?

This was what my parents did, ask questions until they got the one right answer. The answer that would piece it all back into their world view.

For a while, none of my answers were plausible enough. They left them confused, but it was my current state of mind too.

Finally mom dropped her fork. "You're serious about this?"

"I am."

Dad asked, "Is he asking you to sign a prenuptial?"

"No, he seems to want me to have half of everything. My name will be on the paperwork."

Then Mom and Dad said together, "Oh!" And Mom said, "It's like a green card thing. I get it now."

Dad said to Mom, "I just had a meeting with Lady Mairead the other day. She was having trouble with the paperwork, so yes, this makes sense now. Well, when I'm talking business from now on it will be with my daughter, imagine that." He took another bite of his drumstick and the two of them, having somehow figured out the 'why' of my marriage, seemed to have their minds at ease.

Mom said, "You'll be very wealthy, congratulations."

"Thanks Mom." I took a bite of mashed potatoes.

"You said the ceremony was tomorrow? At town hall?"

"At St. Peter's."

"A church wedding." For a moment Mom was confused again but then she shook her head of it. "Since it's for citizenship, your reasonings must be kept quiet. We don't want him sent from the country after all. So I'll just tell everyone it's for love, sound good Katie?"

"Sure. Will you be at the ceremony?"

"Sure, my only daughter and my best client? Your father and I will be in the front row."

CHAPTER 31

I only had to survive the rest of the night. Hayley and I stayed in with some beer and a movie. We had three to choose from. Or we could watch all of them if I couldn't sleep, which was likely. Michael arrived at ten o'clock, pretty drunk from his evening with James and the gang. He curled up in the recliner, finished watching the end of the first movie, and by ten-thirty was snoring.

Hayley crossed her eyes and joked, "If you're lucky you'll get this much romance."

"I can dream."

We put on another movie.

At two in the morning I went up to toss and turn in my bed. My grandma used to tell me to talk myself through what I did know, but everything was an unknown: Magnus, weddings, marriage, the future. I couldn't even begin to start with talking myself down.

I was going to get married.

Tomorrow.

To someone I barely knew.

CHAPTER 32

The following morning everything felt like a last supper. Hayley made Michael get up and go to McDonalds for muffin sandwiches. We ate on the couch and it was poignant, especially after Hayley said, "It's our last morning as roomies!"

I drank a lot of coffee.

I packed my clothes and stuff into boxes and suitcases remembering the day I sat in the middle of my apartment in Los Angeles, attempting to separate my belongings from Braden's while crying and hoping he would take pity on me and love me again. Instead he was walking around the house with a bandaid on his cheek as if he was the victim.

I stripped the bedding off the bed and started a load of laundry. Then I ate lunch, sandwich and chips with a coke. By this time my stomach was flitting and flying around inside my ribcage.

I took a shower. Blew dry my hair. Then Hayley followed a YouTube tutorial for putting it up in a pile on my head, with swirls and twirls and curls. With the pearl crown in the center I looked gorgeous.

Then I put on the dress. Hayley laced the back. My breasts,

generally too small for much notice, were pushed up, having, for once, a bit of cleavage. I put on a necklace but after taking a look Hayley and I decided it wasn't necessary. Just a plain neck, bare wrists, unadorned fingers.

My makeup was perfect.

All those details.

For months I had worked on wedding plans with Braden, and here a wedding was happening in a day and a half and the details were exactly like I wanted.

Hayley drove me to the church. In silence. Because there wasn't much to say, and I was shaking in my boots. Or fancy white satin pumps to be exact.

When we pulled up in the parking lot of the church, I panicked. "What if they aren't in there, what if this is all a—"

"They are in there because your dad's car is here. So see, they're in there."

I tried to stretch the tight front of my bodice to get more air. "Can you go check for me? I can't...what am I doing?"

"First, you're taking a nice long swig of this." She pulled a flask from her bag. "It's medicinal. Next, you're going to sit here while I go look inside."

She left me alone in the car and went up the front steps of the church. I sipped from the flask. Whiskey, strong but necessary. She returned a few minutes later and pulled open the car door and leaned inside. "He's here. Oh my god Katie, he is so freaking hot. Are you ready?"

"I am not ready. I am not at all."

She grabbed my hand, pulled me out of the car, and stood in front of me adjusting a tendril of hair near my ear. "Back straight."

"I don't want to do it. I'm scared, Hayley. What if this is some huge mistake?"

"If this is a huge mistake, you divorce his ass and take everything he owns. But in the meantime, he's standing at the altar waiting. By himself."

"I don't know if 'divorce' is the pep talk I need. I kind of feel like I'm going to throw up."

"You aren't going to throw up, you're going to stand tall. Straighten that back." She pushed my shoulders and I stood straighter.

"Take a deep breath." I drew in some much needed air.

"Who's thought this all through?"

"Me."

"Louder."

"Me!"

"Yeah, you. Who's gonna marry that hot Scotsman and tell Braden he can suck it?"

"Me!" I stretched my neck side to side.

"Who's going to march into that church and come out rich as hell?"

"I'm not in it for the money, but me, I am."

She went to my back and massaged my shoulders. "Who's the bravest girl in the world?"

"I am."

"Damn right you are. You're going to take that Scotsman to bed and you'll figure out where to put his sword later."

"True that."

"You might not know half of what he's talking about but when he says 'Aye' you get all weak-kneed, so you're going to march up those steps and right down that aisle and you're going to say I do. Ready?"

"Ready."

CHAPTER 33

St. Peter's was a beautiful old church, right off Centre Street. The kind of church that sold photo postcards in the gift shop and that tourists walked by and gawked at. It soared to the sky and had beautiful windows. It looked oppressive and important and walking up to it in a wedding dress felt so significant. I paused for a moment at the door, staring at the handle — I was scared out of my mind, but as my grandma would have said, "Pay attention to the butterflies; that's not fear that's excitement. Because you have nothing to fear, only things to do."

Hayley swung open the door and I stared into the big gaping maw of the church.

This church, like most, was dark, barely lit. Soaring ceilings and wide windows didn't help the light situation much but the whole combination made me feel very, very small. I had been coming here since I was a child, not often but on holidays and special occasions. I was bigger now but the height of the place made me feel like a child again.

Plus it was empty. We had it all to ourselves.

It must have cost a pretty penny to get this whole church on such short notice.

My parents were on the left, front row. The priest was facing me. Lady Mairead was sitting in the front row on the right.

Magnus was kneeling in front of the priest, his back to me.

Hayley whispered, "Who's the bravest girl in the world?"

"I am," and I walked down the aisle toward Magnus.

CHAPTER 34

*W*hen I arrived at the altar, Magnus stood and my knees about gave out. He was so handsome, hard jawline, soft eyes, dark and mysterious. He was wearing a tuxedo on his top half with a darker more modern kilt on his bottom half. He wasn't carrying his sword. He smiled briefly, nervously, and then we stood shoulder to shoulder in front of the priest.

The priest prayed and welcomed us. I was instructed to turn to Magnus, and we clasped hands while Lady Mairead slowly bound our wrists together with a silk rope before she returned to her seat.

Magnus bowed his head, so I bowed too and stared down at our hands. He held mine so tight and sure, but mine trembled. I worked to settle their flutter, concentrating on the form of his hands and the strength, the way he held mine, and the heat forming between our palms.

The priest began to speak. His words, the prayers, the solemnity and importance of their meaning filled me with calm and slowed my racing heart. Warmth spread through me.

I was marrying Magnus Campbell before God and family. I glanced up at his face. He was stoic, solemn, strong. Clasping my hands, he made me feel safe.

My arms grew tired but the ropes held us together, or was it his fingers woven around mine? The priest prayed over our hands. He asked if I would be true to Magnus, forsaking all others, as long as I lived? I answered, "I will."

He asked Magnus if he would be true to me, forsaking all others, loving and comforting and caring and keeping, and Magnus said, his words rumbling through my head, "I will."

Then the priest spoke longer about the importance of our decision and the binding union of our lives. He prayed and when he quoted scripture Magnus's voice whispered along. And then the vows began.

Magnus repeated the priest, staring into my eyes, his hands shaking with mine. "In the name of God, I take ye, Kaitlyn Sheffield, tae be my wife, tae have and tae hold, from this day forward, for better for worse, for richer for poorer, in sickness and in health, tae love and tae cherish, until we are parted by death. Tis my solemn vow."

Then it was my turn. I repeated the words back to Magnus, a quiver in my voice, a catch in my throat. "To have and to hold, from this day forward..." I lifted my eyes to his and he smiled — my breath caught. I filled my lungs with the air between us. "...until we are parted by death. This is my solemn vow."

The priest asked Magnus for the rings. We pulled our hands from the knotted rope, leaving it looped over Magnus's sleeve, and he pulled two gold rings tied with a ribbon from his inside breast pocket. The priest blessed the rings while Magnus and I stood, six inches apart, no longer touching. I missed his hands.

A few moments later Magnus took my hand in his. He trembled as he said, "I give ye this ring as a symbol of my vow, and with all that I am and all that I have, I honor ye, in the name of God." He slid the ring onto my ring finger.

The priest handed me a ring. And I repeated the same words and slid the ring onto Magnus's finger.

This was the most I had ever touched him. We had been in close proximity on his horse, rubbing and jostling together. But here, holding his hands, was intimate and forever and intense.

The priest proclaimed that we were married. "What God has brought together, let no man tear asunder."

Then we turned toward the altar, my right hand clasped in his left, and our heads bowed. The priest prayed and read scripture and prayed again. We said amen together at all the important points and rose or knelt when asked.

And then finally, it was over. We turned around to the mostly empty church. A few more words were spoken and my hand was clutched in Magnus's as we walked down the aisle toward the doors of the church.

I was married. I was Kaitlyn Campbell, former YouTuber, believer in the big public life, a past lover of more than one boy, now the wife of a mysterious Scotsman named Magnus.

My parents rushed us. My mother hugged me and carried on about how thrilled she was, how beside herself with excitement. She didn't need to say it. She was in high color, carrying on as if she couldn't believe it actually happened, which was a little embarrassing for me. Did she think I was making it up? Did she come to the church to watch me fail?

Dad shook Magnus's hand, hugged and kissed me, then announced he would bring paperwork to be signed tomorrow. Meaning I would have my name on a fortune within hours.

They were all coming to my new house where Zach was making a wedding meal.

You might think the dreamlike trance of the day would be

broken by now, but no, still going. And I hadn't even kissed him yet. I thought that was the main part of every wedding, yet here I was, not kissed. My hands had been bound to his though, in many ways that was way better.

He was speaking with Lady Mairead, the side of his face angled and intense.

Lady Mairead turned to me. "Kaitlyn Campbell, I will see ye at home. Your parents are giving me a ride." She clasped my hand in hers. "Thank ye."

"Oh, no worries, I mean, you're welcome." I had forgotten I originally did this for her because I could only think of Magnus now and what I had done for him.

She and my parents left, and then Hayley hugged and kissed me. She led us outside as it dawned on us that her car was the only vehicle left.

She said, "I should have thought this through. I could have had a temp here with a car. Hmm. Okay, in a pinch, I'm your chauffeur."

She opened the car door for us, and I slid in and then Magnus. She closed the door and ran off to check we hadn't forgotten anything in the church.

Magnus still had the silk rope looped over his arm. He slid it off, coiled it into a small circle, and fit it over my hand to my wrist as a bracelet. Then he pulled my arm, up under his own, and pressed his lips to my temple and lingered there. I listened as he breathed me in. "Ye have married me then, Kaitlyn?"

"I have Magnus, I married you. Did you marry me?"

"Aye, I have, forever." The words vibrated on my skin.

Hayley appeared and climbed in the driver's seat. "Okay — to Magnus's? Am I invited to dinner too? Michael?"

I laughed, "Michael's probably there moving my stuff in, right? So definitely." Then I glanced at Magnus, "I'm sorry, I just — can Michael and Hayley come eat dinner tonight?"

"Tis your house too Kaitlyn, ye decide."

"Yes, come to dinner."

CHAPTER 35

*W*hen we got to the house, my parents made us stand on the deck while they took pictures of us in pseudo-wedding poses, side by side, holding one hand, strained smiles. I supposed we would like to have them someday.

Zach roasted lamb and served it with mint. There were also turnips and potatoes, to which Magnus exclaimed, "Neeps and tatties, well done!" as well as some citrus and berries because it was summer and Zach wanted to lighten it up. For dessert there was a beautiful wedding cake, two round layers with white icing covered in flowers. He explained that he bought it because we did not give him enough time to bake one. Though he would have.

He said, "And it's chocolate cake, you're welcome, Katie." There was also sorbet, heather ale, and champagne.

Magnus and I sat beside each other at his big dining table. A key part of any wedding plan is the dress the bride puts on after the ceremony. I had forgotten the need for such a thing. So I stayed in my wedding dress, which was over the top for the living room. Yet so luxurious —white damask in folds around me, with my dark, handsome husband in a tux beside me. He was hanging on my every word, watching me constantly, completely. We leaned in toward each other. I batted my lashes. He smiled a lot.

Hayley and Michael joined us, my parents, and Lady Mairead. Waiting for the first course I noticed Magnus tug at his bow tie. "Tis too tight."

"Just unclip it."

He fumbled with the back of it. "Daena have a clip."

"Lean in." He raised his chin. I pulled the ends, untied the bow, and left them dangling undone beside his buttons. Then, because I liked the proximity and the touches and the being the-person-who-touched-him-there, I unbuttoned the top button of his shirt, opened it off his neck, and stroked down the fabric, starched, cotton, expensive. It was the most intimate thing I had ever done with him — at the table in my wedding dress, untying his tie, unbuttoning one button of his shirt.

His eyes lingered on my face the whole time. By the time I sat down I was flushed. Bordering on hot.

Zach and Emma served the meal and brought in platter after platter of food and asked if we needed anything. They stayed close by joking and laughing as they handed the plates of food around.

After serving us they served themselves and joined us at the table, sending food out for Magnus's security team. It was equal parts traditional, the way Magnus had a staff, but also very modern how his staff shared the food and the space with him. I liked it and supposed it had a lot to do with Magnus, his kindness that he didn't need to feel superior.

The dinner was festive and fun but the space between Magnus and me was charged with electricity. We barely touched. His fingers brushed mine here and there as we ate. It was much like those moments when you're first dating someone, trying to bed them, but so different too because there wasn't any downside. No 'what ifs', only anticipation.

He was mine. Forever and ever mine. And I hadn't even tasted him yet.

CHAPTER 36

$\mathcal{M}$y parents left and Lady Mairead went up to her room to bed.

We sat for a bit longer, enjoying another beer and more conversation with Hayley, Michael, Zach, and Emma. Then Hayley came up with an idea to stage photos of us in our wedding clothes, sprawled back on chairs, surrounded by plates of half-eaten food and half-empty drinks. Zach and Emma had done some cleaning already, so they dragged out dirty dishes and set the table again to look post-feast. Hayley told me to lean in against Magnus's chest, holding a big slice of cake in my fist, his hand around a whole bottle of wine. Part of the roasted meat in front of us. It looked like some kind of neo-rococo last supper, ornate and beautiful, a little decadent, and very funny. We laughed a lot and all agreed that those photos of our wedding were our favorites. Then, before I knew it, Hayley and Michael were up grabbing their things, saying goodbye, and leaving through the front door.

Zach and Emma cleared plates from the table and poured us each another drink. I was stuffed. Our chairs were very close to each other, yet we still weren't touching. I leaned back and tried to get a deep breath but my bodice had grown tight with the food. I tugged at the base of it. Magnus shifted his hand to trail a finger along the bottom edge of my bodice, so close to my hip, back and forth, slowly, mesmerizing, then his finger went up under the edge of it and gently pulled, barely, slowly, drawing me closer, promising more. My breath caught.

"Would ye like tae go tae our chamber, Kaitlyn?" He asked quietly.

I shook my head.

"Why nae?"

"I'm scared." His finger continued to travel back and forth along the lower edge of my bodice.

"You are scared of me?"

"No, it's just, I think I'm scared of the moment, you know?"

He nodded. "Aye, I know. I feel it too."

His fingers trailed up my side and across my shoulder and faintly, lightly, down my arm, giving me shivers.

"I think twill be all right," he said quietly, seriously.

"How do you know?"

He smiled softly. "We canna stay here, there is cleaning that must be done and our bed is much more comfortable."

I nodded and stood. He held my hand and led me to the bedroom, just off the main living area.

"You sleep here now?"

"Aye, since ye slept here. It smelled of ye for a time."

"Really? You're going to give me a complex."

"A complex?"

I stood in the middle of the room while he adjusted the window screens and turned on a table lamp, throwing the room into a dim light.

"Make me insecure — because you keep talking about how I smell."

"You smell like nothing and everything at once, I canna describe it." He opened a top drawer, showing me my underwear in small stacks. I hoped Emma had done the folding instead of Michael and Zach. But also, whoa, someone put my clothes away.

Magnus sat on the bed. "You look verra beautiful."

I blushed. "Thank you."

I was still wearing my pearled headpiece, so I went down the small hallway, through the frosted glass sliding door, past the closets that I would need to explore tomorrow, to the gigantic master bathroom. I paused for a moment. My toothbrush there beside another strange toothbrush in a strange bathroom, my husband's, forever more. I reminded myself to breathe, pulled the crown off, yanked out the bobby-pins and hair-bands, and ran a brush through my hair.

When I returned, the room was darker. Three cylinder candles burned on the bedside table. He stood. "Come here, Kaitlyn."

"I like it when you say my name. I mean, I like that it doesn't have 'mistress' in front of it anymore." I stood in front of him. His eyes were intense on my face; I felt awkward. "You lit candles."

"Aye, Emma assured me ye would like them."

"I do, they smell good." He slowly trailed his fingertips down my sides to my waist and gently turned me so he could untie my bodice. His fingers shook as he worked at the lacing.

"Do you know what the scent is?"

He was quiet, working on the laces. "She said tis called Hot Amber."

"Yum, I love — is it going okay back there?"

He sighed. "I am tryin' tae concentrate."

"Ah, sorry." It took him a long time because it was complicated and tight, but then slowly he worked his fingers into the tight laces, the fabric folds, and taking his time spread open the back of my dress. He looped a finger under the capped sleeves and with excruciating slowness pulled them off my shoulders and down. The entire dress fell in a giant puff of white around my knees.

He offered me a hand for balance while I stepped over the pile, and he shoved it away with his foot. I was facing him, mostly unclothed. He sat down on the bed. Then he reached out and ever so slowly, bit by bit, pulled my panties down to the ground. "Can ye stand there for a moment?"

It was hard to know what to do as his eyes traveled around and over my naked body. I wanted his touch so desperately. I was arching forward with my breaths, doing this thing I did where I couldn't be still. He was as still as a rock, concentration and focus, but I was struggling against my need to climb in his lap, bringing force and energy and movement.

He grinned. "You art a breeze ridin' wisp. You daena wiggle so much when ye were clothed."

I pretend whined, "I can't help it, this is too long without you touching me."

"Tis now?" He grasped my hips and pulled me forward to stand between his legs. "Ah, much better." He ran his hand down my back, my ass, my legs. Until I couldn't bear it anymore. I pulled him to standing and began working on the buttons of his tuxedo shirt. My fingers brushing the shirt linen stretched across his firm chest. I yanked it down his arms and tossed it to the side. And ran my hands up and down the ridges along his abdomen.

The kilt was more complicated. It wrapped. I found the latch and it dropped to the ground. He sat and removed his boots which took a second. Then he asked, "Kaitlyn, will ye come tae bed now?"

I nodded and joked, "Aye."

CHAPTER 37

*H*e shoveled under the covers, giving me my first glimpse of my husband's full form in motion, muscles taut, holding my hand, pulling me along. We arrived in the middle of our luxurious bed, under a cloud of a comforter, surrounded by too many, too high pillows. And we snuggled close, wrapped, front to front.

And

oh

my

god

I was touching the length of him, my chest pressed to his. He wanted me; he was pressed on my stomach, and he was holding me so strong and sure, his breath warm on my cheek. His hand traveling slowly down my back and around my buttocks and then up slowly along my side. He pulled a breath away and watched his hand as it moved up my stomach. The caress so light and electric that I arched toward his fingers. His hand paused at my breast. His voice rolled from somewhere in his chest, vibrating against my skin. "May I touch ye here?"

I breathed out, "Anywhere."

"Och, aye." His hand drifted along my curves, checking to see if I was telling the truth. His hand followed along the curve of my bottom, caressing up the back of my thigh, raising it to his waist, around and into the folds between my legs, and down my thighs and back up again. He closed his eyes. His brow drawn in intense concentration. He placed his mouth against the edge of my neck, hot, lips, wet, whispering — "I want ye, Kaitlyn. But I daena want tae scare ye."

I wrapped my hands around the back of his head, my head against his lips — *I'm not scared* — I arched forward and with my leg wrapped around his waist I brought his hips closer to mine. "I want you too."

He looked into my eyes. His were wild, his brow hot, his hair tousled. "I dinna think ye would want—"

"That I would want you?" I ran my hands down his back inching him closer, myself wanting him more and more. My lips were close to his ear. "I do, I want you."

"I daena want tae hurt ye..."

I ran my fingers down his jawline. "You won't." His hand played between my legs, and I was losing the ability to think or speak.

His hot breath was in my ear. I tasted the salt on his cheek. His lips on my neck — *you won't* — I ran my hand across his wide shoulder, caressing along the broad muscles — *I want you* — and slowly massaged down his side to his buttocks and staring into his eyes, my breaths heaving, I pulled him inside me.

He moaned, closed his eyes, and rolled on top of me, filling me, pushing inside of me. I wrapped my legs around his body and pulled him in, more, harder, more. His breath was hot on my neck, pushing and pulling against me. His chest pressed to my skin — his moan — his words — *you are tremblin'* —

I caught my breath — *what?* — I lost the meaning of his words between the thrust and pull of our bodies — *really?*

Aye — the touch of his teeth pressed near my throat's pulse — *as if ye are frightened o'me.*

I looked him in the eyes for — so briefly. I couldn't keep looking. His eyes pulled me inside out. I clamped them shut. "I'm not afraid of you."

"Good, but still you tremble when I enter ye." He shoved into me hard and fast full of force and power. He nibbled on my throat. "You art a'flutter."

"God — Magnus." I moaned and arched toward him. He inhaled me with his breath. He pulled out of me and touched between my legs. "You tremble here, like ye anticipate me, ye want—"

"I do," I gasped. "I do want."

He entered me again with a rush and ran his lips down my cheek. "You want me gentle?" He shoved hard, deep, rough.

"No." I pushed against the headboard, motion against force. My legs pulling me up, forcing him down — close in — *I just want you* — faster and faster — *god oh god oh god*— waves rushed through my body, shaking me through. Magnus pounding between my legs until he climaxed with a groan and relaxed down onto my body.

He lay there heavy on me, soft within me, for a long time. His breathing fast, then growing slower and slower. His mouth on my shoulder. His voice vibrating on my skin. "Tis the way it goes then?"

My eyes wide, I asked, "Magnus, was that your first time?"

"Nae." He gave me a sheepish grin. "Twas the first time in a bed, changes the operation of it." He put his mouth back on my shoulder. "Twas my first time with you. It changed the meanin' of it." He pulled a hair breadth away. "Am I crushin' ye?"

I wrapped my arms and legs around him tighter. "No, I like you here."

He leaned his cheek to mine and then rested his mouth on my neck, just under my jaw at the edge of my throat, my heartbeat against his breath. And then slowly he rubbed his cheek along mine, his lips up to my lips, and kissed me, for the very first time, soft and sweet. I wrapped my fingers through the back of his hair pulling him closer. The kiss was lingering and awesome, tastes and moans, licks and nibbles. The scent of amber floated around us and when it was done I looked up to find him staring down at me. And we stayed there for a moment looking deep into each other's eyes.

He nodded. "Aye Kaitlyn, ye have married me."

I sighed. "Aye Magnus, I did." I had to look away the feeling was so intense, deep. I concentrated on pushing a bit of his hair behind his ear.

He shimmied down my body. With a hand firmly holding my breast, he kissed me on the bottom edge of my ribs and nuzzled his forehead into my chest. With his other hand he firmly gripped my buttock. "Tis all mine?" His voice sounded muffled, pressed to my diaphragm.

"Technically speaking."

"Good, I plan tae live here now."

"In my breasts?" I laughed.

"I could eat my meals here." He kissed my breast causing me to arch toward his mouth. "And tis a pillow so I can sleep here too." He snuggled his cheek into my skin.

"It might get boring after a while to live in bed, sleeping and eating, but I'm game to try."

He chuckled, held in my arms but holding me too. "I canna believe I would get bored with ye." The room was peacefully dark. The candle flickers cast dancing shadows. Our voices low and deep, meant only for each other.

I entwined my fingers in his hair, wrapping and twisting a curl around my finger, brushing hair from his sweaty brow.

We laid there like that for a long time. The amber scent wafting around us. I was thinking about all the firsts — we had just made love, undressed each other, seen each other naked for the first time, then we kissed. And—

"Did you do this with James Cook?"

I startled, "What? Why do you ask that?"

His cheek pressed to my chest, his voice a rumble. "I feel I need tae know. And I need ye tae be the one tae tell me."

"Oh." That's why he had been so quiet. "I don't think we should talk about it. I—"

"Usually when I ask ye something, you answer."

"But this is not the same as 'how does the light switch work.' This is—"

"If I dinna ken this about ye, but you do, and James Cook knows this about ye, and I dinna, then I am made a fool."

"Oh. Yeah, I guess I can see that." His arms tightened around my back, holding me tight and still.

I spoke it into the air between us. "I have done this with James Cook. I also did these things with my fiancé, and... But that was my past and we shouldn't dwell on it because there's no going back. Honestly, I didn't know you were coming."

"Aye." He lay quietly, his heartbeat in a constant rhythm on my stomach "And ye dinna marry these men, Kaitlyn?"

"No, only you."

He raised his head and shoulders above me to look at my face. Candlelight flickered across his pained expression. "So you dinna vow tae them that ye would never bed another man?"

"I didn't make any vows, but when I loved Braden I wasn't with anyone else. When I loved James I wasn't with anyone else. I stopped loving them when they chose other people. It's complicated, I guess. But it's more like an agreement than a vow." I stroked my fingers down his wide shoulder. "Are you worried I might break my vow to you?"

"I daena wish tae be made a fool."

"We are new to each other and until we have spent more time together we won't have proof of our truthfulness, but I won't lie to you Magnus. And I meant my vow today. I will not be with another man." My voice caught. "Just please don't break my heart."

He pressed his lips to my breast, just at my heart. "Mo chroí, a chuisle mo chroí."

"What does that mean?"

"It means you are the beat of my heart." He rolled to his side and I snuggled into his arms. "I have made a vow before God that I am yours. And you are mine. But more, I have made a vow here," he took my hand and placed it on his chest.

I nodded.

"And now I have made a vow here." He brought my hand down to the space between us. "And here." I laughed when his hand dove between my legs. "I will remind ye of my vow many times a day, mo reul-iuil."

I ran my fingers down the side of his cheek. "I am super glad about your enthusiasm for your vows. This bodes well for a very happy wife."

"I have one more question and I will be done of Master Cook and other cock-full half-men." He raised up on one elbow and hovered his strong hand over my stomach. "How is it ye haena borne them children?"

"I'm on birth control." When he looked at me blankly, I explained, "I take a pill, it makes it so I can't get pregnant."

"You daena want children?"

"I do, someday, but we can talk about it, and when we want to I can stop taking the pill. But until then, we can do more of this." I rubbed my hands down his back and his hand relaxed, the weight of it on my stomach was a comfortable pressing.

"That would be good. No bairns, until I figure out this trouble with Lady Mairead's husband."

"Are we done with the questions?"

"Aye, you will soon tire of telling me about the world. I will need tae shew ye something, tae ride, or I will train ye tae fight with a dirk or a sword."

I grinned at him. "I actually think I'm already in training with your sword."

He chuckled. "Mo reul-iuil, your wit is marvelous."

Our bedding was shoved off the bed in all directions. The sheets twisted under us. Pillows tossed about. I loved that we were so new, languishing in bed together, getting to know each other in the darkness of our room.

He propped his head up on his elbow. And then, because I was curious, I asked, "Did you mean you've only ever had sex up against walls?"

"When you are young at court without much standing, ye must take what is offered ye."

I laughed. "It sounds like you had a great deal of standing."

His chuckle vibrated along my side.

"And I know you're joking, the queen is not going to stand for all that fornicating in the halls." I raised my brows. "See what I did there, 'stand for it'?"

"I did. Tis verra funny."

"But if you haven't much experience with beds, then you probably haven't really been fully naked with someone?"

"Nae. Tis much too cold for it in drafty stairwells."

I huffed. "I'm totally irritated that James took you to that strip bar."

"Why?"

"Because now in your head you're comparing me to strippers."

He shook his head slowly, solemnly. "Put your arms up."

I stretched long, raising my arms above my head. Shoving a pillow away.

He ran his hand all along my body. His fingers trailing up and down and around, lingering on my stomach, traveling to my breasts, tickling and caressing, as if he was memorizing me. Investigating me, exploring, causing me to wriggle and dance under his fingertips.

It was so electric and slow and thoughtful that there was a chance I would internally combust.

Finally he murmured, "Tha thu breagha, mo chridhe."

My voice was much like a gasp when I asked, "What does that mean?"

"You are beautiful, luminous. I try tae get my eyes used tae looking at ye but I fear ye blind me tae everythin' else."

"Really?"

He paused his hand in mid-glide down my body. "Aye, Kaitlyn, tis true. I have never touched anyone like this. Nae body has ever allowed me tae. I daena think there would be a way tae compare ye."

"Oh." I was losing my ability to think again. His fingers caressed the soft side of my breast, then trailed to the peak and gently pulled, making me arch to his mouth. He nibbled and sucked and then his hand plunged between my legs. He pulled me closer with a triumphant smile. "I want ye again."

I laughed. "So soon?"

"When I touch ye wriggle and move, corrachag-cagail. How can I help myself?" He made to roll on me, but I pushed him to his back and climbed on him, astride, pulled him inside me and sat down deeply. I rocked and shifted and moved on him. His hands curled around my bottom, lifting me, pushing me closer and pulling me away.

I pressed my palms to his wide firm chest and it was long and delicious and slow. I arched back and felt him so deliciously deep and finally so desperate and intense, looking down at him with power and control and then filling with him. I lost my breath, then my mind and my heart, and with a rush I loved him. The feeling raced from my heart and roared down my stomach and warmed me, hot and sweaty, and when I collapsed on him it was a full collapse leaving me vulnerable and breathless.

He rolled me over, climbed on, and finished — his lips on my shoulder, his breathing heavy in my ear, my moans in his. There was no going back to Kaitlyn alone — I was his.

He rose up, shook his hair, elbows beside my head, his full body on mine. The delicious weight of him holding me still and down. In my past I always had trouble with my want — wanting closer, more, touch me please, but he was there, here, everywhere, always. "You art a braw wife, mo reul-iuil. I like ye verra much."

I wrapped my hands around his over my head. "I like you too." He pressed the side of his cheek down to my mouth and I tasted him, salty on my lips. "Maybe later we can add licking to our fun bed romp?"

He smiled. "I think I would much like that."

"Me too, definitely but alas we'll have to wait for another rest." I wiggled my hips against his softness.

"Give me just a wee moment," he joked.

He rolled off and offered his arm so I could curl along his body.

I asked, "When did you know you liked me?"

He was quiet for a moment. "The first night I saw ye. I will never forget it, twas a full moon and..." He raised his face to look at me with a grin.

It took me a second to get his meaning. "Oh my god Magnus, did you see me naked?"

"A fine bonnie lass in the streaming moonlight racing with her buttocks out for the whole world to see."

I groaned. "I'm so embarrassed. What did Lady Mairead think?"

"Ah, she assumed ye were a prostitute, but I said tae me'self, there is the sweet, modest girl I am going tae marry."

"I'm so embarrassed, and also, what the hell — you *married* me." I sat up and held his hand in both of mine, opened his fingers and spread them wide, his palm flat. I brought it to my lips and kissed the warm center. Thick pads, hard calluses, strength and work. When I traced the back of his fingers they folded forward, less curling, more bunching, muscles and sinews, grip and power. I massaged my hands up his arm, measuring and assessing, veins and taut and firm and curved, across his chest, down his stomach, admiring and exploring. "This is all mine? All of you?"

"Och aye." The corner of his mouth pulled into a smile. "Though I think I may have the better of the deal, ye have better parts." He reached between my legs causing me to giggle and squirm. "And we can do this anytime we want tae?"

I nodded. "Oh yeah."

His brow drew together. "I had been told twas nae of interest tae most women."

I scoffed. "Whoever told you that did not know how to do it right."

He chuckled. "Twas my brother."

"Probably don't ask him for advice going forward."

"I winna. Did I do it a'right?"

I laid back down beside him, curled on his chest. "Definitely, that writhing and squirming was me wanting you again, all of you. More. And soon as you've rested for a bit. We have all night to practice together at this sport, we can go slow."

His chuckle vibrated against my chest. "Much like in the caber toss, I must begin with the smaller trunk first?"

I laughed. "No, in this sport you should always start with a nice big trunk."

He laughed outright. "I have tae introduce ye tae my Uncle Baldie some day."

"Will you take me to Scotland?"

"I would wish tae but it may nae be possible. And this first time I must go alone."

"When would you?"

"Soon, I must away afore Lady Mairead." He kissed me on the neck then swept the blanket away. "And I'm hungry." He climbed from the bed, found a pair of flannel pajama bottoms in a drawer, tugged them on, and tied the drawstring. "I'll ask Chef Zach tae serve us some cake."

"He'll be up in the kitchen?"

"Nae, but he will be a listenin' for me and up as soon as my door opens."

"I'm going to stay here, in bed, with all these awesome pillows." I stretched out luxuriously. "Will you open the screens a bit so I can see the dunes from bed?"

He adjusted the screens for me, opened our bedroom door and walked halfway across the living room toward the kitchen, when Zach's voice called from the top of the stairs. "Magnus, did you need something?"

"Aye, Kaitlyn and I wanted cake."

"Sure, give me just a moment."

"I'll check with the night watch." Magnus slid the living room sliding door open and stepped outside to murmur with his security man. Our security man, I supposed. Though why on earth did we have a man on watch all the time? The truth was though, they made the house seem like the safest place on earth.

Soft sounds came from the kitchen as Zach cut slices of cake, opened the refrigerator, poured something into glasses, and offered to carry them for Magnus, who refused, opting instead for carrying it himself. While I snuggled into our nest bed. The AC was cranking. The comforter was perfectly warm. The pillows were perfect. And I had gotten married, just hours ago, had made love twice, and really, deeply fallen for my husband, and hadn't slept at all last night, so all of this night-time-ness was lulling me to sleep. My eyes grew heavy and my mind drifted away.

Magnus placed the tray with a giant slice of cake, two forks, and some champagne on the nightstand. He whispered, "Kaitlyn, are ye hungry?"

I whispered back, "Sleepy."

"I will see ye in the morn."

The last thing I remembered as I fell asleep was Magnus sliding into bed beside me, fluffing a pillow to prop himself, and bringing the plate to his lap.

CHAPTER 38

*I*t was still night when I woke, or early morning, and storming outside, loud and booming. Lightning streaked across the sky. The light was grey, the wind tore across the dunes, the sea grass whipped and bent in the gusts. It was spectacular to have that much weather outside and be safe and secure inside.

I squiggled over to Magnus who was flat on his stomach and snuggled against his back. I kissed his shoulder and stroked down his side. He didn't move. I rubbed up and down along his side and then because he wouldn't wake up, coughed to see if I could jar him awake and pretend like I hadn't.

It was sort of lonely to be in his bed without him talking to me. And it had been a few hours, plus our wedding night.

I whispered, "Magnus? Magnus wake up?" He remained immobile. "Magnus?" I sat up and shook his shoulder, and finally shoved him to his back, lifeless.

Blood rushed to my head and I went from sleep to full panic in a second. "Magnus, oh my god, Magnus?" I put my ear to his chest, his lungs. "Magnus?" Two fingers on his neck. I pressed and waited. There was a heartbeat, light, shallow breaths. "Magnus!" Completely unresponsive.

I jumped from the bed, raced to the dresser, and dug through drawers for a pair of boxers and a T-shirt. "Magnus, Magnus wake up?" I yanked the clothes on. "Magnus, you're scaring me, get up, okay?"

I raced for the sliding door, yanked it open, and stepped on the porch. The security guard was in a chair at the other end, and I couldn't remember which one it was. "Hey, I need help, Magnus is..." His head lolled forward on his chest, "Hey! Hey! Help." A lightning bolt streaked across the sky directly for the beach in front of the house, I pulled into the room, slammed the door shut, and raced for the living room. "Zach! Zach! Emma!" I climbed the stairs two at a time to the second floor and banged on the door of Zach and Emma's room.

There was no sound from inside, so I shoved the door open. They were both in bed, television flickering, the volume completely down, not moving, not responding. "Oh no, oh no, oh no." I raced down the hall past the nurse's room, she had gone to her own home to sleep. Lady Mairead's door was locked. I banged to no avail.

I raced back down the stairs to our room and climbed on the bed. "Please wake up Magnus, please, wake up. You're scaring me." I shook him and then rubbed the side of his face. "Magnus, everyone is asleep. No one will wake up. Magnus help me. I don't know what to do." Should I call 911? What would they do, would they wake everyone up? Somehow? Could I Google how to wake up a whole household of unnaturally sleeping people?

"Magnus? Please?" I massaged down his arms to his fingers and then his calves to his feet, not even an extra breath or a moan or anything like waking. What had happened? My eyes swept the room. The cake. There were two crumbs on the plate, the rest, eaten. The glasses of — I sniffed a glass — champagne were mostly finished.

I returned to the porch. The wind whipped my hair, grabbed at my clothes. I bent into the wind to make it to the security guard's position, finally remembering his name was Jim — something. "Jim! Jim!" He had a plate with a half-eaten slice of cake under his seat. He also had no roof over his head and rain was headed up the walkway. Jim was a lunk of a man. There was no way I was moving him, dragging him inside.

I spun around taking in the deck. At the far end was a table with a standing umbrella. The wind gusted so hard it almost knocked me from my feet. I grabbed the umbrella, pulled it from the table, struggled to keep it from ripping free of my hands, and carried it racing to the security guard's chair. I shoved the umbrella stick into the slats between Jim's side and the chair and angled it toward the storm. Then I struggled mightily to open it against the wind. "Jim! Jim! Wake up you mother fucker, wake up!!" He was the worst freaking security guard in the world. What the hell was going on? The umbrella was open and it was not a good plan. What if the umbrella attracted lightning?

As if to scare me further, lightning raced across the sky and struck a bush in the dunes between my walkway and the neighbor's. Crap. But, there was nothing I could do. Jim was an easy two hundred and forty pounds of dead weight.

I needed someone to help.

I raced back up the stairs to Zach's room. "Zach wake up. Wake up." Emma's side of the bed had a plate on it with a couple of cake crumbs. But Zach's was empty — maybe they shared, maybe he only had a bite — "Zach?" I stood over him and shook his shoulder, then I shook it harder. "Zach!"

He mumbled something.

"Zach!" I yelled into his ear. His eyes fluttered open but then closed again. "Zach, I need your help, something is wrong with Emma and Magnus, please, help me." His eyes fluttered open.

"Katie?" Then they closed again and he was back dead to the world.

"Did you eat cake? Zach?" His eyes opened briefly and he looked around then closed them again. I raced into their bathroom, grabbed a cup near their toothbrushes, and filled it with water from the sink.

I brought it to Zach, tried to rouse him to drink, and then in a panic just threw the whole thing in his face.

He spluttered. "Fuck Katie, what was—"

I was probably terrifying. My hair and eyes wild, the color drained from my face. "Something happened. I think something was in the cake. Oh my god, Zach, something is wrong with Magnus, he won't wake up, Emma won't wake up."

He turned confused to Emma and shook her shoulder. "Emma, baby? You okay?" He sat up, groggily rubbed his eyes, and looked around. Then back at Emma. "Baby, wake up?" He looked at me, his eyes unfocused and his mind still confused. "What happened?"

I burst into tears.

"Zach help me. What should I do?"

He swung his legs off the bed with a groan then dropped his head into his hands. "Tell me again?"

"The cake. The cake, something was in — I need to go back downstairs, something might be really wrong, Magnus isn't — stay here and try to wake Emma."

I raced to our room, dove onto the bed, and began shaking Magnus's shoulder again. "Magnus!" This time his breathing changed. He shifted. "Magnus!" I kept shaking and massaging and cajoling him to wake up. Pleading with him to *please*. Slowly seeing more and more movement.

Zach appeared. Wobbly and dazed. "Did he wake yet? Emma is coming around."

I was on my knees on the bed beside Magnus, clutching his hand in mine, pleading for him to please wake up. I said, "The security guard is asleep too—"

"Jim is fucking asleep, are you kidding me?"

I massaged and shook Magnus's shoulder. His eyes were fluttering.

I asked, "Have you checked on Lady Mairead?"

"She's not down here? What the fuck is going on?"

The sliding door opened and Jim, sopping wet, staggered in. "Is everyone okay? Something knocked me out hard. There's a storm, and an umbrella was stuck to my chair."

Zach said, "Jim the whole house has been knocked out, Magnus is still, I'm going back to Emma." Jim rushed behind him up the stairs.

Magnus's fingers wiggled in my hand. I knelt over him. "Magnus, please wake up. I need you to stop sleeping because you're really scaring me."

A few minutes later Jim returned. "How is he? Emma is awake, groggy but awake."

"He's not waking, not yet."

"I'm implementing a full Lights Out, and a search for Lady Mairead."

I had a full edge of hysterical panic now. "I don't know what that is, what is it? I don't know how to—"

Jim said, "Just stay here, try to wake him." He turned off the lights and left.

I sat on the bed, in the dark, hovering over my husband, whispering. "Please wake up Magnus, something happened and I don't know what to do. Please wake up."

Zach came in, sort of stumbled to the bed, and sat on the

edge. "Katie I'm sorry I'm not much help, I'm trying to get my wits about me. He'll wake up in a moment, if we have."

"What was in that cake?"

"I don't know, I swear Katie, it wasn't me."

"I didn't think you—"

The motorized shades buzzed closed, then the whole house powered down. Zach said, "I need to go back to Emma, so she's not scared."

Zach's footsteps crept up the stairs and the security guard came into the room and stealthily checked the closets and under the bed.

I pressed my lips to the back of Magnus's hand. "Please. You're scaring me."

CHAPTER 39

A while later, after what seemed like forever, Magnus mumbled, shifted, and mumbled again before falling back to sleep. Then a bit later he groaned, thrashed for a moment, and startled awake at the sight of me, sitting cross-legged, staring down at his face, frantic with worry.

"Kaitlyn?"

"Magnus, oh my god, I think someone drugged the cake. We can't find Lady Mairead—"

Magnus groaned and swept the comforter aside, but when his feet hit the floor his head and torso weaved to the right. He collapsed back down to the bed. "How long have I been out?"

"Hours. Everyone was, the security guard, Emma, everyone. Magnus, who did it?"

"Was there a storm?" He attempted to sit, holding his head in his hand.

"A big storm, lightning, thunder, wind. I was trying to get an umbrella over Jim—"

"You were out there? During the storm?" He stood and

wobbled a bit but made it to the dresser and held on; his body weaving dangerously.

"Should I call the nurse, ask her to drive over to check you? We should make sure you're okay."

"I'm fine. I have tae talk tae security." He left for the living room. I collapsed back on the bed in relief. That had been a freaking terrifying experience. Adrenaline coursed through me. I said to myself, "That was the scariest thing that ever happened to me." And then I burst into tears.

CHAPTER 40

I recovered myself and went to the living room. Zach and Emma were at the table. Magnus and Jim had raced down the boardwalk to the beach searching for Lady Mairead.

Zach said, "Katie, I would never drug you guys, I swear. I don't know what happened."

"I know Zach, I'll talk to Magnus about it, but I don't think he would ever suspect you. Emma, are you okay?"

"Head hurts. I took some aspirin. But Zach promised a big healthy breakfast, so?" She looked at him expectantly.

"Yeah, I'll make some food for everyone, yeah definitely. I just, you'll talk to him Katie? I really don't want to lose this job."

"No worries, I'll talk to him if I need to."

"Thanks." He went to the kitchen. "How do you like your eggs?"

Through the window I could see Magnus and Jim standing on the dunes, staring out at the ocean, and looking up and down the beach.

I said, "Fried but thick, like the plasticky egg they put on an

English muffin at McDonalds, with American cheese? And a lot of coffee. But not the fancy kind, the regular kind of coffee."

Zach looked at me with his eyebrows raised. "I have eggs. I can probably pull that off. But with cheddar cheese because seriously, American cheese? But hey, you're the boss. But I would like to add that pancakes are on the list of possibilities, fucking, excuse me, waffles, if you want them. Or crepes. With blueberries. And the coffee is fancy. I'll put your favorite on my shopping list." He poured me a mug of coffee and brought it to me with cream and sugar.

Magnus came to the door, slid it open, and stormed in. "Chef Zach I will need tae speak tae ye in a few minutes. Emma, I am verra sorry about this, are ye well?"

She nodded.

He leaned over and kissed me on the forehead. "I will be upstairs searching Lady Mairead's things."

"Do you think we've been robbed?"

"Nae, I think Lady Mairead has been involved." He jogged up the steps.

I turned to Emma, my eyes wide. She said, "Well, he told us not to trust her."

"Oh man, what the—" I followed Magnus up to Lady Mairead's rooms. I found him on his knees yanking a drawer from her dresser and pouring it out on the floor. The room was full of art — paintings, sculptures, plates and candlesticks stood around the edges, some leaning layers deep.

He sifted through the pile then poured out the next drawer and shoved his hand around through the pile. "What are you looking for?"

"I dinna ken, anythin', paperwork, trinkets, artifacts. If I think tis important—" He finished with the last drawer and sat back on his heels with a sigh.

"Let's go tae the office."

The office had already been searched by the guard. Magnus rubbed a hand down his face and collapsed in Lady Mairead's desk chair, a pile of papers and effects in front of him, all the drawers open.

I pulled a chair up beside the desk.

"It looks as if Lady Mairead is gone, nae, tis nae exactly right. I know Lady Mairead is gone, and she has made it so I canna follow her."

"Why not, like your passport or the ticket or something?"

"Aye."

"So what are you going to do?"

"I will have tae wait." He put his forearms on the desk. "The trouble is, I daena have any idea what is happenin'. I canna help."

"Maybe she doesn't need help. Maybe she's right, maybe she can handle this, and you're better off here."

He sat quietly for a moment. "Lady Mairead's husband is a verra dangerous man. He would like tae know where tae find me. I am worried he may convince her tae tell him where I am and how tae get tae me."

"Why does he want you so badly?" I was twisting my shirt, worried.

"Because he wants revenge but also greed. And evil spite."

"Lady Mairead sounded like she wanted to protect you. Just because she went back doesn't mean she'll tell him where you are."

"You have seen her face. He can be verra persuasive."

I sighed. "You could buy a new ticket, get a new passport, you have the money..."

"I have much tae tell ye about, but — my head is verra pained, and I have pressing problems. I need tae hire a new security man. Jim is leaving."

"Really?" My heart sank.

"He has been here temporarily anyway."

"He doesn't like it here?"

"I think Lady Mairead poisoning him has changed his mind on it."

"I can't believe she did that."

He shrugged. "Tis her way. I need ye tae call Mistress Hayley and tell her tae hire Master Peters for my security."

"Master Peters, who, Quentin? Why?"

"I have been thinking on it for a while now. He is military trained and—"

"But *Quentin*? He's never been that smart and he—"

"He has been tae war. He knows a great deal about weapons and battle. You daena think he is a good pick?" He squinted his eyes.

"I don't know, he's just kind of a troublemaker."

"Aye, he has trouble with the law, but he also has a fighting spirit. I believed him tae be your friend?"

"Kind of, he's in the same friend group, but he's more James's friend." I huffed. "I'm not being very fair I guess. I'm still kind of pissed because he hid that James was sleeping with other girls from me because of the bro-code. He's a big believer in the bro-code."

"Ah, he is loyal. Tis also a good trait in a guard."

"Loyal to James though, I don't think it will be a good idea."

He leaned back in his chair and watched me for a moment. "Tis how ye see it? Because I am grateful tae him for the service he did ye the other night. If you remember it was Master Peters who helped ye discover Master Cook's true nature. He told me he was nae comfortable with Master Cook's behavior tae ye."

"He did?"

Magnus nodded. "Tis enough for me tae trust him. I would like him tae start today."

"Okay that makes sense."

We sat quietly for a moment. He was sprawled in the desk

chair. I was staring down at my folded hands. "That was our first discussion about running the household," I said. "I think it went pretty well."

"Aye."

"We've had a lot of firsts in the past twenty-four hours." I was trying to be calm, matter-of-fact, grown up, but my chin was beginning to tremble. "I just — It's been less than a day since I married you, and already I don't know if I can — what if something happens to you? It was so scary, I thought you died." I sobbed into my hands.

Magnus knelt in front of me and wrapped me in his arms. His head bowed beside mine. He dried my eyes with his fingers and tucked some of my hair behind my ears.

"I don't know how I went from getting married to you, barely knowing you, to this, so scared something might happen to you."

"We art bound, mo reul-iuil, tis a magic."

I nodded. "I didn't know Lady Mairead wasn't to be trusted. You never told me. I'm really sorry I signed a contract with her and sided with her against you. I didn't know."

"I dinna tell ye. Tis nae your fault. And Lady Mairead is wrong about many things but marrying ye was nae one of them."

He climbed back to his chair looking tired and worried. "I haena lied tae ye though, tis dangerous for ye tae be Kaitlyn Campbell. And tis likely I will nae survive—"

"Magnus, please don't."

The worried look had grown heavier, his face wore a pained expression. "I know ye are strong enough, ye must be ready for what comes."

I chewed my lip. Ready for what? How could I possibly be ready for something dangerous?

"Will ye be?"

"No."

He watched me quietly.

I felt like a petulant child, so I said, "I can try."

"Tis all I can ask."

The clock on the wall ticked, it was familiar from the day I was here signing the marriage contract with Lady Mairead.

"How are you feeling?"

"My head hurts, I am verra hungry, but I suspect Chef Zach will remedy that in a moment. First, I want tae show ye this."

He twisted in his chair and leaned low to a cabinet and opened the door revealing a safe. I kneeled beside him and he showed me the combination and how to open it. Inside were more jewels and some gold. There were rolled up papers on top, yellow, legal pad pages.

"Is that..."

"Tis your contract with Lady Mairead."

"Oh. And you have more gold, more jewels?"

"Aye, we have kept some for emergencies."

He closed the door of the safe and asked me to open it. Then he locked it and asked me to open it again and then again. "Will you remember the numbers?"

"I will."

"Good." He seemed relieved. "Let's go for breakfast."

At breakfast Magnus explained to Zach and Emma that Lady Mairead had put a sleeping potion in the wedding cake so she could steal away unnoticed.

Zach remembered hearing footsteps earlier in the night but they weren't Magnus's, so he assumed they were Jim's and didn't get up to check.

"I dinna believe she would do this. She has returned tae Scotland. I thought we were still discussing the plans, but she apparently believed we were done with the discussion."

Emma asked, "Will she be back?"

"I daena believe she plans tae return, and we should behave as if she will remain in Scotland. We should begin, after breakfast, which is delicious, Chef Zach, with running through our morning exercises and the house security drills."

He turned to me. "Kaitlyn, will ye call Mistress Hayley? Also we will nae longer need the services of Lady Mairead's nurse."

CHAPTER 41

orty-five minutes later we were all standing on the beach. I had called Hayley already. She had answered with, "Hello, married chick, how's it going, still flat on your back exchanging vows?" She giggled merrily.

I said, "We took a break for sustenance before the next round, and oh my god, it's — whoa."

Her giggle grew to a cackle. "Awesome, I can't wait to hear stories."

I told her we no longer needed the nurse, but I wanted her to call Quentin and offer him a job and ask him to start right now.

"Quentin?"

"Yep."

"The guy who rarely takes anything seriously and is always a piece of work?"

"Is going to be the head of my husband's security team. If he wants the job."

"He is out of work, has been for months. Okay, I'm calling him now. He's going to be psyched. Today?"

"Yep."

"I'll call you later after I figure this out."

Then I asked Emma what exactly this "security drills" thing would entail. She told me to wear yoga pants because it would be, "kinda excercisey and swordfighty." So I put on yoga pants and a crop-top tank.

Magnus had a small pile of bamboo training swords. He and the other security guard, who arrived for the morning shift, went first, sparring in a circle. It was thrilling and cool and a little dangerous to watch. Magnus was good, and he was well matched with the guard, who from the looks of it was the best of us all. I rooted for Magnus. Then Zach and Magnus fought. Finally, the guard returned to the house to keep watch, and Zach and Emma ran through some forms together. Magnus gave me a real, heavy blade. "Tis a dirk, Kaitlyn, I want ye to wear it under your—" He raised a brow and grinned. "You haena a place for it."

"I can keep it in my bag. Show me how to use it."

He taught me to grab it, pull back, and thrust forward. It was exciting to thrust toward him and have him deftly push my blade away. Then he'd ask me to do it again.

I was exhausted. I hadn't exercised in a while, and it was aerobic and repetitive. "Again, Kaitlyn!" I would grab my blade, swing, and thrust. He would deflect and tell me to try again.

Zach and Emma returned to the house, and it was our turn to swordfight. He showed me how to do a basic attack swing and a defending stance and then had me do it over and over and on...

Finally, out of breath and with wiggly arms, I collapsed on the sand in a sprawl.

He stood over me, casting a shadow across my stomach. "Twas verra good, Kaitlyn."

I grinned up at him, squinting in the sun. "Am I ready to defend myself?"

He chuckled sadly and shook his head. "Nae, you arna close."

"Really? Because my arms are really tired, I'm super sweaty, and I think I tried really hard."

"You tried, but if someone comes at ye consider runnin' instead of fightin'. You need more lessons." He offered a hand to help me up and slung the bag of gear over his shoulder.

I walked ahead of him, then turned, and walked backwards. "What or who exactly am I fighting?"

"Nae body, you arna fightin' anybody because I shall be right there tae protect ye.

"You know, here on Amelia Island there isn't a lot of need for swords and drills and grandiose statements like 'I'll protect you.' Back in LA even, I had a pepper-spray canister in my bag, but soon forgot where I put it, and it doesn't matter. People are mostly good, you know."

"Mostly. Some are nae so. Twill be good for ye tae know how tae fight so you can if needs be."

"You look like you can use a shower. Want to shower with me?"

"Och aye, verra much."

CHAPTER 42

*O*ur master bathroom was really large. There was a spa-style tub with jets, a double shower, and a closet that was almost as big as my kitchen back in LA. I turned the water to steaming hot and stripped off my clothes. "Coming in?"

He watched the steam pour into the air. "How did you do this?"

"You don't know how to work your shower?"

"When you shewed me tae use the room ye dinna explain this part. My showers have been freezin', or hot as a cauldron at full boil. I heard Zach and Emma talkin' about how perfectly warm the water is in the third bathroom, and I guessed I dinna ken tae work it right."

"You could have asked Chef Zach to show you?"

"Aye, but I am asking them tae live here on my lands, under my protection. I dinna want tae tell them I dinna ken tae do it."

I said, "You push this handle down. When you push it up, you aim it for here and let it run until it's warm. This direction is cold. This one hot."

While I taught, he pushed his kilt to the ground, pulled his shirt over his head, and stepped in after me with a large hand on my hip. He spun me around and we kissed, steam rising around us. "Or I could just ask ye tae turn it on for me every time." He grinned and pulled my hips close to his.

I squirted shampoo into my hand and gestured for him to lean forward. I rested my elbows on his shoulders and massaged the shampoo into his hair. "Who bought you the shampoo?"

"Emma. She purchased all these ointments for me." He closed his eyes and moaned. I ran my sudsy hands down and around his rear, feeling his form, rounded and taut and slippery and — I lathered up my own hair while his hands were busy up and down my back and sides and then I pulled the shower head from its holder and sprayed his hair and then my own. I arched back to get mine perfectly rinsed and he folded toward me, "I want ye, mo reul-iuil."

I teased, "I can tell. Here's the hard part though, showers have the potential to be awesome but are also notoriously diffi—"

There was a knock on the outer door of our bedroom. Magnus stopped still and listened. Emma's voice reached us. "Katie, your father is here with paperwork. He says you have a meeting with him?"

I opened my eyes wide. "I forgot Dad was coming from the bank." I slammed the shower off, grabbed two towels, tossed one to Magnus, called, "It will take me a moment, I'm still changing from the workout!" and pulled Magnus's hand to the bed.

I dropped back and pulled him on top of me; there was no way I was missing out on this moment. He caught on immediately and entered me with a breathless rush. I held on, steamy skin, his hair the scent of lavender mixed with that scent he carried around always, musky and sexy. My legs wrapped around his back, deep breaths in his ear. His mouth heavy on the edge of my neck.

He was fast. It was intense. His moan at the end made me

feel powerful, desired, loved. Could it be? He hadn't said it, not really, and love takes time, right? But this was really, really liked. And I really, really liked him too. Deep.

He pulled away and wrapped the towel around his waist. "Would you turn the shower on for me again?"

I was sprawled naked on the bed, an arm behind my head, a grin on my face. "Is that why you married me, to turn on the shower for you?"

"I married ye because I canna live without ye, mo reul-iuil. Tis nocht to do with the shower."

CHAPTER 43

My father brought stacks of paperwork and one of the local lawyers. It looked like we would be at this for a while. It was basic name-changing and adding me to the accounts, or so I thought, but in reality Magnus signed absolutely everything over. The lawyer asked about joint ownership, but Magnus asked if it meant we would both have to sign for withdrawals and deposits, and yes, there was a requirement that both partners signs for major changes. So he asked to have me made the primary account holder. Just me, alone. And so, form after form, Magnus signed off, and I signed on. Lady Mairead's name wasn't on any of the contracts which was good, but it seemed kind of final that he was giving it all to me as if he wouldn't be around to need it.

This was an astonishing amount of trust. He was giving me everything, no questions asked. My father and the lawyer still spoke to him as if he was in charge though, crossing the paper-work to him, deferring to him, barely noticing my questions.

It was past one o'clock when Dad and the lawyer left. That's how long it took for me to make a fortune. I was rich. Not just by marriage but on paper, official-like.

Zach was motioning us toward the kitchen where he spread lunch. Sandwiches, warm, melted, cheesy, yummy, exactly what we needed.

During lunch Zach said, "Tomorrow is Fourth of July, Magnus, would you like to have a barbecue?"

"I daena ken, would I?"

I explained, "It's the American celebration of our Independence. We blow up massive quantities of fireworks, have barbecues, and drink all day. Probably starting tonight. I actually expect the invitations to start any moment now." My phone rang — Hayley. I said, "Hold that thought," and answered.

"Hey babe, Quentin is on his way"

"Perfect, thanks."

"And tonight Michael, James, me, and the whole gang want to give you a little wedding reception at the Cafe in the courtyard. Starting at four. We'll buy all your drinks."

"Let me ask Magnus, just a minute." I held my hand over the phone. "Hayley and the gang want to throw us a party to celebrate our wedding at a restaurant. It won't be a late night."

"Would you like tae go?"

"I would."

"Aye then, I could go out for a few hours."

"Your head feels better?"

"Much. Chef Zach always makes me feel better. And other things." He grinned.

I returned to the phone. "Yes, we'll come but probably closer to five. It will take me a while to get ready." I remembered to ask, "Hayley, what are your plans tomorrow for the Fourth?"

"Nothing, maybe James's house?"

"What if we had a cookout here?"

"That would be great, will Zach grill?"

"You know it."

"Perfect."

I hung up and told Zach, "Yes, a cookout tomorrow, possibly ten to twenty people."

He asked, "Hotdogs, burgers, steaks, or chicken?"

I picked burgers and suddenly Zach and Emma and I were planning the menu for our party. I made the shopping list. They were going to do the shopping and literally everything else. I was very happy with this, being the decider not the handler of everything.

In my relationship with Braden I came up with the ideas for each video then made them happen, buying the supplies, writing the script, even handling the tech issues when they came up. From idea to implementation it was always me doing everything, and at the end of the day, though I was only twenty and Braden and I were partners, I got to figure out how to feed us both too.

Braden was pretty traditional in that he didn't give a shit how he got fed as long as someone fed him. Sadly my care-taking freed him up to spend his time dating someone else.

I scowled down at my sandwich.

Magnus noticed and asked quietly, "What is it?"

"I was thinking about something, not a good thing, not you — Thank you for trusting me with your accounts, your money, everything. I hope I can figure it out. I'll have to learn how to manage it all."

He held out his hand and squeezed mine. "I figure ye are more qualified tae run the estate than I am, since I dinna ken half what your father was speaking of."

"Do you understand only half of what I'm talking about too?"

"Nae, you are easy tae understand. Ye speak with your eyes."

"I do? Whatever does that mean?" Emma took my empty plate to the kitchen.

"Means... I am nae certain. I can tell what ye mean though many of your words I have never heard afore."

"So like, you get me. That's nice; I like being got. I think I get you too."

He looked down at his plate. His smile seemed sad. He fiddled with his fork overlong and seemed thoughtful about something. He said, "I will need tae spend some time with Master Peters when he arrives. Before I get ready for the party."

CHAPTER 44

I showered again and this time put some effort into the work that needed to be done. Hair removal, scented drops, lotions, a pedicure. I put on a silky pale blue party dress. I worried it was overly dressy for the restaurant we were going to but it fit the occasion — my wedding reception.

He had spent a couple of hours talking security with Quentin and rushed in to get dressed.

Emma had laundered his linen shirt. He wore a kilt of course. From the looks of his drawer he owned four now. Where did he get them, did they sell kilts in Jacksonville, or were they ordered online? He spread the long tartan fabric on the floor, kneeled beside it, drawing it into pleats, then laid down on it and wrapped it around his waist.

"Well, you aren't getting dressed in a hurry."

"Tis why we wear it all the time. I imagine twould be easier tae pull up a pair of pants."

"And what is that called?" I asked as he fastened on the bag thingy he often wore at his front.

"A sporran."

"What do you keep in there?"

"Wee bits and pieces of things." He opened the top and pulled out his bank card with a grin. Then he sifted through it and pulled up the shark tooth I gave him the day we went to the Fort. "You kept it? That's so sentimental."

He nodded. "Aye, Kaitlyn Sheffield gave me the tooth of a monster, I plan tae keep it tae guard me."

"I'm Kaitlyn Campbell now."

"Och aye, ye gave me a monster tooth. I had tae marry ye. I'm nae a fool."

I pulled my bare feet up under me and sat on the bed watching him get dressed. Strapping on his belts — one around his waist holding the sporran, another holding the sheath for his dirk. He slid the dirk into it with a fondness that was kind of thrilling to watch. He was so gentle and kind and good natured for all these armaments.

He picked up his coat, pulled it on, and buttoned it up the front.

"It will be hot for so many layers."

He nodded like he didn't hear me. "I might need it, I winna know."

Then he pulled out a wider belt with his sword's sheath and strapped it across his back. There was a steel circle at his chest, leather straps pointing in three directions, the sheath centered on his back. He picked up the sword that lay on the floor beside our bed, swept it over his shoulder, and shoved it into the sheath.

"What is that sword called?"

"Claymore." He ran his hands through his hair. He had grown quiet, his expression was pensive.

I pushed my feet into a pair of strappy, overly high heels encrusted with rhinestones.

"You can walk in such a verra high shoe?"

"Boy, can I." I strutted, catwalk style, across the carpet and back.

He chuckled. "Och aye, ye can."

"It's cool with you that James will be there tonight?" I checked my makeup in the mirror.

"James Cook is the easiest man in the world. He is much like my uncle and my cousins. I am used tae men like him."

I grabbed the keys to the Mustang off the dresser and we went down to the car.

When we entered the garage, Quentin was waiting for us. I said, "Oh, is he coming?"

"Aye, for protection."

"Fine, but—" I jangled the keys. I really liked driving the Mustang, and it was mine now, officially. Mine. I had been psyched to drive it. My own, really nice, fast, sexy car. It was a convertible. It wasn't sensible at all, unlike my Prius in almost every way.

Magnus smiled and said to Quentin, "Kaitlyn wants tae drive."

Quentin said, "Yes sir," and slid into the back seat as I climbed in behind the wheel.

"So, you're working for us now?" I looked at Quentin through the rearview mirror.

"Yes ma'am."

"What the hell, Quentin, I am not your ma'am. I'm your exact same age. I've been in school with you since first grade. You have to call me Katie, same as always."

"Okay."

Magnus twisted around. "And I would like tae be called Magnus."

"Yes, sir. I mean, yes, Magnus — sorry guys this is going to take some getting used to."

I rolled my eyes. "Yeah, totally." I pulled the Mustang out of the garage. I got to drive. I looked awesome. My new husband was hot. The party was all about us. Quentin called Magnus 'sir.' Plus, I had a designated driver for the ride home. The day had started out scary as hell but this night was getting our honeymoon back on track.

CHAPTER 45

*I*t was still daylight out, and would be for a while. It was hot but not terribly. Eighty-eight degrees instead of ninety eight. In Florida you learn to be grateful for a few degrees of cool. And shade. And the bounteous awesomeness of AC.

The restaurant was in the historic downtown just off Centre Street on a little side street that barely anyone went down. The restaurant was popular though, the food delicious, the ambiance good. The outdoor patio filled an entire lot and was surrounded by a low two-foot brick wall. Open air, it was strung around and through with little white lights. At night it had the feel of a grotto although I didn't really know what a grotto was. But even during the day the patio was nice, shady, cool, because huge oak trees grew right up out of the middle of it. Their roots busted up the pavement all around. The tables, about twenty, were all a bit tilted one way or another because of the marvelous trees.

It had long been my favorite restaurant in the area. We were directed right to the patio where James, Hayley, and Michael had reserved six tables for the entire crew. Everyone I knew and then some were there and cheered when we walked in.

As soon as we got to the table the bartender, Rob, bee lined for us, "Hand it over."

Magnus sighed. "Tis always the same in these places. What if I need it?"

"If you need it, you just ask for it. But seriously, it's Fernandina Beach; you don't need a sword. Promise."

Magnus handed the sword over but kept the sheath on his back, which was so hot, the straps stretched across his wide chest. The bartender continued to stand, hand out. "My dirk as well? Fine." Magnus unsheathed the dirk he wore at his hip.

"Jeez man, these are heavy." Rob carried them away and put them behind the bar.

James had his arm around a girl I didn't know. I was introduced to her and then quickly forgot her name because it was James, ex-boyfriend, *philandering*-ex-boyfriend. Plus I was a bride. Brides got to not care about anyone else; it was in the handbook. If he introduced me to her at a second event, I would remember her name then.

Michael poured us beers from the pitcher, and then everyone held up their cups, "To Katie and Magnus and their super fast, overly convenient, arranged-marriage!"

I said, "Hear hear!"

James called across the table, "So how're you liking marriage, Magnus? Is our Katie giving you her green card?" He chuckled like that was a great joke.

"Aye, I like it verra much. She's a bonnie lass."

I chugged the last half of the beer and swiped my arm across my mouth. "I think what Magnus is too polite to say is yes, I've given him the ol' green card and would give it to him again right now if there was a spot with some privacy." I leaned down to look under the table.

Magnus, James, Michael, the whole table burst into laughter.

Hayley said, "I don't want to interrupt your honeymoon, which sounds awesome so far, but Magnus, I need to borrow Katie tomorrow, so I can hear all the steamy details."

I said, "You're coming to our place tomorrow for July Fourth, anyway. We'll sneak away and I'll tell you all about it."

Magnus began a conversation with James and Michael about hiring Quentin and how he made Quentin sit just outside the restaurant in the car. They all thought that was hilarious. I was poured another beer, and Hayley and I turned our conversation to living in my new house. Amazing, of course, because I had a staff. I never knew anyone with a full-time staff.

Hayley said, "I have a staff at work. But I don't get to order them around all day long, and I don't get to demand things twenty-four-seven. Having them around at night must be pretty weird. I mean, Zach lives there now. Emma. It's like you're running a little hotel."

"It's way better than a hotel; they make ice cream for us at midnight if we want it, and I don't have to worry about the bill. It's not weird at all. It's awesome. The security guards work in shifts and go home to sleep."

"What happened to Lady Mairead?"

"OMG I forgot to tell you, she left last night..." I glanced at Magnus. We hadn't discussed whether the story was one I could share. And it crossed my mind that it would freak Hayley out. It was frankly unexplainable. It might also expose my new husband to undo scrutiny. I didn't even know everything about him, yet.

Hayley asked, "How'd she get to the airport, Uber or something?"

"Yep, weird, huh? Magnus said she probably won't come back, so yeah, I'm the woman of the house now."

"Well, I'll tell you what, girlfriend, that is the best news for you. You do not want your mother-in-law living with you. That would totally suck." She raised a glass. "Let's chug."

We both gulped down our beers and laughed merrily.

Magnus turned his attention back to me. "My head is beginning tae hurt from the noise."

I tore strips off napkins and wadded them up. He leaned forward so I could tuck them into his ears. "Have your ears always been so sensitive?"

"'Tis a recent issue."

James poured another couple of beers for us. The girl he was with leaned across the table to yell, "James tells me y'all got married for his green card? I would never be able to do that. Are you going to live together or just pretend to be married?"

Hayley said, "She's not pretending to be married, it was in a church." She rolled her eyes and gave me the 'see what I have to deal with' look.

"Well, James told me it was just business..."

I raised my brow at James. "Really, you have a lot of opinions for someone who doesn't know how to keep their pants zipped up."

He shrugged. "You should know. You were unzipping them just a few weeks ago."

He glanced at Magnus, "Sorry man, habit. Katie and I have a long history due to the fact that I was there first."

Michael's eyes went wide. "Shit James, the guy carries a sword. Keep your shit together."

All eyes were on Magnus.

He shrugged. "I am aware of your long past history with my wife. But there is something ye need tae know about me. I was born of men with titles. My father, I am told, is a king. My uncle is an Earl. My mother is a Duchess. My whole life I have been ruled by men who rule simply because they were there first. But see, they will die. Or they will make the missteps of fools. And when they do, then I will take their crown and it will be my turn tae rule as a king."

"What is that supposed to mean, are you saying you'll rule Katie?"

Magnus chuckled "I think Kaitlyn is most unruly. I mean it daena matter that ye were anywhere first, I am there, now, best."

Michael fell forward on the table laughing.

James smiled. "Well, you are right about one thing, Katie being unruly."

I grinned. "I can be ruled, if the person is firm enough. Magnus does very well in that respect."

Michael laughed so hard he fell out of his chair. "I wish Quentin was here he would be dying."

Magnus nodded and looked down at the empty plate in front of him. He said quietly. "I would wish tae add, Master Cook, ye have a long history with Kaitlyn Sheffield, and I know she values your friendship verra highly but in the future I expect ye tae show my wife, Kaitlyn Campbell, the respect she deserves."

James nodded. "Yeah, yeah sure, I get that."

Magnus nodded. "Thank ye."

Everyone was quiet, looking from James to Magnus, though they seemed to have come to an arrangement that they could deal with.

Hayley said, "Okay, now that we've been interrupted, what were we talking about?"

Magnus asked, "I wanted tae ask ye Mistress Hayley, do all women here speak with the same kind of mischievous tongue as Kaitlyn?"

Hayley said, "No way, Katie is a one of a kind. She has been saying crazy shit like that since forever."

"It gets me in so much trouble." I shook my head. "I try to keep it cool, but if I see the joke I go for it. Can't stop myself."

Magnus said, "Tis a wonderful wit, I marvel that such a boisterous voice comes from such a wee bonnie lass."

James said, "Here's to Magnus and Katie, a woman with a sharp tongue, a man with a sharp sword, and a marriage of convenience."

They all raised their glasses and drank robustly. But Magnus shook his head. "Aye, tis most true, but the marriage is nae for convenience... I have vowed more."

He turned in his chair to me and said slowly with meaning, "Kaitlyn, mo reul-iuil, is ann leatsa a bhios mo chridhe gu bràth."

My heart swelled.

Hayley whispered, "Do you know what he said?"

"No, but I can see what he means by his eyes."

Magnus grinned. "It means I like ye." He grabbed the pitcher of beer off the table, "Slainte!" And chugged more than half of it down. Then he passed it to me, and I finished off the last.

After that the conversation grew less testy and more fun.

Hayley, Michael, and James talked about past parties and adventures, and I joined in, and we laughed and told Magnus all about our wild youth, and he and James were even friendly.

His hand reached out to mine and rested on my knee.

When he got up for the bathroom, Hayley waited until he was gone and said, "Oh my god, I'm dying. I wondered if the church was just an act but he is so into you. This is like, *real*."

"It is, it — I can't explain how real it is. I feel so—"

"You're speechless. James, Michael, she's speechless."

"I really like him, I mean, that's weird because he's my husband, and I can barely get used to that but you guys like him too, right?"

"I do, he's hot, he's really nice, and he's rich as hell. And he seems to like you a lot, so I'm a huge fan."

Michael said, "Well, he didn't kill James after that 'I was there first' comment, so he's got to be some kind of superhero. Maybe he has an ass repelling tool. I would have punched a guy for saying that about my wife."

Hayley laughed. "You don't have a wife!"

I turned to James. "What about you?"

He nodded. "I think he's great. I just don't want you to get hurt."

"How's he going to hurt me?"

"You know, something about him isn't right — his back story. I talked to you about it at the kickball game."

"Because he doesn't know anything about soccer—"

"Football."

"Football, maybe he's just not—"

Michael said, "Katie, he didn't know anything about soccer. Even kids living in the mountains of Afghanistan know soccer. Kids in the Amazon know soccer."

James corrected him. "Football. And he wears a freaking sword." He leaned back and flicked a napkin away. "I like him, I do, and that's all I'll say. He can drink me under the table, plus he carries a sword. Also he's your husband, apparently."

Magnus was headed across the patio toward our table.

James said, "Plus, it's a wedding party. We're celebrating your future life together. Right Magnus? Friends forever?"

Magnus said, "Aye. I am happy tae know ye." He sank into his chair as the waiter brought trays of appetizers and placed one at every table. Magnus studied one of the trays. "What's this then?"

"Mozzarella sticks, careful, super hot inside."

He bit into one and puffed and grimaced because I was indeed right. Then he smiled, chewing. "This is delicious! Could Chef Zach make this dish?"

Michael overheard. "He could, but he won't. That's junk food. He likes his food pretentious and hip."

Magnus said, "I think he will be jealous I tasted something he didn't cook. You will come tomorrow, to our house for the four month of July party?"

James grinned. "The Fourth of July, man. Independence from Great Britain. When we fought against that King, what was his name?" He watched Magnus waiting.

Magnus looked blank for a second. "Was it Charles?"

James squinted his eyes. "King George."

Michael, totally oblivious to the point James was trying to make, said, "How did you remember that?"

"It's been crammed down my throat since I was five."

Magnus said, "I suppose in England we daena wish tae talk about losing the New World. I haena remembered it."

James said, "Yeah, that's probably it."

We ate heaping piles of mozzarella cheese sticks and a blooming onion. It was twilight, the little twinkling string lights glowed over our heads, and the scented citronella torches wafted around the patio. Cicadas hummed. It was still steaming hot though, even with night coming on. "You don't want to take off your coat?"

"Tis possible I may need it." He straightened the front where it clung to his body. He looked very handsome in it. Broad shoulders, angled jaw line.

"You got your dirk back."

"I did. On the way tae the necessary room, I went tae the bar and explained tae the bartender that wearing my dirk was a part of my whole suit. Without it I am just a man in a skirt, with it I am a true Scottish Highlander at his wedding party. He relented but would nae give me my Claymore. I daena ken."

I jokingly rolled my eyes. "Makes no sense, it's only five feet long."

An elderly couple interrupted us. "Excuse us, Dearie, we overheard that this is your wedding party?"

I said, "It is."

"My husband and I have been watching from across the patio, and you're looking at each other just the way I remember looking at my dear Arnold, fifty-five years ago. Right, Arnie?"

Her husband said, "Aye."

I said, "Oh, are you Scottish?"

Arnold said, "American now but Scottish in my blood. You're Campbell clan?"

Magnus said, "Aye."

"I'm Clan Munro. Wore my kilt on my wedding day too. And if you keep looking at her like this, you'll have a long and happy life, my friend."

His wife said, "Ah yes, it warms my heart to see two young people in this much love. May your hearts stay full, your bed happy, and your voices kind."

"Thank you," I said, a bit weepy about it all.

She and her husband congratulated us once more and left the restaurant.

Magnus said, "Kaitlyn, I think tis time for us tae go as well."

Hayley said, "Stay! One more thing — you guys need to dance. I'll take pictures!"

"Dance?"

I said, "Yes please can't we stay, please?" I batted my eyes. "After a wedding the bride and groom have a sworn duty to sway in circles together in front of their friends and family. Just once, maybe twice. We'll leave after? Maybe after another drink?"

Hayley said, "I'll go request your favorite song." She ran away without even asking what it was.

Magnus's hand rested gently on my thigh. I loved a big strong hand so stilled and gentle, I wrapped his in both of mine and held it tightly.

It washed over me again that he was all mine — this felt so much like a first date that I had to keep reminding myself.

"I am nae certain I know how tae dance."

"Honestly, all you have to do is put a hand on my hip and smile like you're enjoying it. I'll do everything else."

Hayley came buzzing back with the newest super sexy Rihanna song playing through the patio's sound system. "See? Anything by Rihanna, your favorite. For years."

"It is, isn't it?" I held out my hand to Magnus and led him a few steps away to an open space where the weekend musicians usually sat and played.

I faced Magnus and stepped closer. I drew his hand around my waist, centered it on my lower back, and began to rock to the music. Our other hands entwined and he held them to his chest. His lips on my forehead, my hips swaying. His hand lowered on my back, holding, a little pressing. I said, "See? Easy, just count the beat..."

He said, "Tis nae easy. Tis hard tae count now I know how wee the undergarments are under your dress." For that I pressed closer and swayed a bit more.

"Tis hard for me too, now I know what's under your dress."

He threw his head back and laughed. "Ah, Kaitlyn, you art a won—" His eyes went to the sky and he stopped. "What is — a storm?" He looked wildly left and right.

I said, "And horses."

"What?"

He pulled the paper wads from his ears as the front legs of a giant horse with a man in a dark cloak yelling "Ha!" bounded over the low wall crashing down against a table. The table flew to the side. Chairs tumbled and crashed. The horse's back legs hit the patio with a rush. People screamed and ran for cover. The horse tromped and spun — huge, menacing, trashing the patio all around underfoot.

The horse's legs tipped tables and smashed chairs.

In the sky above a bank of clouds rolled, roiled, and rumbled higher. They were the color of dark gray, almost soot black, and were climbing. Lightning arced. A flash struck the road right in front of the restaurant. People scrambled away, diving over the wall, as a second horse with a cloaked rider crashed over and trampled and spun in circles. The wind was blustering around. The two men were yelling. The horses destroying everything in their path—

Magnus grabbed my arm, hard — twisting it. He shoved me toward a low wall. A flung chair crashed into us, knocking me to the ground, right behind an overturned table — Magnus landed on me with a crush. Pain shot through the side of my thigh as it landed on a metal table leg with Magnus's full weight on top of me. I screamed, loud. Magnus gripped both of my hands, painfully, "Kaitlyn, Kaitlyn! Shhhhhh, daena be afeared, shhhh-hhh, I will come back. I will do whatever it takes tae get back tae ye." His face was an inch from mine, his whole weight on me, pressing. His hands gripped around mine. His voice beseeching. "Nae matter what, I am trying tae come home tae ye, I—"

I screamed again as another chair crashed onto his back. "Shhhh, daena be afeared." I clamped my eyes shut.

"Kaitlyn, look at me, I need ye tae run and get my sword. Stay low, slide it tae me. Okay?"

I nodded.

He climbed up from my body and looked out from behind the table top. Then he jumped and ran at the men on horseback, unsheathing his dirk as he raced. In three steps Magnus leapt with his blade raised.

I scrambled up, checked my path, shoved a chair out of my way, and ran, in my heels, across so much overturned furniture, broken dishes, spilled glasses, picking my way, ankles twisting, repeating to myself, "Go, go, go, get the sword, go."

Behind me Magnus roared as he fought.

I swung myself under the bar. "I need the sword!"

Rob, the bartender, glanced up from where he crouched, eyes

wide, and gestured with his head toward the sword on a shelf a few feet away. I scrambled to it, grasped it with two hands, and dragged it to the ground. It was so fucking heavy. Why was it so heavy? Using momentum, I swung it beside me and half-dragged it around the bar.

Magnus was close, facing away. One, two, three, I hurled it toward his feet. The sword slid, then stopped short by about three feet — I burst into tears.

Magnus lunged at one of the men, then deftly jumped to the side, three steps, bent for the sword, swung it in an arc behind him, and roared forward, swinging wildly.

The first man dropped from the horse, swinging in return. Their swords clanked, metal on metal, sharp scraping sounds, clank, crash, crank, crashing, wind howling, people screaming. The wind whipped the tree limbs, flying paper in gusts. My hair was wild in my face.

People cowered all around the edges of the outer wall.

I slid to the ground and shoved myself backwards to the bar, cowering around my knees while I tried to breathe.

Thunder crashed. The air sizzled as lighting struck a chair leg. It electrified, popped up like corn, and banged to the ground. The whole place smelled like fire.

I peeked around the bar as Magnus roared forward, swinging his sword wildly.

Quentin jumped over the lower wall, crouched low, and ran to my side. "You okay?"

"Do something, please, please, do something!"

He peeked out from behind the bar. "Can you follow me to the wall?"

I clutched at his shirt sleeve. "I need you to help him, Quentin, help him!"

"My orders are to keep you safe."

He yanked me up by my forearm and pushed me toward the

opposite side of the patio. In a low run I raced toward Hayley, Michael, and James. I tripped at the end, stumbling, and someone's hands grabbed me under my arms and yanked me over the wall, scraping my thighs.

Quentin scrambled over the wall just behind me but my view was this: Magnus doubled over. The man he was fighting brought his sword down in an arc, hitting him with a blunt blow. Magnus stumbled under the force of it, his knees and hands hitting the stone patio. Magnus had almost been killed. Ohmygod, ohmygod, Magnus was going to be killed.

James to Michael on one side of me, "You concealing?"

"Nah man, it's a wedding party. It's at home."

James said, "Shit, mine's in my glove compartment."

Quentin on the other side of me pulled his pistol. "I just need a clean shot."

Hayley was hunkered down right behind me, her phone to her ear. "Yes, I have an emergency. Yes, there's a sword fight with horses at the Cafe on Third Street."

The wind whipped my hair in every direction. I said to Hayley, "Don't get him in trouble, it's not his fault."

The man swung his sword around to attack again, but Magnus recovered his footing and arced his sword up. The force of it set the man stumbling off balance. Magnus swung around with his dirk driving the man to the ground.

Magnus dropped onto him, holding him down by the throat, and thrust his hand in the man's sporran. He sifted through the contents, tossing them away, diving his hand into the sporran again. He yelled into the man's face, "Where is it!"

Magnus stood, looked wildly left and right and focused on the second man on horseback now on the road in front of the restaurant. Magnus ran in two big leaping steps to the wall, bounded over it, and charged the second man with a bellowing war cry.

I yelled, "Magnus!"

The second man swung his sword down. Magnus ducked just in time, narrowly missing a blow to the head.

James said, "We've got to help him, man."

The wind was whipping around the street, leaves, paper, debris spinning. He and Michael ran across the patio toward the front of the restaurant. Quentin stood. "Katie, don't move, stay right here," and ran after them.

Magnus and the man on horseback were in a full spectacular sword fight. Magnus swinging up, the man carving down, the horse turning and stamping, and making that crazed screaming sound. The first man stood, climbed back on his rearing horse, and jumped it over the wall to the road to join the fight.

Magnus was lunging and backing and ducking — dust and sand spun in gusts around his body. He stumbled back three steps and the man on horseback deftly turned and charged him. Magnus dodged out of the way, twisted, but the man slashed his sword down on Magnus's left shoulder. Magnus yelled in pain and stumbled, clutching his shoulder, dragging the sword behind him. A bloom of blood red appeared on his sleeve. Two men were circling him now, two horses rearing, two swords arcing toward him.

Magnus charged the second man on horseback, bellowing, using momentum to drag his sword up in an arc — a forceful blow aimed at the man's side. The man jerked sideways, dropped his sword, but was able to hold the reins.

Magnus swung his sword up and slid it into the sheath on his back. The man turned his horse around and charged again.

Quentin yelled to Magnus, "I've got a shot! Want me to shoot?"

Magnus whipped around. "Take it, now!" And Quentin fired, hitting the stranger in the shoulder. The man jerked backward then slumped forward as Magnus grabbed the reins and yanked the horse's head sharply to the side, drawing it to a shriek-ing, trampling halt. Then Magnus swung up behind the rider. In one second he had his dirk at the man's throat, his other hand diving into the man's sporran as their horse raced away with the first man on horseback thundering just behind them.

An arc of lightning flared around them as they disappeared down the street. The storm rose and roiled and thundered. Light-ning flashed and for a terrible moment the storm grew even more frightening, cutting our visibility to zero with gale force winds. Then suddenly it rolled and rumbled and rushed away.

I scrambled to my feet and yelled at James, Michael, and Quentin, "Get him, oh my god, get him!"

"We'll find him Katie," James called. He and Michael dropped off the wall to the road and raced down the street.

Quentin returned to my side.

"Shouldn't you go look for him too?"

His jaw was set, firm, security-guard-business-like, but his eyes looked as confused as mine. "Magnus told me not to leave your side."

CHAPTER 46

The air still smelled burnt. The sky had the glowing pallor of an extreme weather incident, green, like some shit just went down. Sirens were wailing from a near distance. Dust was settling. Rubble was adjusting and falling.

The bartender stood and called out. "Anyone hurt?"

Restaurant diners climbed up from their hiding places, carefully picking places to step. The place was trashed, food, plates, glassware, blood, grime. One of the horses had left a pile of horseshit right in the middle of it all.

The wails of the sirens were close, just around the corner. Then three police cars screeched to a stop along the front of the restaurant. Police rushed the patio.

The bartender, the chef, and the manager met them at the front gate and tried to explain.

The world had gone slow-mo around me.

Hayley was clutching my arm. My hands were shaking. I knew this much. I had hands, they weren't behaving right. All my blood had rushed to my head, and my ears had stopped working — buzzing like an hour after a Foo Fighters's concert. My eyes were searching around, independent of my brain, my body, my other senses. I was disjointed. Discombobulated. Undone.

I heard the bartender say, "One of our patrons. Yes, he's a local. It was his wedding party. Two guys assaulted him and they went off that way. That's his wife over there."

He pointed in my direction.

My head was spinning.

I stared in the direction that James and Michael had gone.

Hayley's voice emerged from my fog. "Where do you think they went?"

An ambulance and a fire truck pulled up outside. The police voices on the radio said, "We have a sword fight, apparently on horseback."

Across the patio over the wall in the middle of the road another police officer was walking around a small puddle of Magnus's blood. Magnus was hurt. He needed an ambulance. Where was he?

James and Michael returned, doubled over and out of breath. They spoke to the police out in the road, pointing in the direction they had already checked.

I convinced my feet to walk toward them. James shook his head. "We didn't see him Katie but the police are sending out a car."

A police car sped away as he said it.

"But he went that way. They were right there. You didn't look hard enough. Oh god." I clutched my face, holding onto my jaw trying to get it to stop chattering.

James said, "We looked. We went as fast as we could. There was no sign of them. Who were those guys?"

I shook my head.

Michael said, "What if they went toward the docks? Let's get your truck, James, and go look. Officer Brand, do you need us any more?"

"No one can leave until we've secured the area."

What followed took hours.

There were gold coins on the ground that were unexplainable, so there was a mystery, a trashed restaurant, a missing husband.

I wanted to see the coins, the sword that the first man left behind; there was a familiarity to them that I needed to investigate. But they were impounded before I could calm down enough to ask.

Quentin stood beside me the entire time. He answered questions, a lot of questions, because he had discharged his weapon in downtown Fernandina Beach. Reports had to be filed.

I needed to pee but he asked me to please hold tight until he was through. He didn't want me out of his sight for some reason. I asked him, "Do you think Magnus could be home already, waiting for me?"

"I don't know, I hope so."

The questions the police asked of me were the most difficult. How long had I known him? Did he tell me he had enemies?

Yes, he paid for security around the clock, plus he was armed. Yes, he had enemies. I don't know why — maybe because he was royal? Yes.

When asked to elaborate I couldn't because none of my answers jibed with what I knew about European politics.

So I repeated it again as if repetition would make it real. He was a royal. That was true. His enemies were because he was a royal. James corroborated. So did Quentin. If enough of us agreed it might be true.

The police set up a command center. A helicopter was called in. Cars were searching and reporting back. Police were bustling around. And then later, much later, I was asked if I would be available for questioning the following day.

"But you'll find him, right? Before tomorrow? He couldn't

have gone far — he was injured. The other man on the horse had a gunshot wound. They were all on horseback. Where would they be? He..."

I trailed off because the faces of the men and women around me looked so blank, completely noncommittal, kind of hopeless.

Finally, we were free to go. I said goodbye to everyone. James hugged me in a bear hug. "Michael and I are going to keep looking Katie. I don't know what happened to him but we'll find him."

"Call me, as soon as you know anything?"

"Of course."

I hugged Michael and then Hayley for a really long time. "That was so scary! Katie, where did he go?"

"I don't know. That was..." It had been terrifying, abrupt, and physically hard. My adrenalin had pumped through my body then left so drastically that I felt like throwing up. And it was way dark out.

I checked my phone, dead. *Great, what if Magnus was trying to —* he wouldn't though. He didn't have a phone. "Do you know what time it is?"

Hayley said, "Eleven-twenty."

"I'm so tired."

"I know sweetie, you go home, try to rest. James and Michael will find him. When you wake up in the morning, he'll be there."

Quentin led me to the Mustang. He talked nervously. "I was out here, feet up on the dash. He told me what to look out for but I didn't really think he meant it, you know? Jeez, I can't believe I shot someone, and then there's nothing. Jeez. He's just gone. Gone."

He helped me into the back seat and raised the roof.

Then he drove in silence until I asked, "What were your orders exactly?"

"He told me to listen for a storm and if there was one to come to the restaurant. He told me to guard you. No matter what. And that I shouldn't intervene unless I was at a distance with a good clean shot."

"I don't understand why protecting *him* wasn't your job. What did he think would happen to me? They were clearly after him."

He sat quietly for a few minutes but kept glancing in the rearview mirror at me, like he was uncomfortable.

I asked, "What? Tell me."

"I got the impression I wasn't really protecting you but guarding you to keep you out of it."

"I'm not that hotheaded. I'm not going to jump into a fight with swords."

"I don't know, I think he knew he was leaving and didn't want you to follow him."

I humphed angrily. "How the hell would he be leaving? From the middle of Centre Street, an island, on a horse? He doesn't have goddamn wings. Or even a phone to call an Uber. Did you call him an Uber?"

"No Katie."

"Yeah, so that's just speculation. I don't want to hear any more about him leaving me. That's just not fair and don't you dare tell the police that; they'll stop looking for him. I can already hear it in their voices. They think he left me — he married me and left me. Well that's not what happened."

I glowered out the window, then added, "His last words to me were, 'I'm coming back.'"

He said, "Yeah Katie, I won't mention it again." He turned up our street. "But think about it, he said, 'I'm coming back,' like he knew he was leaving. That's all I meant. He kept saying things that sounded like he was."

I glanced at his eyes, irritated, partly because it was true. Magnus had been saying goodbye since we met. The whole reason we got married was because he wanted to leave and Lady Mairead wanted him to stay. Well, guess what, it didn't work. I didn't work. I wasn't enough.

We pulled into my driveway.

When I opened the front door of the house, everyone rushed me with questions. Apparently Quentin had called the other security guy, and he told Zach and Emma. but now it was up to me to give the blow-by-blow.

Two hours ago, on pure adrenalin and agitation, I would have been up to the chore and then some. I probably would have embellished and dramatized it. Now, exhausted, scared, and broken, I wasn't up to the task. Quentin told them all about it from the moment he arrived, so they didn't hear about how I stuffed wads of napkin in Magnus's ears so he didn't hear them coming. How I begged him to stay longer at the restaurant though he wanted to leave and come home.

How a freaking horse leapt over a wall in downtown Fernandina Beach and just about killed us. How I almost got Magnus killed.

Or maybe I did.

Because he wasn't here.

What the hell happened — my husband got into a sword fight and disappeared on the back of a horse?

While Quentin told them the story, I listened. And it sounded crazy. Like a movie that involved superheroes and villains-with-robotic-appendages crazy. Fernandina Beach was a super small town; how could this be the kind of thing that happened here?

I asked Zach. "Do you think he left me?"

Zach lightly tapped his fingers on the table. "He kept mentioning that he needed to leave but it was an 'if.' I don't think it was about you at all, but I don't know. I know it was a strong if." He dropped his head to his hands. "He told me I would stay on to cook for Lady Mairead. Now neither of them are here. I — Katie, do I still have a job? Emma and I really liked it here and—"

I said vaguely, "We'll talk about that tomorrow..." and stared down at my hands thinking about all the decisions I would need to make. It had only been that morning when I signed all those contracts. I was in charge of Magnus's fortune, and he was missing, and...

Zach's face looked worried.

I said, "You know that's unfair; I'm sorry. Magnus thinks the world of you, of all of you. Of course you still have jobs." I took a deep breath. "None of this matters though because he'll be here any minute now. Worst-case scenario, tomorrow."

Quentin asked, "Katie, could I go out looking?"

I said with as much snark as I could muster, "I don't know, you think Magnus is okay with you leaving my side?"

He chewed his lip, then said, "Katie, I've only had this job for a few hours. I did the best I could. I followed his orders because it was my job to."

I glared at him for a moment, but I couldn't stay mad because it was a hundred percent true. "Yeah. You're right, I just, I'm pretty overwhelmed and... I'd appreciate it if you'd go looking, thank you."

Quentin stood from the table and headed for the front door.

Zach jumped up to get me a cup of chamomile tea and some aspirin.

Emma said, "The police, James and Michael, Quentin, they're all looking for him. He's on horseback, they'll find him."

"Yeah, that's the only thing that makes sense."

I took a sip of tea and realized I needed to get into bed or I would pass out right there on the table.

CHAPTER 47

I woke up hours later. My brand new wedding bed, empty. The room was too cold, bare, lonely. There was a hum, practically an echo. I breathed in a scent of him, deep and big and mysterious and sexy and—

A whole night had passed. I had gone to a party to celebrate my marriage and came home alone. It felt like a dream but I was ready to wake up now. *Please.* Tears slid down my cheeks, I curled in on myself and sobbed until I couldn't cry anymore.

Then I knew this — I had to get up. I had to run things. I had to meet with the police and my dad and come up with a new list of household work for my employees because I was in charge now. Magnus had picked me for this. To take care of things when he was gone.

And I didn't understand it, but — I remembered the weight of him on me, the sharp pain on my thigh, and his words: "I will do whatever it takes to get back to you." He was gone. I had no idea where but that part of me that had been filling up with him had gone startlingly empty and lost and terribly sad, but I was the woman of the house now. I had to lead.

CHAPTER 48

*W*hen I emerged from my room, glancing around, hopeful that something happened, maybe a surprise. I felt it in my bones that there was nothing new. It was clear from the faces, sympathy frowns on everyone there.

Zach cooked me oatmeal pancakes with nuts and yogurt, drizzled with syrup, plus coffee. It was delicious and necessary. Quentin was back from searching and hadn't found Magnus or any sign of him. The police were still looking and planning to interview me today. Also, I needed to call my mom and dad and tell them.

I should call Grandma though she wouldn't be any help. I felt spacey, disconnected, untethered.

My phone was lit up with notifications: Hayley, James, Michael. Texting they didn't know anything yet.

And so that's how I spent the day — I dealt. Friends, police, staff, my parents, my new house, life, fortune, piled up on top of the basics — I ate when Zach put a plate in front of me. I drank when a cup appeared. I showered when I caught a whiff of my underarms and thought I might spare everyone the agony. Plus, he might come home, right? I should be ready.

I did these things the first day.

Hayley, Michael, and James came for dinner and held my hand while I explained how I was feeling. Kind of lost. Really scared. Very heartbroken.

James tried an intervention. "I think you need to consider the very real possibility that the boy left you. I'm sorry Katie, you deserve so much better, but he—"

"No. He didn't leave me. Not on purpose, he—"

James's face grew irritated, his brow drew down. "Katie, you have to face reality."

"No, I don't. I got married two days ago and my husband meant it. He gave me everything he owned, and he wanted to spend the rest of his life with me, I know it. I just know it." I sobbed into my hands before Hayley bustled me off to my room where I cried myself to sleep.

Second day? Scarier. Because the conversations stopped. Because the first day he could come home. Now he was gone.

By the end of the week he was way gone.

The following week it was hopeless.

People began speaking about him in past tense.

People gave me the sad looks they saved for widows. And probably I was one.

Trouble was, everyone considered me a widow but also assumed I should start moving on. Because I hadn't known him for that long, not really. The marriage was actually arranged. There hadn't been enough time to get truly invested.

Hayley, week three, walked with me out to the beach and sat beside me on the sand, and said something like this: I should think about getting back out, seeing people, and I told her to shut up. I told her I had really fallen for him. And that he was coming home. He wasn't dead.

That's what I said.

I barely believed it though because this felt a lot like he died.

I got a pile of books on money markets, investments, and tax law thinking I needed to study up. I got another stack of books on art history because there were paintings in Lady Mairead's office, or rather, my office that seemed important. Old and historical. I needed to get them appraised but couldn't attest to where they came from or how they got to be here. I needed to ask Magnus about them. Find out their story because all my guesses sounded crazy. And they seemed very valuable.

But beyond studying, I was pretty damn bored without needing to do any of the normal life upkeep.

Emma ran errands and did anything else I wanted. She also cleaned and laundered the clothes. Zach cooked. I sat around feeling sorry for myself, occasionally reading books about how to be a money mogul or Renaissance painters.

I also spent a lot of time out on the beach. I took up jogging again. Quentin followed behind for safety though neither of us knew why. It was simply Magnus's orders and until he returned and told Quentin to stop we just kept following them to the letter. I searched for shark teeth during low tide and filled a little jar with the tiny black triangles and a few random big ones that I was very proud of. And I sat. At the top of the dune looking out on the ocean, at the horizon, and occasionally up at the sky watching the clouds, studying the wind patterns, waiting for another storm. Because in the weeks I had been waiting for Magnus to come home, I had learned something.

The men from the wedding party had been carrying coins. Those coins shared a lot in common with the coins my husband owned. The coins his wealth was built on. Magnus Campbell had the best collection in the world of coins and jewels that shared those qualities.

The police interviewed me about the coins, how odd they were. I told them they had been stolen from my husband. So that was the motive: theft of antique coins.

They were searching for the attackers, thieves, for him.

But I had stopped looking because I wasn't sure how to continue. I had a hypothesis. It wasn't one that made sense, or that I could explain without sounding crazy or delusional. So I kept it to myself.

It went something like this, the coins were age-dated 1600-something. As were Magnus's.

So this is what I believed: Magnus was somehow from there, from that time. That he had traveled forward to this time somehow. And he was back there, now. It was the only thing that made sense though it made no sense at all.

Because it was impossible.

And so I hid my hypothesis. While looking for proof beyond. Magnus didn't know the rules of football. Or Magnus had never used a flushing toilet. Which might be proof enough if it weren't proving something that was categorically undeniably completely impossible.

That's why I didn't tell anyone about my suspicions. I let them go on believing he was missing. He was. I let them go on wondering if he had left for Scotland. Probably. I let them think he might be dead now. Because it was true.

I just had to wait for him. Remembering his assurances — "I will come back, I will do whatever it takes to get back to you," and hoping what he had somehow made possible, he could do again.

I hoped. Because without hope, without the ability to do what is impossible, he was the past. And it broke my heart to think about what that meant. That in the history of the world there was a Magnus Campbell and now there was a Kaitlyn

Campbell and once they loved each other but now he was nothing more than a grave. Where would that be, a dusty church-yard in Scotland? It made me cry whenever I thought of it. Was he dust? God, my heart was breaking. He was dust to me.

What had he said, the night we discussed our plans to marry? It chilled me to the bones — "I'm nothing but a dead man, there's no changing that."

CHAPTER 49

I wandered out to the end of the beach walkway and sat on the dune, looking out over the wide white sand past the deep Atlantic Ocean to the far horizon. I took this view while I was thinking about him, but I couldn't sit here like this for long. I went to the sand and searched for shark teeth because it was simpler. Searching cleared my mind, Zen-like. I had been waiting for him for eight weeks. Sixty-one days. Just over two months. Over one thousand, three hundred, fifty hours.

Was I a widow?

There would be a time, soon, when I would need to decide. Because searches for lost husbands couldn't go on forever. And if I needed to search the past — I didn't know how...

I stared out over the ocean trying to wrap my head around the impossible. Magnus had traveled through time and space to get here. And now he had gone somewhere else.

I wanted him to do it again.

I was asking the impossible to happen twice.

Technically impossible but I had watched a Ted Talk on the possibility. What if there were threads of time, woven and wrapped, tied and unraveled, and what if my Magnus had climbed away like an aerial artist, suspended over his own time into my time? Could I lower into his? No, because it was ridiculous, impossible, and frankly made me sound insane just thinking about it.

I ran on the beach. It was about three quarters of a mile to the pier and then I ran back. I stopped twice, walking and searching for shark teeth. Usually Quentin trailed me but some days I was chatty, or he was, and we would run beside each other talking and laughing. Like today, talking about the new Will Ferrell movie and speculating about the next Avengers movie.

When we returned to the house, Quentin jogged up the walkway while I stayed on the beach, looking for shells. Then I sat on the dune, staring out over the horizon. It was about ten in the morning but so hot I had a sheen of sweat on my skin already.

The beach was growing crowded, Labor Day weekend, last hoorah of the summer and all. I had been invited to James's house for a cookout. All the gang would be there and they were a good crowd. They took good care of me. Kept me laughing. Tried to get me out of the house. But they also didn't mention Magnus. Because it was weird, uncomfortable and what should they say — sorry your man disappeared that night?

They were there, they saw it, and it was weird as hell.

They kept looking for him that night because it wasn't possible he disappeared into thin air. But that meant something much more tragic happened and... No one knew what to say about it.

It would be easier on everyone if I would simply decide to call myself a widow.

Hadn't that been what Magnus wanted? He had made sure every bit of money, paperwork, and all the contracts and leases were in my name. The final actions of someone who was dying.

"Aye, Kaitlyn. I am a dead man."

A little girl on the beach was running toward her mother's towels. Her father had brought a shovel to the beach, a big, full-size shovel, and dug a little swimming pool in the wet sand near the lapping waves. The little girl, maybe two years old, had been sitting in it, splashing, and now wanted her mommy to join her. Would it be possible to dig to the past, like some Journey to the Center of the Earth movie plot or something? *Maybe Dwayne Johnson would know, did he have a Twitter account?*

— a deep dark cloud about a mile up the beach billowed up. I stood. A rumbling fury of a storm cloud, climbing the strata from beach to sky. It was a big storm, from nowhere, and there was a surging, flashing, sizzling, an electrical storm at its front edge. I yelled up the walkway, "Quentin! Quentin! A storm, Quentin, a storm! I'm going!"

I took off at a sprint to the north, weaving through all the beachgoers as they raced away from the storm to their cars and trucks.

A few minutes later Quentin called my name from behind. I turned to look without breaking stride, and he waved at me to keep going.

We had never discussed this. Our protocol was if Weird Shit Happens lock down the house. We didn't know why but did it anyway and then felt sheepish about it after. Like that was stupid to lock down the house and go quiet because of a thunderstorm.

But I knew in my heart of hearts that the storms around Magnus's comings and goings weren't normal storms. They had an unexplainable quality. They materialized from nothing and grew to giant heights. They billowed clouds that behaved like smoke and were the color of coal fire. There was a blustering, gusting wind. And finally, an arcing electrical storm underneath. This one was acting just like that.

I was out of breath by the time I was at all close, stumbling, holding my side. Full blown stitch there now, but ahead of me under the electrical storm was a pale lump of what looked like a lifeless body. I forced myself to keep running.

The storm gathered itself up and retreated as quickly as it had arrived. And as I gained on the body I got scared because it was lifeless and other people were gathering around but not getting too close. The body was pale and naked and a man, and as I crunched through the shells and arrived finally, full of gasping breaths and heaves — it was Magnus, oh god, naked, on his side, fallen, and very very very not looking alive.

I collapsed to my knees beside him. "Magnus?" His forehead had a gash across it. Both eyes were black and his lip fat and split. "Magnus?" There was blood, a big angry wound on his shoulder, and his earlobe was torn. I wiggled his arm, "Magnus?"

He grimaced, coughed, and bloody phlegm dripped from the corner of his mouth. A stranger on the other side of him said, "Look at his back." I rose up on my knees to look over. It was gouged with deep hacking wounds, up and down and across and over and over and blood and—

Quentin ran up. He whipped his shirt off over his head and draped it over Magnus's midsection, his phone already to his ear. He looked around at the growing crowd. "Did you see anyone, anybody, who left him here? Anything?"

The people shook their heads, all blank stares and whispering.

I dropped my face to the sand eye to eye with Magnus. "Hold on, we're calling an ambulance. Hold on Magnus, please."

His head nodded, grinding in the tiny shells. I grasped his hand and from it rolled a metal cylinder. About the size of a small energy drink can. It was warm. I shoved it into the waistband of my yoga pants and pulled my shirt over the bulge. He nodded again, barely noticeable.

Then he made a croaking sound from deep in his throat, and he stopped. "Magnus?"

I felt for his pulse, nothing, but I was no expert. Behind me Quentin's voice grew excited on the phone, "We need someone right now!"

I shoved Magnus to his back, in the sand and crushed shells, and started my best imitation of a chest-pushing CPR. I couldn't really remember how to do it. It had been four years but I started because I had to. "Does anyone know CPR?"

No one stepped forward, so I went on, terrified that it was me, my shoddy memory of a lifesaving technique that stood between Magnus and no pulse.

Sirens from way far off were screaming, coming closer, and I kept pumping, counting, begging. "Please, Magnus, please." Until from down the beach a lifeguard truck was flying toward us, and over the boardwalk two paramedics were racing over the dunes, and finally they all converged on Magnus. I dropped away as they set about trying to save his life.

"Will he live?"

They answered me with a brusque, "Step back, Ma'am."

"Yes, of course, but his back, he's injured on his back."

They glanced under his shoulder, put a mask over his face, lifted him to a stretcher, and hustled him away.

CHAPTER 50

J rode with the ambulance to the hospital. He had been brutally beaten and whipped. His heart had freaking stopped but everything was started again. He was alive. He just wasn't awake.

Everything relied on him waking, safely.

No one could believe the brutality. And of course, they began an urgent search for his captors but he hadn't spoken yet. They had no clues, nothing to do except comb the beach where he was found. And wait for him to be well enough to explain what happened.

I was pretty sure there wasn't anything they could find.

After he was wheeled away for hours, Magnus was wheeled back, still unconscious, and deposited onto his stomach on a bed in a private room. I was told that he wouldn't wake for at least three hours. A large bandage covered his entire back. His face was haggard. His body devastated. Most of his skin had a purple tinge just under the surface or in places an angry deep red. His gashes had been bandaged. His deep cuts, including the earlobe, had been stitched so that most of his skin was covered. A tube of

IV fluids stuck into the back of his hand. The beep beep of a heart monitor filled the room.

He slept for hours, while I watched.

Emma called. "I heard, is he okay?"

"Yeah, he will be eventually."

"Zach and I are coming, can we bring you food, anything from home?"

"I need a change of clothes. My bag, my wallet. Yeah, some food would be good. I haven't had anything since breakfast."

"We're on our way."

A bit later, Quentin knocked on the door, and let Emma and Zach into the room. They hugged me, gave me a bag with sandwiches, cokes, chips, and my favorite chocolate bar. Also a change of clothes, a pair of drawstring pants and a T-shirt without a tight neck, just what I needed. Basically pajamas. Zach and Emma stayed in the room watching Magnus sleep for me, while I went in the bathroom to change and clean myself up a bit.

I gave everyone in the hall updates. Quentin, Zach, and Emma hung out until visiting hours were over at about seven. I planned to stay the night in the room. Hours had passed and he still hadn't woken up. Thankfully Emma remembered my toothbrush.

I pulled my chair up to Magnus's bed and fell asleep at 9:30, holding his hand. My head resting on his mattress, my forehead pressed against his arm still waiting for him to wake up.

CHAPTER 51

*J*ust past midnight, he shifted. Then he blinked. I pressed the call button for the nurse and three bustled in to perform a bunch of procedures. After they left, Magnus's voice emerged like a croak. "Kait..."

I grasped his closest hand. "Hi Magnus. Welcome home."

His cheek pulled back in a sad attempt at smiling. I clutched his hand as he drifted back to sleep.

My head jerked up. Three hours had passed. The room was dark, except for the glow of the lights, quiet except for the hums and beeps of the machines. I had been deep asleep but Magnus was squeezing my hand. I wiped drool off my cheek and looked up. Magnus's face was pressed heavy into the mattress and we were almost nose to nose. He whispered, "I needed tae see ye."

I kissed his fingers and tucked his hand to my cheek.

He asked, "Can ye get closer?"

I wanted closer too and figured I could slide under him easily

278 | DIANA KNIGHTLEY

enough. It was wishful thinking though, the easy part. I pushed his shoulder up and shimmied under halfway. He was a heavy weight along my side. My arm stuck under his chest.

He said, "Raise your arm," and with a groan and a strained expression he lifted while I brought my arm up and under his forehead. "Am I too heavy for ye?"

"No, I need the weight of you. It feels good."

He buried his face into my underarm. "It hurts terribly." His shoulders heaved with sobs.

"Oh, oh — Magnus, are you crying?" I wrapped around his head. Oh no. I held him, the parts I could touch, as tight as I could. I kissed his hair and held him. Spasms rocked his body.

"I'll call the nurse, have her bring some pain meds." I pushed the button beside his bed.

It took a few moments before a nurse appeared. She quietly said, "Is he awake?"

"He is and in a lot of pain."

She asked, "Mr Campbell, how is the pain, scale of—"

He gasped, "Terrible."

She adjusted the bag on the pole beside his bed. "Mrs. Campbell, this will take a few moments; then he'll be able to sleep again."

"Thank you."

I held him quietly, scared, in the dark for some long moments until slowly his large mass of muscle bound shoulders began to relax, to soften, and grow heavier on my body. He groaned and then sighed. "Tis a wee better now."

"Good." I relaxed my grip on his arms.

He burrowed his face into my side, his voice a whisper. "I missed the smell of you."

I said, "I ran for a long way to get you, and I'm sweaty and..."

He inhaled deeply. "Kaitlyn is alive, the smell of ye means you art alive. I worried I would nae find ye again."

I burst into tears. "You almost died."

He remained quiet, still. I wished he could hold me while I sobbed under him, but I wasn't lying when I said I needed his weight. Having him heavy on my side helped.

After a long cry, I wiggled to the side and flailed to get my fingers on a tissue from the bed stand. I wiped my eyes and nose, sniffling and wet, and wriggled back under him. I used the dry side of the tissue to wipe his cheek. "What happened to your back?"

"I was whipped." His voice was deep, quiet, and rumbling, vibrating my chest where his head was cradled. "Tis a long and complicated story, Kaitlyn — Lady Mairead is the keeper of three — I dinna ken what they are called. They are verra precious machines. I daena understand their power, but I know they are dangerous. They can transport a body beyond the world of flesh and marrow to an otherworldly time. Like a vessel. Tis a power that in the wrong hands could end wars but might also begin them."

His body spasmed for a second, "Where is it?"

"You gave it to me for safe keeping, I have it in my bag, here, by the bed."

His body relaxed. "My sword?"

"You didn't have it. You didn't have anything with you."

His forehead, rubbed on my skin as he nodded. "I remember."

"You said there were three, Lady Mairead has the other two?"

"Her new husband, Lord Delapointe wanted the vessels. She kept them from him for a time but he is a brutal man." Magnus grew quiet in the darkness of the room. He was breathing heavy but seemed determined to go on.

"Delapointe has a black heart. He believed he could force Lady Mairead tae give him the vessels, as he forced her tae marry him, but she would nae relent. He accused her of witchcraft,

280 | DIANA KNIGHTLEY

sentenced her tae death — I had tae fight tae save her and in doing so I have killed his brother."

"Oh." I couldn't think of a thing to say, it didn't seem real.

"Twas a mistake to do it. There was nocht else tae do but run. I brought Lady Mairead here with only one of the vessels. While we were away, Lord Delapointe uncovered the hiding place of one and has been using it."

"That was the men who came to the restaurant?"

"Aye, those were his men. I have been his captive. He meant my whipping to be a warning tae my mother she should give all the vessels tae him. Then last night someone I dinna recognize passed me one and I was able tae escape my cell. I dinna ken which vessel it is. I am nae closer tae finding all three."

"Have you seen Lady Mairead?"

"I haena seen her, she remained hidden."

"That's probably good, right? She is hiding a vessel. She's probably going to take the one from her husband, then she'll bring them both here."

"There is a chance she has one. There is a small chance she will do the right thing but I canna trust her."

We lay quietly for a long time, I stroked my fingers up and down his shoulder, the one place that seemed uninjured.

Finally I asked, "Magnus, what year is it for you?"

He shifted slightly and inhaled and exhaled deeply. "Tis the year of our Lord, one thousand, seven hundred, and two."

I nodded. Because I was relieved to be right and happy to have it finally out in the open, but why was I nodding? That was terrifying, crazy — three hundred years ago? That's where this man was from. Three. Hundred. Years. "Really? How is it possible?"

"I daena ken. I only ken tis true."

"Oh. Thank you for trusting me, for telling me."

"We are tied by a vow, a name, and this — the vessels are verra dangerous. When I go back—"

"You'll go back? Magnus you can't. You can't go back. You almost died, and I have no way of knowing if you're alive and—" A tear rolled down my cheek. "You've been gone, and I didn't know if you were alive or how to find you, and it's been so scary."

"I have been on the other side of that fear. I dinna ken if I could get back."

"You did though, but can't you please stay?"

"I have tae find the vessels and protect them."

"But you could live here, just forget it, stay here and not worry about it." I hated how I sounded, pleading, insecure.

"Kaitlyn, I dinna ken if that is possible. I have turned time tae be here, broken natural law. Tis verra likely witchcraft, and if I have used witchcraft I am nae longer deserving eternal salvation. I may be a lost soul. Am I tae live here as if I winna born three hundred years ago? I am nae assured of my life when I am in this time."

I was shaking my head against his forehead, silent tears streaming down my face.

"I fear the laws of god and nature will catch up tae me. What is the price they will extract? How will I pay for crossing time, and with what, my life and my soul? When will the payment be due? I have no assurances here. If the natural order has been disrupted, tis up tae me tae set it tae rights."

"It's not all your responsibility, Lady Mairead—"

"Kaitlyn, imagine if one of your weapons ended up in my time?"

I chewed my lip considering. I only knew of time travel from movies. There was always a downside to messing with the natural order of things as Magnus had said. I could agree it was dangerous but his broken wounded body weighed heavy on my heart. He almost died. It was too dangerous for him to take on so much. "Can we just — I can't think about you going back. You're hurt. You have to heal. Please stay until you're better and then please, we need to talk about it first."

"Aye, Kaitlyn."

We stayed quiet for a few moments. The sounds of the room surrounding us, the soft hum of the air conditioning, the beep of his heart monitor, a light with a barely distinct buzzing sound was driving me crazy, so it must have been driving Magnus mad.

He said, "I knew I wanted tae spend my life loving ye but my life is from three centuries past. I am here in this hospital, but I am nae alive this year. There may well be a gravestone with my name etched upon it, yet tis improbable — an airport has been built atop, burying me more still. I am a dead man, tis nae done in fairness tae bind ye tae my life when I am nae alive."

"Don't Magnus, don't speak of it — you are. You're flesh and blood in my arms and I don't know what kind of magic it is, but I know you're really here. I can feel you. Please don't talk anymore of fairness. I married you, and you married me, and you promised to give me your full life. You promised. I mean to hold you to it."

A chuckle rumbled low in his chest. "You have used my words."

"I did. I may have signed a contract. I may have agreed to marry you through your mother. I may have entered it without knowing you at all. I still don't. But I mean to hold you to it. I find myself tied, heart and soul, and I can't bear the thought of being without you."

"I canna bear it either, mo reul-iuil."

I turned my lips to his hair and breathed in his scent. It made more sense now with the truth between us that lingering scent of dust and wine. I had discovered it the other day in a candle with the smell of musk, patchouli, ylang-ylang, and frankincense. It had taken me back to Magnus or brought him forward to me. He smelled of the scents of a deep dark past.

He burrowed his face further in under my arm and quietly said, "I want ye, Kaitlyn."

"Jeez Magnus, you're incorrigible — here, in the hospital?" I glanced about me. A nurse would be in here any minute, plus Magnus could barely move. "What are you thinking—"

He chuckled.

"Oh, you're joking! I half-believed you for a moment."

"From my scalp tae my feet I am either in screaming discomfort or, thankfully, numb. I'm in nae condition."

"Your heart monitor would probably alert the nurses, anyway."

"'Tis what this incessant noise is?"

"It's to make sure your heart is pumping because it stopped earlier."

"I must have scared ye."

"You did."

"What else happened?"

"Your back is terribly cut up, you're bandaged. You have many bruises internal and external and your heart — you're dehydrated. On your other arm there is a tube for dripping liquids into your blood stream. You may be missing part of an earlobe."

"I will be far uglier. My other parts though, they have made it unscathed?"

"If you're asking about your family jewels, yes. You were naked when you arrived and they were present and accounted for. I would assume that in a few days they'll remind you of their existence."

"Good, I have future plans for them with ye, but for now I am verra tired. I am going to fall asleep but worry I might crush ye."

I kissed the top of his head. "I'll climb out." I shimmied out from under him. "I'll sleep right over there on the couch. If you need me just ask, okay?" I pulled an end of the couch from the wall so that I was angled to see his face better. "I'm glad you're home."

But from his deep breaths and still body it sounded like Magnus was already asleep.

∼

The end.

∼

but please read on for the first two chapters from book 2...

TIME AND SPACE
BETWEEN US

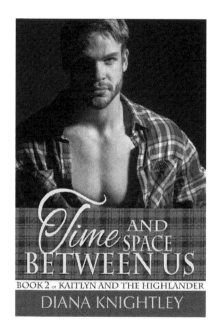

CHAPTER 1

I was still licking the hunks of chocolate lava cake off my fingers from our dessert when Magnus, sitting on one of the kitchen stools, took my hand and pulled me closer between his legs.

It was still a little awkward to kiss him. There weren't a lot of places on his body that weren't painfully injured. I couldn't touch him without causing him to wince.

"Are you feeling better?" I pressed closer, keeping my hands on his thighs, off his back.

"Och aye." He ran his hands up the back of my thighs to my panties. He pulled my hips closer.

"Would you like your massage?"

In answer he led me to our room, our bed.

I helped him peel his shirt off his back, not easy with so many bandages. Then I dropped his kilt to the ground and took a deep breath to steady myself.

I missed him. I wanted him. It had been way too long.

As he crawled to the middle of our bed, I pulled my shirt off, unfastened my bra, and slid it down my arms.

He dropped face down on the bed, but turned in time to see me shimmy my shorts and panties down. His eyes went wide.

A smile spread across his mouth. "You are disrobed mo reul-iuil, tis markedly different from yesterday's massage."

I poured a dollop of oil into the palm of my hand, grinned, and climbed astride his lower back. I massaged across the top of his wide shoulders. The whip marks there weren't as deep. I pressed down the side of his arms. Up and down, pressing and pulling. Wherever I could touch where the skin wasn't marred. He moaned happily as I burrowed my fingers into a tightly bound muscle and spasmed when I accidentally grazed an especially angry looking wound. "I'm sorry."

"Nae matter, Kaitlyn. Tis painful, but I feel clear for the first time in days, turadh."

I pressed my hands along his left tricep. "Remind me what that means?"

He groaned with pleasure. "Turadh, the clouds have broken."

"Oh. God, I love it when you say things like that — in Gaelic, right?" I pressed my palms to his triceps and wiggled my hips on his back.

He growled and rose up, bucking.

I squealed as I slid off his slippery back to the bed.

"Tha thu breagha." He pinned my wrists and climbed on my body. "Is ann leatsa abhios mo chridhe gubrath."

"Oh my god, Magnus, that is fucking hot."

"Mo reul-iuil..." He shoved hard and fast up into me, desperate and intense, holding my arms above my head, his mouth pressed to my neck. My moans started low but grew as he rocked and pushed against me. His body had been sitting idle and broken, but now strong and powerful. His forehead butted against my cheek; his breath filled my ear. "You art mo reul-iuil."

"Oh — oh — oh my god," I arched against him with a moan as waves rolled through me. He held on, riding, his voice a groan. It rumbled up from his chest as he finished and collapsed on my body.

We both lay still. Panting. Slowly catching our breaths. Kissing the spots of skin closest to our mouths. I wriggled my wrists free from his grip and clasped around his hands. I kissed and nibbled his neck.

Then he kissed me, slow. His tongue flicked around my teeth, teasing my lips.

We stared into each other's eyes.

"I missed you so much."

"Och aye." He kissed my lips, the tip of my nose, my chin. "I can tell ye have been wanting me, ye are talking to God." He chuckled, kissed my neck, and rolled off me to his side.

I curled up beside him. His strong hand on my hip.

I loved him more than I ever believed possible, but the last thing he said just before he fell asleep was, "I would bide here forever if I could."

I knew in my heart that loving him wasn't enough to convince him to stay.

CHAPTER 2

The next morning Magnus was sitting on a deck chair, leaned forward, elbow on his knees, making imaginary marks on the thin layer of sand between his feet. Quentin, now his number one security guard, was nodding, listening, occasionally asking a question.

Magnus was leaving.

I knew it because of what he said when I talked to him about the estate while he was still in the hospital: "Tis good Kaitlyn, how ye have caused it to grow, verra good." His words were proud. As if he was a parent watching a child start out in a life they couldn't really share in. He was watching me grow our estate, not for us, but for me, alone.

He told me again that he was leaving soon. I begged him to stay. We ended the conversation with an uncomfortable agreement — there was no way to agree, so we wouldn't talk about it anymore.

So I had no idea what his plans were and that sucked.

But I couldn't imagine how to start the conversation. And I was frankly scared to. As if asking would make it real. Ignoring it would keep it improbable. But I needed to know, needed to get it out into the open.

I had to talk to him.

To beg him to stay.

So I planned, plotted, and carefully deliberated, and decided to bring it up in the office, in a dignified adult way.

But I forgot or disregarded all that planning and brought it up right after making love. In the middle of the night with silent tears rolling down my cheeks, already distraught. Childlike, wrapped in his arms, tears pooling on his chest. "Please don't go."

"What's this then?"

I clutched his shoulders, being mindful of his wounds. They were jagged, red, a few still open and sore. He told me the whip marks didn't hurt that much, that he could lay on his back, that I didn't need to be gentle. But his back looked so angry, painful, and deeply, deeply wounded that I felt like it was a reminder why it was too dangerous for him to return to Scotland. He couldn't see it. Maybe that was why he was so determined to go.

"You're leaving and you don't have to... you don't."

"Ah, Kaitlyn, ye know... we have discussed this—"

"We haven't, we haven't discussed it. Not enough. I don't know why. Not really. And you're making the plans without me, and it's just like with my—"

He shifted his head and his hand that had been stroking my shoulder paused.

"What are ye saying?"

I sobbed. "That just like everyone else, you're leaving me and lying to me about it and — am I not worth staying for?"

Magnus huffed. He tensed, then rolled out from under me, and sat on the edge of the bed. His bandaged back turned to me.

He sat there for a moment, facing the wall of windows. Very quietly.

Panic hit me in the gut. He had turned his back on me.

He said, "Tis nae fair."

"What isn't fair?" I reached for his hand.

He pulled it away and rubbed it across his thigh.

"You are saying this tae me? Comparing me tae your other men, Kaitlyn? I am your husband. I will nae stand for this."

I was too shocked to know what to say. In my imagination this went so much better.

"I know, I just—"

"You are my wife. When I tell ye I must away, you should say goodbye without a fuss. And I'll have nae more of speakin' of other men in my bed."

"I'm sorry I brought up my past. I only wanted you to know one of the reasons why this was too hard for me. I'm sorry."

His jaw clenched. "In the future, here, know ye one thought, your husband, Magnus Archibald Caehlin Campbell has been true tae ye."

I curled up around my knees wishing I could sink away. My voice was so small it shocked me when I spoke. "It doesn't feel like truth, it feels like a lie of omission. Just because you don't lie out loud doesn't make it not a lie. There's a truth you're refusing to say." I looked up at his back.

His face turned to mine. His eyes glaring dark. "You call me a liar?"

"You aren't telling me the truth. From here, in the pit of my stomach, and here in my heart, it feels very much the same."

He turned to the windows again. I squirmed up to the pillow, taking a view of the side of his face. His jaw clenched and unclenched. I had hoped that starting this conversation might be an immediate relief, but no, I felt really terrible and desperate.

He was headed out the door and my hand was on his back shoving him through.

"You are a woman, ye will try tae convince me tae stay. You canna understand why I must fight. You see my wounds and want tae heal me, and ye want me tae hide here. Just as Lady Mairead—"

"If we're not to talk of men in your bed, I would appreciate not comparing me to your mother in mine."

Magnus let out an appreciative chuckle. Then shook his head.

I continued, "I do want to convince you to stay. Explain to me why I can't. I'm listening. If you'll listen to me."

His head hung. "I daena want tae leave ye. I canna talk of it without changin' my mind, and I must nae change my mind. You want me tae listen tae ye, you plan tae beg me tae stay, but ye do, every moment." He reached behind to take my hand, wrapping it in his. "Your smile begs me. Your body, your laugh, ye dinna need words, Kaitlyn. I am nae strong enough tae hear them."

"Then stay."

"I canna."

"Then tell me why."

And so he did. Sitting on the edge of the bed, lit by moonlight shimmering on his darkness. He exposed his shadows. He told me about his home, or lack of a home, in Scotland, the cusp of the eighteenth century. He had spent his youth at Balloch Castle, but when he was nine years old he had been sent to London to live with an uncle. He had been to court. Had lived and played with royals. But he had always been one of "the Highlanders," not fully trusted, not really fitting in.

Then his Uncle Baldie sent for him because Lady Mairead

was missing, abducted. Suddenly, after growing up in a life of wealth and civilities, Magnus was thrust into danger and intrigues. "I lived at Balloch again. I trained to fight alongside my brother, with my cousins, but winna fully trusted for many reasons: My father was a foreigner. I grew up in London. I was Protestant. And maybe worse — the son of Lady Mairead. Twas a blight on my reputation."

"That must have been really hard."

"I dinna think on it much, there were feuds to fight." He gave me a small half-grin.

I squinted my eyes. "You like fighting?"

His eyes twinkled. "Tis hard to like something that may end me, but I am verra good at it. And is braw tae fight alongside my brother. There are troubles brewin' though. My clan is split in their minds and hearts. The next fight will be cousin against cousin. Up tae now I have been in the middle. They believe I am on both sides and nocht at all. Tis difficult tae prove my allegiance and is harder still tae prove my independence. But I must always be provin' m'self tae stay alive."

"Your own cousins are a danger to you?"

"Och aye, I have a great many cousins. Some are like brothers. Some are dangerous. A few are villainous."

"I have three cousins, they live in Alabama. I don't see them much."

"TIs good if they are villainous," he joked.

His face grew serious again. "I was sent to search for her in France, until finally Lady Mairead was found, in a castle in Scotland, married to Lord Delapointe. She sent for me. She made me take a binding oath tae follow her commands. Then she asked me tae recover one of these vessels from its hiding place and bring it tae her.

"I did as she asked, but when I returned with it, Lord Delapointe met me at the gates and fought me for it. Twas my first indication that the vessel was very valuable."

"That's awful."

"It was, in the ensuin' battle I killed John Baldrick, the brother of Delapointe."

"His brother?" My eyes were wide. "Have you killed many people?"

"Enough that we shoudna speak of it." He looked down at his hands. "Lady Mairead met me on the field of battle tae take the vessel. As her hand clasped around it she spoke a numerical incantation. I was fearful and begged her nae tae perform spells, but she continued, and I was dragged here tae Fernandina Beach, the year 2017."

"You must have been terrified. That night you met James, you didn't know where you were or anything about the world you were in..."

"Twas terrible. But then I met ye, and you introduced me tae coffee, and after that twas all okay." He chuckled. "The truth is I am used tae being in places that are nae mine. I haena had a home in many years. I daena fit any—"

I pulled his hand to my heart. "This is your home Magnus. You belong here. You are my husband. This is true. I know it." I smiled. "I know it here." I drew his hand down between my legs. "And here."

He groaned happily. "I would live there if I could." He drew his hand away and turned back to the windows.

"Thank you for telling me. But it all sounds so complicated and dangerous; I still don't know why you have to go back."

"That is why I am nae talkin' tae ye about it."

"So what do you want me to say?"

"Kaitlyn, I want ye tae say, 'Aye master, I will do as ye wish,' and be done with it."

I flicked the sheets, pissed. "You're kidding me right? I have never in my life said anything like that to any man, and I'm not going to start now." I lay fuming. "I mean you've met me right? I'm Kaitlyn Sheffield, and I don't just take orders—"

"Your name is Kaitlyn Campbell, and ye will take orders from me—"

"No I won't."

"Let me finish. I would say — you will take orders from me as my wife, but as your husband I winna give them. Nae like that." He scrubbed his palms down his face. "I knew what kind of woman ye are when I married ye. I knew Kaitlyn Campbell dinna take orders. Lady Mairead warned me. She said ye winna be a woman under my control, and I said that was good. I like ye with the fire in your throat and passion in your heart, but you asked what I want ye tae say and I answered — I want ye tae submit tae me. I know ye winna, so instead tis better nae tae talk of it."

"I want you to be able to talk to me about anything."

"I canna trust that ye will listen and nae beg me tae stay."

I huffed, threw the covers off my legs, swung my feet to the opposite side of the bed, and stood. "So you don't trust me and I don't trust you. That's a fine piece of horseshit of a marriage." I stomped into our bathroom and wanted to slam the door, but guess what, frosted, sliding glass. So I crossed my arms and pouted like a big baby for a few moments and then stomped back into the room.

~

He hadn't moved. He was still sitting, staring at his hands between his knees. The skin on his back cut and injured, his head hanging down.

And I softened.

Oh.

"What do you need me to do?"

"I need tae talk tae ye about it. I need your help with something — tae be able tae trust ye tae help me go."

"Oh god Magnus, I'm so sorry." I dropped to my knees in front of him and clutched his hands. "You can trust me. I'll just — I can just listen. I will. Tell me." I laid my forehead on his hands and tried, really hard, to listen through my breaking heart.

"Delapointe wants all the vessels. If he finds them all it will make him verra powerful. There are three; he knows I have one. Lady Mairead still has one. The other is in his hands. Ye have seen the cuts on Lady Mairead's cheeks. He will torture her if he is given the chance.

"Also, I have killed his brother. He swore tae kill me, but he dinna. Instead he kept me locked and bound and beat me — he drove me close tae death. He only allowed me tae live as bait so Lady Mairead would come tae him."

"He knows I have one of the vessels and I have used it tae escape. He will follow me here. Then he will kill me. But he may wish to see me suffer first. And if he discovers you... I canna allow that tae happen. And that is the story of it — why I must go. Because living here is nae the end of it."

I looked up at him. "It sounds like you have to."

"I do Kaitlyn." He smiled sadly. "I must." He shook his head. "Our marriage is nae horseshit."

"Yeah. I know. I say stupid things sometimes. I'm trying to be better. To listen more."

He swept his arms around my back and pulled me up onto him, leaning back on the bed, me on top. He put his arms behind his head and I sat on his waist looking down. I loved this view: his bicep close to his ear, his shoulders bound with muscles, his chest wide. His eyes were appreciative, but he couldn't look on me for long, instead he focused on my thigh, my hips, kept his eyes cast down.

I asked him once, from this position above him, what he saw when he looked up at me — he answered, "An emanating light bursts from your skin. I must take ye in pieces, else I might cry." Then he chuckled.

I considered it a joke. But also a little bit true. He often mentioned how much light I emanated, which might have been the corniest compliment in the world if not that he was so dark.

His darkness was a reminder he was not truly alive anymore in my time. My brightness was a reminder I was not alive yet in his.

My happy thoughts faded as I remembered him talking about how he was living on borrowed time, and maybe he had gone against the natural order and might have a price to pay.

I bent down and pressed my cheek to the side of his. "What was it you needed help with?"

His hands pulled my hips closer to his. "I wish I could talk tae ye about it now, as ye are in a willing mood, but I find myself with a deeper desire."

I kissed his lips and his tongue slid into my mouth as he pulled me closer. His hands massaging over my chest and down my sides, over my hips and thighs until I raised up and sat down on him with a small gasp. I folded down and we rocked against each other. Pushed and pulled. It was sweet and slow, but tears mingled with my sweat and dripped onto his face because he was leaving. Always leaving.

~

When we were done, he pulled away to try to see my eyes. "You are crying, Kaitlyn?"

I nodded against the stubble on his jaw.

"Can ye tell me?"

"I just promised I wouldn't say anything."

"I dinna ask ye nae tae speak, I asked ye nae tae argue."

I sobbed. "It feels like every moment with you is saying goodbye."

"Tis true," he said quietly.

Our darkened moonlit room was still, our voices quiet under the soaring ceiling. Our bed rumpled from love making and just a little over a week ago had been empty. For eight weeks I had been alone. And would be again.

I sobbed and he held me until I was done.

Then he said, "I think all men have this problem — we must consider each and every day our last. We are all of us saying goodbye and if ye consider our good fortune, Kaitlyn; I am married tae ye in a second life, three centuries in the future. Our future, our goodbyes, mayna be as final as some."

I said, "Yes, that may be true." To wipe my eyes, I squirmed off him for the tissues on the bed stand, left there from all those nights crying myself to sleep while he was gone.

He adjusted up to the pillows and I joined him. And we lay there together, me wrapped on his whole body. He said, "I canna sleep, would ye come tae the office with me?"

I hope you enjoyed the first two chapters of book 2. Continue reading Magnus and Kaitlyn's adventure and love story (much of it in 18th century Scotland), by following this link:

Time and Space Between Us

THANK YOU

There are many more chapters in Magnus and Kaitlyn's story.

If you need help getting through the pauses before the next books, there is a FB group here: Kaitlyn and the Highlander Group

Thank you for taking the time to read this book. The world is full of entertainment and I appreciate that you chose to spend some time with Magnus and Kaitlyn. I fell in love with Magnus when I was writing him, and I hope you fell in love a little bit too.

As you all know, reviews are the best social proof a book can have, and I would greatly appreciate your review on this book.

Kaitlyn and the Highlander (Book 1)
Time and Space Between Us (Book 2)
Warrior of My Own (Book 3)

Begin Where We Are (Book 4)
A Missing Entanglement (now a prologue within book 5)
Entangled with You (Book 5)
Magnus and a Love Beyond Words (Book 6)
Under the Same Sky (book 7)
Nothing But Dust (book 8)
Again My Love (book 9)

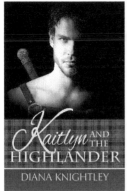 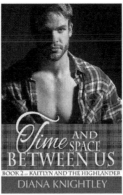 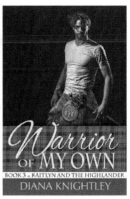

SERIES ORDER

Kaitlyn and the Highlander (Book 1)
Time and Space Between Us (Book 2)
Warrior of My Own (Book 3)
Begin Where We Are (Book 4)
A Missing Entanglement (now a prologue within book 5)
Entangled with You (Book 5)
Magnus and a Love Beyond Words (Book 6)
Under the Same Sky (book 7)
Nothing But Dust (book 8)
Again My Love (book 9)

Can he see to the depths of her mystery before it's too late?

The oceans cover everything, the apocalypse is behind them. Before them is just water, leveling. And in the middle — they find each other.

On a desolate, military-run Outpost, Beckett is waiting.

Then Luna bumps her paddleboard up to the glass windows and disrupts his everything.

And soon Beckett has something and someone to live for. Finally. But their survival depends on discovering what she's hiding, what she won't tell him.

Because some things are too painful to speak out loud.

With the clock ticking, the water rising, and the storms growing, hang on while Beckett and Luna desperately try to rescue each other in Leveling, the epic, steamy, and suspenseful first book of the trilogy, Luna's Story:

Leveling: Book One of Luna's Story

Under: Book Two of Luna's Story

Deep: Book Three of Luna's Story

SOME THOUGHTS AND RESEARCH ...

Some **Scottish and Gaelic words** that appear within the books:

Turadh - a break in the clouds between showers

Solasta - luminous shining (possible nickname)

Splang - flash, spark, sparkle

Dreich - dull and miserable weather

Mo reul-iuil - my North Star (nickname)

Tha thu a 'fàileadh mar ghaoith - you have the scent of a breeze.

Osna - a sigh

Rionnag - star

Sollier - bright

Ghrian - the sun

Mo ghradh - my own love

Tha thu breagha - you are beautiful

Mo chridhe - my heart

Corrachag-cagail - dancing and flickering ember flames

Mo reul-iuil, is ann leatsa abhios mo chridhe gubrath - My North Star, my heart belongs to you forever
Dinna ken - didn't know

∾

Characters:
Kaitlyn Maude Sheffield
Magnus Archibald Caelhin Campbell
Lady Mairead (Campbell) Delapointe
John Sheffield (Kaitlyn's father)
Paige Sheffield (Kaitlyn's Mother)
James Cook
Quentin Peters
Zach Greene
Emma Garcia
Michael Greene
Hayley Sherman
The Earl of Breadalbane
Uncle Archibald (Baldie) Campbell

∾

Locations:
Fernandina Beach on Amelia Island, Florida, 2017
Magnus's castle - Balloch. Built in 1552. In early 1800s it was rebuilt as Taymouth Castle. Situated on the south bank of the River Tay, in the heart of the Grampian Mountains

∾

*At one point Magnus spoke with thous and thees and thy and thine and it was lovely but a lot confusing. In the 1700s those began to go out of fashion, so Magnus is forward thinking that he uses you and your.

ACKNOWLEDGMENTS

My Facebook page was kicking it for a while there. My friends and family weighed in on questions like, "What should my Highlander's name be?" And "What would James call the Scottish National Football Team?" And "Which restaurant in downtown Fernandina Beach should I destroy?" Then we took the conversation over to Kaitlyn and the Highlander, my FB group and they answered even more questions for me, like "Were kilts too cold for a Scottish winter?"

There are too many people to thank, but thank you to Nipuna Devi Dasi for her input on using rendered goose fat on clothes for warmth (needed in book three!), and her suggestion that Magnus would be mesmerized by a flushing toilet. True, he is.

Speaking of being mesmerized, thank you Anne Leyden for mentioning that Magnus would be *ahem* excited by women's lingerie (Magnus's last words to Kaitlyn are, "Tis hard tae count now I know how wee the undergarments are under your dress.") And bandaids (these play a big role in book 2.)

And thank you to David Sutton for coming up with the

name, Magnus, it's excellent. Also for weighing in on many things from Scottish customs (housing in the eighteenth century really helped with book 3) to Amelia Island customs (Pirate's Punch!) to Millennial customs (your advice against the keg stand was right on), your suggestions helped me so much.

Thank you to my brother, David Cushman, for your advice about the restaurants, chef-styles, bars in downtown Fernandina Beach, and especially the story about Puttanesca. That was a nice touch. Lady Mairead liked the story very much.

I'd like to thank Paige Alvarez Hanks for checking over my wedding scene and giving it the okay, I'm touched you took the time, thank you.

Thank you to Kevin Dowdee for being my support, my guidance, and my inspiration for these stories. I appreciate you so much. And thank you for revisiting Scotland with me on our honeymoon. That was awesome.

Thank you to my kids, Ean, Gwynnie, Fiona, and Isobel, for listening to me go on and on about these characters and accepting them as real parts of our lives. When I asked, "Guess what Magnus's favorite flavor of ice cream is?" They answered, "Vanilla," without blinking an eye. Also, when I asked, "What is Magnus's favorite band?" They answered, "Foo Fighters." (necessary in book 2) So yeah, thank you for thinking of my book characters like a part of our family.

And a huge thank you to Isobel Dowdee for putting your care and attention to the pages. Your suggestions, advice, knowledge, and opinions are always so amazing. I'm blown away by how you make the story better and better.

ABOUT ME, DIANA KNIGHTLEY

I live in Los Angeles where we have a lot of apocalyptic tendencies that we overcome by wishful thinking. Also great beaches. I maintain a lot of people in a small house, too many pets, and a to-do list that is longer than it should be because my main rule is: Art, play, fun, before housework. My kids say I am a cool mom because I try to be kind. I'm married to a guy who is like a water god, he surfs, he paddle boards, he built a boat. I'm a huge fan.

I write about heroes and tragedies and magical whisperings and always forever happily ever afters. I love that scene where the two are desperate to be together but can't because of war or apocalyptic-stuff or (scientifically sound!) time-jumping and he is begging the universe with a plead in his heart and she is distraught (yet still strong) and somehow, through kisses and steamy more and hope and heaps and piles of true love, they manage to come out on the other side.

I like a man in a kilt, especially if he looks like a Hemsworth, doesn't matter, Liam or Chris.

My couples so far include Beckett and Luna (from the trilogy, Luna's Story). Who battle their fear to find each other during an apocalypse of rising waters. And, coming soon, Magnus and Kaitlyn (from the series Kaitlyn and the Highlander). Who find themselves traveling through time and space to be together.

I write under two pen names, this one here, Diana Knightley, and another one, H. D. Knightley, where I write books for Young

Adults. (They are still romantic and fun and sometimes steamy though because love is grand at any age.)

DianaKnightley.com
Diana@dianaknightley.com

ALSO BY H. D. KNIGHTLEY (MY YA PEN NAME)

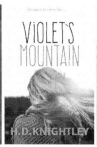

Bright (Book One of The Estelle Series)

Beyond (Book Two of The Estelle Series)

Belief (Book Three of The Estelle Series)

Fly; The Light Princess Retold

Violet's Mountain

Sid and Teddy

Made in the USA
Middletown, DE
15 December 2020